SWIMMING *Back to*
TROUT RIVER

❧

a novel

❧

LINDA RUI FENG

SIMON & SCHUSTER

NEW YORK   LONDON   TORONTO   SYDNEY   NEW DELHI

Simon & Schuster
1230 Avenue of the Americas
New York, NY 10020

First Simon & Schuster hardcover edition May 2021

SIMON & SCHUSTER and colophon are registered trademarks of Simon & Schuster, Inc.

For information about special discounts for bulk purchases, please contact Simon & Schuster Special Sales at 1-866-506-1949 or business@simonandschuster.com.

The Simon & Schuster Speakers Bureau can bring authors to your live event. For more information or to book an event, contact the Simon & Schuster Speakers Bureau at 1-866-248-3049 or visit our website at www.simonspeakers.com.

Interior design by Carly Loman

Manufactured in the United States of America

10   9   8   7   6   5   4   3   2   1

Library of Congress Control Number: 2020942157

ISBN 978-1-9821-2939-2
ISBN 978-1-9821-2942-2 (ebook)

To MYZ

PART I

Two Children of Trout River

THE TRAIN THAT WAS DELIVERING JUNIE TO TROUT RIVER WAS just pulling out of the station and gathering speed, and already the compartment was filling up with cigarette smoke and the gregarious sound of sunflower seeds being cracked open. This was 1981, when trips traversing the length of China took days, and the passengers, having waited for that first lurch of the train, now sprang into action. They poured each other hot water for tea from a communal thermos stabilized inside a metal ring beneath the window where Junie sat on the lap of her mother, Cassia.

Cassia too was set into motion in her own way. She began to tell Junie over and over again to listen to her grandparents, as if some urgent and collaborative task awaited them at the end of the journey. The cadence of that litany—*listen to them, they know what's good for you*—merged with the rhythmic rattle of the train until the two sounds became indistinguishable. To Junie, who was five and wasn't otherwise prone to premonitions of loss, it seemed as though something unprecedented was about to happen, and it made her almost afraid, until the scenery outside the window began to change. Junie had never seen so many dewy rivers and paddies, or so many trembling shades of green, and they exerted a tug on her that the snowy landscapes of her birthplace had never done.

Throughout their trip, passengers in adjacent bunks, noticing Junie's empty trouser legs, asked Cassia about them, believing themselves to be striking up a conversation with a somber woman who needed company. But Cassia pretended not to hear them, and after this happened a couple of times, no one asked again.

She knew that if her husband Momo were here, he would never ignore these proddings. He always educated his inquisitors, sometimes even chided them in outbursts, saying something like, *Many forms of human locomotion are possible.*

Momo was a believer in possibilities. That was the best thing about him, but also the worst.

Earlier that year, Momo left for graduate school in America, and it was understood that in a year or two Cassia would follow. The night before his departure, he managed to borrow a violin that someone, somewhere, had made into a size that fit a child's fingers.

It seemed to Cassia that an absurd amount of craft went into making such a miniature instrument—something that even for adults was a luxury, and even contraband not long ago, during the Cultural Revolution. The fact that it was made in the first place presumed a kind of child prodigy who would, against all odds, make all this arcane skill worthwhile.

But Momo didn't think it absurd, and his impending absence from Junie only made him more determined to start her on music—not just any kind of music, but the kind that had shaped him in his university years in a way Cassia didn't fully understand. In the wee hours of the morning before his departure, he insisted on giving Junie a last-minute violin lesson. After some cajoling and a tussle, it ended in a tantrum and tears. Cassia thought his desperation pitiable—what had he been thinking? But she also knew she could never match his aspirations for their daughter, who was born with nothing below her knees—no tibias, no feet. Where her legs ended, the skin was smooth and the shapes perfectly rounded and unapologetic.

But Cassia rarely touched her there.

Unlike Momo, right now, she was determined to accomplish something very practical: to deliver Junie into the hands of her in-laws, to ensconce Junie in Trout River where Momo had grown up, and to make herself dispensable as a guardian. Whatever Junie would become—and Cassia could not fathom it any more than she could her own future—it had to start with this.

Outside the rattling train compartment, the gleaming railroad tracks merged and separated like undulating steel snakes. She pressed her mouth close to Junie's ear, as if she was sharing a conspiracy with her: "Remember that time when your dad was little and Grandma thought a tiger snatched him up?"

Junie's eyes lit up with laughter, as if she'd been reminded of a successful stunt pulled off by someone her age.

"Don't laugh," Cassia said. "Promise to never make your grandparents worried like that."

Before they boarded the train, Cassia had scraped her memory for tidbits from Momo's boyhood—things they'd talked about during their courtship and the early years of marriage. She was planning to impart these tidbits to Junie, through repetition and review, to allow for a seamless transition into this new ecosystem and new life.

She knew she had a lot to compete with—the scenery outside, the chatter and laughter of strangers inside. Over the rest of the journey, she began to take more liberties with the stories, until they became expansive like a rustic saga. It now involved not just tigers (too remote and menacing) but also sparrows (which he caught during the lean years), plus a river turtle that he befriended (to show Junie that not all animals were food).

It was the closest Cassia had felt to Momo in a long time. After all, wasn't it true that to love someone is to figure out how to tell yourself their story? She could almost see him in his prepubescence, running through the feral paths and brimming with vitality that had no place to go. When she imagined him like this, unformed and far from invincible, it was much easier to forgive him for his absurd optimism.

As the train trundled south and crossed first the Yellow River, then the Yangtze, and eventually entered the long mountain tunnel toward Trout River, Cassia even thought that this was how the two of them might start over, if starting over was still possible.

⚘

On the day that Cassia was to return up north without Junie, she took a walk over a stone bridge with Junie riding on her back. It was autumn, and underneath them, the river that gave the small town its name gurgled with shifting pitches and rhythms in a way that Junie thought resembled singing. She shook Cassia's shoulder to point this out, but Cassia did not seem to relish the river, or anything at all.

Cassia stood out against the fluid movements and chatter of Junie's grandparents, more like a dam than a rampart. Junie could see that something about Cassia made her not belong in Trout River. But the way the world was laid out here amid the water and leaves made sense to Junie in a way that life with Momo and Cassia did not—for example, how Cassia was always worried about something they couldn't see. Or the way Momo pressed Junie's fingers down on the cold violin strings even though she told him it hurt—and the way he got angry when she fought off The Violin Monster and broke it by accident.

For the time being—this was what the adults all said about her being here, but Junie didn't think that this was a temporary arrangement. She heard this in Cassia's tone, in the urgency and finality of her admonition: *They know what's good for you.*

Junie did not cry when they said good-bye to Cassia.

That night when she began life with her grandparents, Junie watched Grandpa wash his feet before going to bed. For most of his life, Grandpa had been a carpenter and tinkerer, though only his age, and not his occupation, was evident from his submerged feet.

Junie scooted over toward him on her knees, reached into the well-worn tub where his feet were planted, and poked at the gnarled sinews and bones in them.

"Your legs grew roots, Grandpa," Junie said, "like those trees by the river!"

He looked at her, then down at his own feet.

"Do you think my legs will grow roots like yours, when I'm older?"

Grandpa now looked over at Grandma, and the look they exchanged was one passed between long-married couples that allowed them to synchronize backstories and action plans. Grandma shuffled over to scoop up Junie from the floor. She plopped her down onto her knees.

"It doesn't work like that," she told Junie, but the question seemed to have put her in a pensive, though cheerful, mood. As Grandpa dried his feet, she told Junie that the universe was full of transformations, some of which we could see, but most of which we couldn't. She said that the philosopher-poets from ages ago talked about *zaohua*, the Fashioner of Creatures, the Shaping Mutator, the unseen forces that turned animals into plants, minerals into animals, and people into anything imaginable. These metamorphoses were more creative than we can put names to, because they erased forms but invented new ones too.

Yes, Grandma answered, the philosopher-poets thought that a person could turn into a cricket's arm.

Yes, maybe even a mouse's liver!—in a manner of speaking.

"But the idea is that we don't always know, you see, what the Great Transformation will turn us into," she told Junie.

It would be years before Junie could fully understand what this meant.

Seven, to be exact.

⚘

Near the center of the village, the river changed all year long. Sometimes the current had a palpable heaviness to its texture and its sound too. Sometimes the river was so flat and opaque that when she rode on the back seat of Grandpa's bicycle as they crossed the stone bridge, Junie could imagine tossing a pebble at it and thought it just might glide clear across the surface. At other times, her eyes got caught by some boy her age squatting at the river's edge, slapping a twig in the water and watching the splashes rise up and disappear into the channel.

Who can say how a child puts down tiny, imperceptible roots in a place? For some, it might have been years of walking barefoot in the damp mountains, from the mud that caked their feet and seeped under their fingernails. Or it might have been from the shifting currents of moisture and breeze, the smell of fungi and moss in their wake, the patterns of leaf fall and resprouting, the regeneration and degeneration of matters vegetal and mineral as they endlessly passed through now one life, now another, until all this became something more than chance, something that imprinted its mark on a child.

Junie's grandparents taught her to read and write at home, and on summer nights the constellations supplied lessons in history and literature. The year she turned ten, Grandpa found one day he could no longer climb the bamboo ladder to the attic with

Junie on his back. So he put her down and climbed up himself, his legs shaky but unafraid. In the attic, he gathered a few of his old carpenter tools and brought them down. The ladder squeaked pliantly under his weight.

He made a kind of rocking horse fitted with four large wheels salvaged from a trolley. Then he carved out two wooden poles of the right length and girth so that Junie could sit astride the wooden horse and propel herself forward with them. The horse shape was to distract her from the fact that it moved without agility or speed. He didn't like the idea of her getting around too far.

Three shallow steps separated the corridor outside their room in the Soviet-style apartment building from the communal court-yard, and Junie soon figured out a way to get down those steps on the wooden horse, by holding on to the banisters and letting the thick wheels bounce down one by one.

From time to time, Junie still asked her grandparents to tell her the story of Momo and the tiger, and they obliged her.

"He's always hated taking naps," Grandma said. "He'd just run out and play."

"So that day when we couldn't find him in the usual places in the afternoon," Grandpa piped up, "we remembered the rumors of tigers coming into the village."

"There was just one, right?" Junie asked, even though she knew the answer already.

"Oh it was a tiger couple," Grandpa said. "Possibly newlyweds."

Grandma rolled her eyes.

"Homeless because they set off all that dynamite in the cliffs," Junie said. She knew that this all led to the concrete-walled apart-ment they were living in now, and the train station too.

"We got all the neighbors out to look for him," Grandpa con-tinued, "for hours."

Junie now held her breath for the best part.

"Then, before supper, someone spotted a rabbit hole in the fence, and if you squatted down and peered into it, there he was—"

"Asleep in our neighbor's garden!" It was Grandpa's turn to roll his eyes.

"With a small bunch of flowers in his hand," said Grandma, "and sunburned cheeks."

Junie released her breath, and a giggle came out with it. It was as if she reached into a hiding place for a favorite toy and found it was still there.

"Momo was too skinny for tiger food anyhow," she said. Junie expected Grandma to correct her, to tell her to use the proper address of "dad" instead. But this time all she said was, "Well, he was skinny, all right."

Grandma could not tell Junie that she hadn't expected Momo to survive his childhood. He was born, whimpering instead of bawling, into a world where Japanese bombs flattened buildings and turned electric wires into clotheslines for severed human limbs. What little hair he had on his crown was the color of dilute tea instead of the normal black. It was as if his hair exhausted itself just pushing out of his scalp, then simply gave up. Grandma knew that even hearty children were plucked off quickly in those years, and she didn't expect better odds for their sickliest-looking son. She delayed naming him for as long as they could, and then simply called him Momo, meaning "no hair."

On the day that the news of Japan's surrender reached them, a pernicious fever and dysentery was making an all-out assault on Momo's small body. All day he purged all the liquid inside him, his eyes shut against the world, until there seemed to be nothing left to purge. Neighbors came to them with the news of the war being over, but Grandma refused to be consoled that day. Thinking it was for the last time, she sat with Momo on a stool and called out his name. A temporary name for a borrowed child. *Momo, Momo, Stinking-Momo, Pooping-Momo,* she muttered over and over, rocking back and forth, while halfway across the world, confetti rained down onto the pavement as couples embraced and kissed.

Besides that fever and the scare with the tigers, Momo had other mishaps that—even in retrospect—brought a clenching to his mother's heart. Like that summer night when they slept on the roof and Momo rolled off the edge of it in his sleep. The house was low—nothing like the buildings they lived in now—but still.

Even by the time he took the name with him to school as his official name, now written with more dignified characters, she still touched him differently from the way she did her other sons. It was the kind of touch that was tender yet ready for a parting.

The family never took note of anyone's birthday—that is, apart from the beginning of each lunar year, when all the children were told they were now a year older. But the day Momo turned twelve, she beckoned him into the kitchen when the other boys were away, and handed him a small bowl of broth. It was an old tradition in those parts, though now mostly forgotten: soup of a small hen for a boy, a small rooster for a girl.

"You have to keep it a secret," she told him.

"Did something happen to one of our hens?" Momo leaned his face into the bowl. Ordinarily, chickens were too precious to be food.

"To mark a gateway in your life," she said. Then she added, "And because now I can stop worrying about you . . . growing up."

Momo's first mouthful made him squint, from the scalding temperature but also from the taste for which he had no words. She didn't know that well after the taste vanished from his tongue, he carried around the bright sustenance of the broth for days. As for the peculiar feeling of milestones, it stayed with him into his adolescence, adulthood, and eventually into his fatherhood, when he understood that a child's birthday was the most fleeting of milestones, when a parent could take the briefest recess on the long road of setting another life into motion.

⚭

On an August night in 1986, there had been a power outage in Trout River, and from sundown, a taper candle lit the room where Junie and her grandparents slept. As was their habit during that stifling time of the year, they abandoned the large bed they shared and instead moved to a bamboo mat in the middle of the concrete floor. In one corner of the room, a coil of mosquito-repellant incense was burning—a green galaxy shape with one of its ends glowing orange—and now it was shedding its third spiral trail of ashes on the floor, a timekeeper for the dwindling night.

Over their decades of life together, Junie's grandparents had perfected a way of talking to each other in the dark, point counterpoint, and in a volume just below the threshold of waking up nearby children. The thoughts spun out this way sometimes went in separate directions, but they always found ways to intersect and stay in motion. They had talked in this way as their three sons grew up and as they left for other places, one by one, with families of their own. But these days, as the couple's world shrank due to the tightening rein of old age, more often they talked about Junie; about Momo, who was the most far-flung of them all; and about Cassia, who they feared was slowly unraveling in America because she'd never written to them since arriving there. The only signal of her presence came at the tail end of Momo's letters, where he always added something perfunctory about Cassia sending her greetings.

"It was a mistake to not let her see the baby," Grandma said.

It was the first and only time she had summoned this thought aloud, something long dispatched into the abyss of Things Families Don't Talk About. But tonight the oppressive heat made her mind less cautious, and it roved far and wide into the realms of What Was, What Will Be, and, along with it, What Might Have Been.

Beside her, Grandpa squinted as if trying to focus on something emerging from the darkness. With one hand, he flapped a fan over Junie's sleeping body. With the other hand, he reached inside his mouth and tried to wiggle a decaying tooth loose. He knew that like the mosquito incense, the number of one's remaining teeth was a kind of timekeeper too.

"What would have been the use?" he mumbled. "The ashes, that child—wasn't even enough of it to fill up a can."

⚘

The next morning, when the troublesome letter arrived, Junie woke up alone on the bamboo mat and found that it had imprinted its woven texture onto the skin of her arm. As she sat up and rubbed her eyes, the day's moist breath was already waiting for her.

Junie washed her face and climbed onto her wooden horse to look for her grandparents, who turned out to be in the courtyard fetching water from the well. Grandpa hovered over the rim with an aluminum bucket tied to a rope, and flicked his wrist to plunge it bottom-up into the well, at the exact angle for its mouth to scoop up the water. With another tug and several pulls, the bucket was back in his hands, now heavy with its new charge. He poured the subterranean water into one basin to keep a watermelon chilled until the afternoon, and then into another containing vegetables Grandma was washing for lunch.

To Junie, this flow of movement and liquid sounds had a whiff of eternity about it, like a melody that you knew would eventually come back to itself and said that the world would always be just so.

The well was off-limits to Junie, of course, and she was only allowed to stand at a distance deemed safe by adults who'd seen how easily any body of water could swallow even an able-bodied child. But even just looking on from her vantage point on the wooden horse, the known world was somehow made intelligible by water, be it the well connected to the river, or the rain that always fell incessantly in the sixth month, or even the exhalation in the noonday air, which brought smells of vines and mushrooms from places she couldn't see.

"There's a letter from your dad and mom today," Grandpa looked up to say. He hadn't waited for Junie to ride with him to the market this morning.

Over the past five years, these letters came to Trout River in envelopes bearing stamps of foreign men with large foreheads. Junie read these letters out loud with her grandparents, but their content perplexed her. (*Momo's doctoral stipend got renewed; Cassia just arrived in San Francisco.*) They were splices and pieces, with their connective threads missing.

Today when they cut open the envelope just before lunch, they found that inside, Momo included a separate sheet of paper addressed "Dear Junie," the first time she had been singled out this way:

I promise you that we will be reunited here by your
twelfth birthday—just a year and a half away! Turning
twelve is a milestone in a person's life, and we will
celebrate it all together.

For emphasis, he'd put dots under the two characters for the word "promise," as if this had been a request on her part that he was granting.

Reunited—there? Junie looked up from the letter and sought the eyes of her grandparents, but their faces portrayed neither surprise nor confusion.

"They mean for me to visit, right?" Junie said. "Not to live with them there?"

There was a pause before Grandma answered: "Your mom and dad want to raise you themselves."

The sound of the cicadas outside rose in volume and seemed to drift into a minor key.

"But why can't I live here with you? Momo grew up here."

A look passed between her grandparents. "Someday Grandpa and I will get old, you see, and won't be able to take care of you."

It was as if the world was going off-kilter, rearranging itself around her, without her. Junie had never thought that at some point in the future, she would sit down with her grandparents around this table for the last time.

"Then I will take care of both of you," she said, "when you get old."

Grandma began shaking her head as if she'd come to the limit of her explanatory powers, but she really hadn't explained anything at all, Junie thought. They were asking her to submit to an order of things that she could not uphold as real.

Her grandparents cleared the table and put the leftover food under a mesh dome to keep the flies away. It was now that time of day when villagers young and old took noonday naps in any position and on any convenient surface available—tables, benches, chairs. Junie and her grandparents lay down on the bamboo mat on the concrete floor together. But Junie lay awake with a tightening feeling in her chest, like a knot that was drawing taut but was also trying to explode too.

The about-to-explode knot said: *There's a world out there trying to lay claim on you. What are you going to do about it?*

She waited until she heard her grandparents snoring beside her, then rose from the mat, and scooted quickly on her knees to reach her wooden horse. She knew she didn't have a lot of time. She propelled herself out the door as quietly as she could. She bounced softly down the steps into the courtyard.

One. Two. Three.

❧

When Grandpa woke up and saw Junie missing, the first thing he did was rush to the well. He leaned into its opening and looked. Once he was certain there was nothing in the water, he gripped the rim of the well tightly with both hands, and rested like that for a moment with his eyes closed.

He hopped on his bicycle and headed toward the fields. Pedaling his bicycle as if gravity was an on-again, off-again thing, Grandpa called out every fifty meters.

Junie! Junie?

The rattle of the metal chains from his bicycle traveled up the dirt road that separated them. In between came the white noise of the rustling trees and the minor key of the cicadas.

He now recognized his mistake, the design flaw in Junie's wooden horse. He had made it to be slow moving, because he recognized in his granddaughter a monkey-like impatience that had been in his son. But he should have made it noisy too, to signal motion. Now he was racing against the lengthening of the afternoon shadows, and if he lost the race, the night that followed would be interminable.

He pointed his bicycle toward the river. By now he was calling out her name without pause.

⚜

Junie hadn't counted on the terrain having so many nooks and crannies that made it harder to propel her wooden horse than on the concrete floor at home. Worse, when she pushed too hard with the wooden poles, one of them snapped, and the remaining piece was too short, so she always ended up veering in the wrong direction.

She made it to the middle of an abandoned field and finally scooted off the wooden horse and sat on the ground. Sweat dripped down her neck, and she muddied herself more every time she took her hand away from the ground to wipe off the sweat.

Junie closed her eyes and imagined herself in the well, with its deliciously cool subterranean water. But it was the river she had to reach, and she wanted to reach it soon, because it seemed like the only hope she had for keeping her world just the way it had been, just the way it should be.

She fought the urge to lay down her head on the ground for a momentary rest.

Clankety-clank.

The rattle of her grandfather's bicycle came to Junie as if in a dream, and startled her awake. She lifted her head off the ground like a woodland animal, and held her breath. Then the call of her name came, across the field between her home and the river, like a growing whisper.

Junie!

She summoned all her strength to answer—*I'm here, I'm here*—then, screwing shut her eyes, began to cry with a vehemence that surprised even her.

For days afterward, the villagers who lived around that field talked about how wrenching that child's cry was. Mothers instinctively glanced at their children, as if to make sure they were still where they ought to be.

When Grandpa came and snatched Junie up in his arms, it was quite some time before she could make herself understood.

"I don't want to go anywhere," she mumbled between spasms of breath. "I want to stay here with you and Grandma, even when you are old, forever and ever—"

Grandpa started to shake his head when he heard the word "forever," but he saw Junie's fever-red cheeks and stopped himself.

"If you send me away, I'll turn," she told him.

Grandpa stared at her.

"I'll turn into a fish and swim back here," she said, pointing to the direction of the river, "from America!"

"From the river?"

"I'll learn to swim for a long way," Junie said. She'd seen America on a map, and it was across an expanse of textured blue. But what was an ocean, after all, but a bigger body of water? And didn't adults say that all rivers drained into the sea?

"We are just going home right now," Grandpa said finally. "Just going home."

It wasn't the answer Junie wanted, but something of her earlier resolve slackened when she heard him say this.

Grandpa put Junie on the back seat of his bicycle and pushed off. As they rode away, neither Junie nor Grandpa mentioned the wooden horse they left behind in the field. It was as if they agreed that it had outlived its purpose.

Junie rested her hiccuping head against Grandpa's bony back as he pedaled on the bumpy road, wobbling and clanking. Across the thin fabric of his sweat-soaked shirt and against Junie's cheek, his ribs rose and fell with his breathing. She recognized that moment as the beginning and the end of something—though she was too young to say exactly what that something was. But she knew, without really knowing she did, that the gossamer threads we put out into the world turned into filaments, and filaments into tendrils, and that what people called destiny was really the outward contours of billions of these tendrils, as they exerted their tug on each of us.

Junie had many questions. About the child who put ashes in a can, for example, which she overheard Grandpa say last night. *Bone ashes.* But for now, what she thought first and foremost was that she didn't know anything about Momo at all, not even as a child her own age many years ago. The tiger story was just a fairy tale, a nice yarn. All of a sudden she found herself too old for this kind of story, because it explained nothing at all, like why he had to leave and go so far away from here, and why he wanted to take her away too.

Behind them, toward a point on the horizon where everything would vanish into the curvature of the earth, the field turned from green to indigo.

Velocity

WHEN THE TIGERS WERE UPROOTED FROM THE MOUNTAIN cliffs, Momo was ten years old. He had heard about them from a fellow they called Hunchback, an old bachelor who lived near the outskirts of the village. He'd gotten up before dawn one day and in the thick darkness saw a silhouette he took for a stocky person sitting by the wooden fence. He greeted the figure with the usual companionable banter, but instead of answering, the silhouette bent down and began walking away on all fours, the bones in its shoulders moving up and down, up and down, as it did so.

"I was lucky it just walked away like that," Hunchback said at the end of the story.

"You were very lucky," said Momo with envy, unaware that his neighbor was referring to escaping with his life and limbs.

In Momo's mind, it was hard to separate the tiger sighting from everything else that was happening: the unleashing of the dynamite among the cliffs where there had been only abandoned ancient graves, the fact that the asphalt road that people had been talking about was finally getting built, and of course the possibility of seeing where that tunnel through the mountain would lead to. So when he mentioned to his parents how he wanted to see what the tiger looked like, it took him by surprise that his mother scolded him with a severity he thought was completely out of proportion, and he ran out of the house, brimming with rage, until dinner called him back.

Like every other boy around him, he rarely wore shoes. He had a slingshot that he used with devastating accuracy against sparrows, which he and his friends then roasted over a spit. He was proud of this and of his agility running on the narrow muddy paths.

But still, so much was denied him just because he was a child. Every day in school, he sat on a rough wooden stool in a classroom where Chairman Mao's portrait smiled at him from above a flimsy blackboard. He was beginning to feel that his whole childhood had been spent waiting for a serendipitous encounter with a tiger, to get his heart pumping. Being in motion—fast motion—helped him get over this impatience, though only somewhat. It was as if he was already building up an escape velocity.

When he was thirteen, his father took him to another town and got his first pair of glasses. On that day he rediscovered leaves— individual ones with outline and texture—on the osmanthus tree in their schoolyard. He took an extra-long road home, risking a scolding, just to savor looking at the leaves, tree after tree. It was also on these walks, when he knew no one was around to hear him, that he started singing to himself. It began as snatches of revolutionary songs he heard on the radio; then he experimented with stretching out the notes in places, adding flourishes to others. He even experimented with substituting his own lyrics. He liked the way his voice asserted itself in the open air, malleable and pure and precise, and he liked to push his voice to its limit.

He was still thin, but in such a way that his body could spring into action when it was needed. His hair darkened and grew more lustrous.

At fifteen, he fell in love with physics, something that was finally able to hold him in prolonged concentration. He liked having the teeming world distilled into just a few laws. Their elegance and power made humankind seem trivial by comparison, and by extension, so did the problems he was beginning to discover with the various indignities of the adolescent body.

He stopped singing now that he no longer could control his voice, though he didn't mind this aspect of growing up compared to other inconveniences. Like many other boys from this time, he had been taught to fear the tumescent longings of his body and to beat them back as if confronted by recalcitrant livestock. That summer, one of the younger boys who swam in Trout River was spotted with an erection. For weeks afterward, the others taunted the boy and called him *liumang*—pervert, degenerate—as if something like this had never happened to them in private.

By the time Momo turned nineteen, his mother seemed more amazed that he survived his accident-prone childhood intact than by the fact that he passed the college entrance exam.

Momo was the only student in his county to gain entrance to a university—any university. That year, 1961, had been yet another disastrous one for crops, and his family's flock of chickens was long gone, as were most of the village's small mammals and birds. This fact alone made Momo's university acceptance seem even more remarkable—a miraculous elevation after two years of belly tightening. This piece of news was brought to his parents by the county's secretary of education. The official—or cadre as they were called—trotted, not walked, to Momo's home, trailed by a few roving children who always knew instinctively when something was afoot in the village.

"Your son," he said breathlessly to Momo's parents when he burst into their courtyard, "is a talent. He is going to—"

When the couple looked at him in anxious confusion, afraid that Momo had wreaked havoc somewhere, the cadre waved the envelope postmarked from Beijing. But this still did not make things clear, so he switched from the local dialect to Mandarin. "He is going to be a robust beam in the architecture of our socialist Motherland."

This proclamation, made in the cadence of broadcast news, caused Momo's parents to stand up even straighter, as if a salute might be called for and they didn't know where to place their hands. The two of them exchanged a look that went through the gradations of worry, inquisitiveness, and, finally, compliance.

Momo was one of the last to find out about the acceptance letter. By the time it caught up with him (he had been trapping wild rabbits outside the village), the news-bearer was trailed by an entire band of roving children, who jostled to see what a newly admitted university student looked like.

A robust beam in the architecture of our socialist Motherland. The luster of that phrase followed Momo everywhere. The engineering major that took Momo in placed a stamp of distinction on him that was wholly shiny and new, because—it was a truth universally acknowledged—the young nation needed to be built and fortified by Science. Few residents of Trout River understood what engineering was, but they grasped the fact that Momo was no longer the sallow-haired boy kept alive only by the vigilance of adults. He now had a new ambition—*lixiang*—to carry out.

The week before Momo's departure, their neighbor came over to see his father. His clothes were spattered with blood.

"I've been thinking that it's only right for us to send him off to Beijing the proper way"—the neighbor gestured toward Momo—"and it's good for the whole village, this honor, and to eat together—"

Momo's father was the first to understand: "Don't tell me you killed your donkey," he said. "You need it for—"

"That old thing was going to keel over any day now," said the neighbor, waving off the remark. "Better for him to go this way, with more glory." He now turned to Momo, his face animated. "Trout River will never be the same again because of you."

In that moment, Momo understood that it had been childish of him to love physics for its own sake, for the elegance of its laws. Rather, it was a way to build things where there once had been nothing. He understood that all of Trout River now waited for him to be that builder; this fact had now set him apart from everyone else here, whether he liked it or not.

On the day of his departure, after he said good-bye to family and fellow villagers, Momo hopped on a tractor that sputtered through the tunnel in the cliffs north of the river where the tigers' lair had been. They took another half day to reach the railway station. Over his shoulder and tied to the bedroll he carried, an aluminum canteen and an enamel mug clanged loudly against each other.

When he reached the station platform, Momo was surprised to see that another small crowd had gathered to see him off—nearby villagers who also wanted to catch a glimpse of a university student. When the Beijing-bound train began pulling away, these villagers, young and old, waved as if they too had watched him grow up. There was only one difference. Their eyes said that they didn't expect him to come back.

A Song for the Troposphere

IN THE FALL OF 1961 IN BEIJING, A YOUNG WOMAN WITH SLEN-
der wrists was one of the first in line to file paperwork for incoming university students. In the rectangular slot designated "given
name," she wrote the character *han* carefully, stroke by meticu-
lous stroke. It meant dawn or, more precisely, the hour just before
dawn. Her name was one of the few things her parents left her.
They had died before she'd started school, too early for her to remember grieving—except when she saw her grandfather, then still
a straight-backed man, crouched over the piano keys and shaking,
in a way that only resembled laughter, but was not.

When the letter of her university acceptance reached the apartment where she lived with her grandfather, Dawn's first thought
was: *My parents would be pleased; I will become an architect.* Then she
thought: *After so many years, I will finally do something useful.*

Dawn wanted to be of use. Her most vivid childhood memories were about music, and although they commanded attention,
in the end they led nowhere. She remembered crouching on the
floor under the piano as her grandfather played it above her. She
was five, it was the year before her parents died, and her grandfather's friend, a Soviet conductor living in Beijing, had brought
the piano into their apartment as a long-term loan. In her mind,
she wasn't just under the piano; it was more like she was wearing it as a cloak. Its vibrations enveloped her, echoed in her chest,
and emanated down to her toes, claiming her, and she hugged her

knees tight just to keep herself in place. If it weren't for her grandpa's legs there looking like pillars, reminding her that there was more of him outside and beyond, she would have thought that the entire world existed under the piano because there, everything made sense.

"If when you play a piece and you feel it right here," her grandpa said, pointing to his solar plexus, "then you're doing something right."

Dawn belonged to that peculiar set of people raised by grandparents out of necessity or convenience. These people, of course, weren't a unified social group, but what they had in common was their older guardians' habits of mind. One generation removed from the enterprise of reproduction, grandparents saw children as genuinely open possibilities. Unlike parents, who needed to see the best parts of themselves duplicated in their offspring, grandparents rarely had such prideful agendas—and for that very reason, they ironically imprinted more of themselves on the young.

Thus raised by those who understood that fledgling lives would continue with or without them, children like Dawn were allowed impractical hopes that parents would've frowned upon. And if these children turned out to be more whimsical and outlandish in their demands on life, the grandparents seldom intervened.

As Dawn got older, she liked the way their apartment filled with people like the Soviet conductor friend, who'd converse with her grandfather in a mixture of Chinese and Russian and throaty laughter, and just as often, he'd get excited about some musical phrase and go to the keyboard to let the piano speak for him. When she turned thirteen, the conductor gave her a violin as a gift, along with her earliest lessons. He was so pleased with her progress that he prophesied that she could soon keep her grandfather in musical company.

But just the year before she began university, in the summer of 1960, relations soured between the two countries, and the conductor friend was called back to the Soviet Union along with all Soviet experts. He had to take the piano with him, and there was now a void in the apartment where it had been. Something about this departure—and the larger rift behind it—troubled her grandpa, she could see.

"We will get another piano," she told him, even though she knew they wouldn't.

He shook his head. "Sooner or later they'll criticize me for playing Russian music," he said. "They're already calling it bourgeois."

"Who says so?" Dawn's voice rose.

"It doesn't matter."

Dawn hated the way the word bourgeois was brandished like a cheap dagger. She hated the way it was used by those who seemed jealous of the additional spark in their lives, which cost nothing extra. After all, her grandfather, who taught Russian and English, earned the same salary as everyone else. They ate the same food and wore the same clothes.

For a while, she worried that Grandpa would make her give up the violin too, but he did not, not even during the year she was studying for the college entrance exam. Now that they couldn't play duets anymore, she practiced harder to play solos for him, mastering pieces of increasing difficulty. Still, even she admitted it was an indulgence, almost as impractical as trying to capture the filaments of melody that floated about in her head every now and then.

Now she would become an architect. Her usefulness to society was about to change, joined by everyone in her incoming university class.

Unlike some of these classmates who crossed climate zones to arrive at the university, she only had to take a long bus ride to reach campus, but it still felt like a clean break with her pre-university past. All around this new country, there was ample room for new buildings and new designs, and architects were needed. In between trunks of trees on campus, dozens of red banners were still strung up to send off the previous graduating class. One of them read: GO TO THE FARM, GO TO THE FRONTIER; GO WHERE THE MOTHERLAND NEEDS YOU THE MOST!

On her way back home, the bus took her past the photogenic main gate of the university. It had a volute arch, a remnant from an age of excess when such flourishes were too much of a preoccupation. The university abutted the ruins of an ancient garden from the days of emperors and dowagers, when Western architecture was a novelty that tickled the imperial family. All of this baroque beauty—marble lattices and all—did not stop the nation from being ravaged in the Opium War, did nothing to halt the marauding foreign troops from setting the expensive gardens on fire. It was said that the flames raged on for three full days.

You can scarcely imagine the beauty and magnificence of the places we burnt, wrote a British soldier during that time.

The burning of the imperial garden is a reminder of the infamy once suffered by our great nation, declared the Chinese history textbooks written in the new era of the People's Republic.

Only one task occupied her mind the entire bus ride, and when she arrived back at their apartment, she ran up the stairs to unlock the door. Her grandpa was still out for his evening walk. *Good timing*, she thought, and headed straight to the inside room. From under his bed she slid out the oblong case and eased it open slowly—How could she not?—like one might ease open a bivalve, bracing against the possible disappointment of not finding a pearl there.

But the pearl was still there: a violin with a warm-hued varnish, nestled inside a cavity lined with purple velvet. Though she'd had the instrument since she was thirteen, the sight of it still astonished her each time she opened the case. She ran the backs of her fingers against the velvet, then the tips of her fingers across the strings. This unleashed five elemental notes that made her heart flutter. The last note, set into motion by the open E string, happened to be the first note in a snatch of melody that rose up in her head earlier, a melody that came to her unbidden—just so—when the ruins of the imperial garden flashed past her field of vision.

Biting her lip, she latched shut the case and took it to the corner bookshelf already overflowing with paperbacks and pamphlets and stacks of stationery. She knew exactly the spot where the violin could fit, wedged between the books and the wall.

She slid the case into that spot and piled more books over it, as if the person most in danger of finding it wasn't herself but some stumbling, nosy stranger.

She took one step back from the bookcase, then another, before spinning on her heels and walking away. Now that she was a university student, Dawn decided, she would start anew. She would study useful things, learn to build things needed for the new nation. She resolved that the violin must stay exactly there, such that each time she returned home, it would take so much trouble to get it out that she'd finally stop trying.

∿

Because it was a perfect evening for doing so, Momo and two buddies left the canteen after dinner, hopped over the stubby wall, and made their way into the ruins of the imperial garden. In those days, in the early 1960s, the garden had not yet turned into a tourist attraction. The ruins, however iconic, were just that: broken stone pillars, overgrown thickets nourished by wood splinters that had once been part of a window lattice or a footstool. It was a de facto playground for the young and insomniac, for those who had energy to spare.

The three of them tromped through knee-high grass to their favorite spot and lay down on a marble terrace built in the Ming dynasty. Using his arms as pillows, Momo watched the sky turn a deeper shade of blue. The stars wouldn't come out for a while yet. As his buddies chatted, Momo thought about what lay beneath their prone bodies: decadence and irrevocable decay. He was not a descendant of that past, no. He was sure that even if he were sent to the very edge of civilization, the future could be wrought from scratch by his own hands.

Since leaving home, Momo had learned that he did not miss the cloying rains of Trout River. Here on the northern plains, he began to get used to a dry clarity in the air. It didn't molder away books and ambitions and didn't encourage an overabundance of clinging plant growth. He liked being able to see a longer stretch of the horizon and feel the force and fluidity of the air.

As it happened, quite often during his first semester at university he sometimes became seized by a sense of wonderment and possibility that bubbled over like an overflowing cauldron. When he was with these friends who themselves had been plucked out of the multitudes and from faraway provinces, he felt a reckless joy, and there was an impulse to pull others into his exuberance. Almost anything could set this off: a line uttered by the teacher in a class, the sight of a red banner on campus, or even (as it did now) the coolness of 400-year-old marble underneath his spine.

From a speaker mounted on a pole somewhere in the distance, Momo heard the faint strains of the national anthem. Something in him was nudged into place by the upbeat melody and yearned for more. He jumped to his feet and pointed to the two friends lying to his left and right. "You are the meteorologist," he said, "and you do oceanography. Just think, with me as engineer, we've got the entire planet covered—land, sky, and sea!"

He pulled each of them up on their feet. "To commemorate this triumvirate of ours," Momo continued, "we must sing something suitably momentous. Are there any revolutionary songs that mention the troposphere?"

There were none, they told him. So Momo braided together melodies from "Song of the Volga Boatman" and the theme song from the movie *People of the Prairie*, and interwove them with his own lyrics.

When he sang it in his tenor voice, the effect was a credible and bracing rendition. Acting as a conductor, he soon got all three of them to sing it in rounds. ("We build dams, break waves, and tame the troposphere!") At one point the lyrics were so fitting yet unfamiliar that his two buddies were rolling on the marble terrace, laughing.

"Who would have thought," the meteorologist said, "that we'd discover a budding musical genius hailing from Trout River."

$\sim$

The piece of news came to Dawn indirectly, like a waft of scent from a distant feast. The university was assembling an orchestra, the news went, and needed string players. She had to verify it with a few more people before she allowed herself to fully ponder it during a semester break when she took the bus back home to see her grandfather.

She had seen the orchestra conductor early in the semester when the faculty held a welcome assembly for the incoming students. She remembered him as an unusually rotund man who sweated even in the cool September breeze.

They were going to hold open auditions in a month, the news went, and every time she thought about that, her heart clenched like a fist.

There was a chilly downpour that day, and when she walked through the door of their apartment, a fire was stoking in the coal stove awaiting her arrival. As she shouted a greeting and walked to the inner room where he was sitting in his wicker chair reading the newspaper, it seemed to her that the apartment had grown smaller.

Then it occurred to her: her grandpa had stopped throwing things away. Piles of newspapers had grown upward like stalagmites. They claimed the space where the piano had been, but also took up floor space that once permitted movement.

She frowned. She was concerned about the consequences of a shrinking space when it came to proper ventilation in this apartment, with him living alone. Dawn had become an orphan because of carbon monoxide. Before they died, her parents were on a trip to survey agricultural techniques in a village in Shanxi. It was winter, and the room they stayed in had a coal-burning stove. The windows were sealed against the cold—much too well, it turned out. Incompletely burned coal produced carbon monoxide that invisibly gripped and suffocated them. Her parents went to sleep in the evening and never woke up.

She went to the kitchen, where she found yet another pile of newspaper and boxes. "Grandpa," she shouted to him, "why are you keeping all these things?"

In his chair, he grumbled but didn't answer.

She began rummaging through one of these piles, intent on sorting out the wheat from the chaff. In a cardboard box full of shoestrings, bicycle inner tubes discarded by neighbors, and rolled-up aluminum tubes of toothpaste, her hand and her eyes simultaneously landed on a folded-up handkerchief, stitched together with cotton padding, that was once a makeshift shoulder rest for the violin.

"Grandpa," she leaned her head into the doorway to say one more time, "why do you keep all these things?"

He waved a hand at her, as if swatting a fly at the edge of his field of vision.

She walked over and stood in front of him with her head cocked, so that he couldn't avoid her gaze.

"You worry about your studies," he said, his eyebrows knotted above his reading glasses.

It didn't occur to her that he might have been lonely, and that sometimes the lonely used things to fill up the space vacated by people. She was too removed from loneliness herself to know that at this point, just as she was still too young to know that death by carbon monoxide was a comparatively peaceful way to go, because dying could more often be a drawn-out process that did not permit dignity in the final hour.

But on this day, she simply felt her grandfather needed a little cheering up. She knew of at least one sure way of doing this, and if this way of cheering him up also scratched a tiny itch that had arisen in her heart, was that so bad?

Just this once, she thought. *Just to see his eyes light up a little.*

She went over to the bookcase and excavated her violin from where it lay buried ("Why did you put it *there*?" he asked). She stood near him and played the beginning of a piece they both liked, which they nicknamed "The Waltz of the Hedgehog."

The piece was based on a Slavic fairy tale and was full of energy and whimsy. It took only a couple of notes for him to recognize what it was, and a transformation instantly came over his face and body. He put his newspaper down on his lap and closed his eyes for a moment. Then he opened his eyes suddenly and his hands rose up into position, and he began playing on an invisible piano in front of him. The two of them kept their eyes glued on each other to keep time, and Dawn could hear perfectly, in her head, the piano accompaniment he was playing. When they finished the last note of the piece, her right hand flew up in an exaggerated arc, and she let out a laugh—she couldn't help it—and he was grinning too.

Now a shimmering, not-damp feeling permeated the apartment.

As with other cases of addiction, a relapse often sent the addict more tightly into the grip of the obsession. When Dawn returned to campus that Sunday evening, she brought the violin with her along with that shimmering feeling. She practiced in a small classroom in a forgotten building on the northern edge of campus. She did this nervously at first, counting down to the date of the upcoming audition, and gradually felt a certain conviction come back into her wrist and hands. And because she wasn't worried about anyone watching, she even began swaying her body a little when she thought it felt right, contrary to what the Soviet conductor had taught her.

Dawn decided to play part of the waltz for the audition, and found that she did not, for the time being, think about its usefulness. At the point of the fastest tempo, when her arm was switching quickly between the strings, she felt as if she had wings and was flapping them up and down, up and down, as though she were about to leave the ground beneath her feet.

Musical Cells

As winter in Beijing turned into spring, the sands of the Gobi desert blew into the city like the collective breath of a barbarian army. When he was finished with classes and after studying, Momo bicycled past the expanse of wheat fields beyond the northern edge of campus. He rode into the gritty wind, head lowered, teeth clenched, eyes squinted shut. He welcomed the onslaught—preferred it, in fact, to having the wind at his back. He tasted the Gobi that way—like he was already going to the frontiers without leaving Beijing.

In the first years of his studies, Momo excelled in his Marxist Principles class and in hydrology. Both made lucid sense to him, and in his mind, he was already a promising engineer at twenty-three, his sleep untroubled and sweet.

The only thing he disliked about university life was noon rest time, a university-wide directive to improve the collective health of the student body—to improve "work-leisure integration," as it was called. From Monday to Saturday when classes were held, libraries and study halls shut their doors for three hours beginning with lunch, so that students and staff could take an "afternoon rest."

But sleeping in short spurts left Momo somnambulant, unfocused, and sullen. At first he tried to read in his bunk bed while his roommates napped around him, but hearing their insouciant breathing and snoring only made him restless, and soon he was slipping out of his dorm, escaping down the stairs.

This was the only time when Momo turned secretive, his movements calibrated for efficiency and stealth. The trick, he found, was to get into the canteen early and wolf down his lunch, then wash up his enamel bowl and chopsticks at the communal brick faucet before others got up and made their languid postprandial shuffle out of the canteen, arms slung over one another's shoulders. By this time he was already on his way, fleeing noon rest.

He learned to keep a lookout for places to spend this time not napping. On days of good weather, a mulberry tree on a field just beyond the northern edge of campus was his favorite reading spot. When it rained, he moved inside a nearby two-story building that people seemed to have forgotten about. There was something diminutive about it, as if it might have been built as part of an elementary school rather than the university. He sat and read on a windowsill in one of its dilapidated classrooms, his bony shoulder pressed against the dirty glass panes that looked out onto the wheat field.

At the west end of the echoing corridor, there was a glass display case. Locked inside it were two plaster busts, one of Beethoven and one of Cervantes. Unlike everything next to the case, the busts weren't covered by dust. This was the first sign that the building was being used.

The second sign came on the first warm day in the spring. Momo was reading under the mulberry tree when he caught a strain of music carried on the breeze from the two-story building. The melody was thin but resilient, like a spider's silk loosened and swaying. He found his mind filling in the gaps in his hearing, and his legs began moving involuntarily, taking strides toward the source.

He stopped between two tree saplings near the first-floor window and oriented on the melody. Something about it made him want to open his mouth and sing, even though he knew that no human voice was capable of carrying that very tune with the same agility and lightness that was demanded.

The melody came to its end, paused as if taking a breath, then repeated itself. Momo skirted around the saplings and walked briskly into the building. He stood in the middle of the corridor with his head aslant, certain that if the music began again, he'd be able to pinpoint its source.

To his disappointment, he heard nothing more.

⚬

Momo went back to the building every day the following week. He squatted down low in the corridor on the first floor, always in the same spot below a windowsill. In this position of sustained waiting and susceptibility, he read halfheartedly, but always with his ears attuned to a signal. For the first time, he noticed not just the sound of leaves rustling outside, but its periodicity, and how much it sounded like water, like waves. It felt oddly like the time he got his first pair of glasses, except now for his ears.

Then on the Saturday of that week, he finally caught something: a door hinge creaking, the scraping of chairs on the floor. He held his breath, triangulating the position of the sound. Someone had gone into a classroom at one end of the building that he knew was usually locked. He sprang to his feet.

From outside that classroom, he looked through the glass on the door and saw a young woman standing with her back toward him, amid small desks in disarray. Under her chin, she clutched an instrument he knew was a violin. In front of her was a wooden chair, and on its back was something rigged from a pair of chopsticks and twine that allowed a piece of paper to be leaned against it—a makeshift music stand.

He was finally at the right place at the right time.

The violinist now lowered her head, as if she was straining to hear a whisper from her instrument. She drew the bow across the strings and produced two notes simultaneously. Momo could tell that they were of the combination of frequencies that produced resonance that was pleasing. She tweaked something in the neck of the violin with her left hand and the notes began to change and become more consonant. He was so amazed by this—by the fact that here were the same elegant rules that once drew him to the study of physics—that the term *constructive interference* temporarily escaped him.

When she seemed satisfied with the adjustments, she stood up straight, and, as if getting a cue from an invisible conductor, began to play. The opening phrase was like a Chinese rhyming couplet: it brought forth a context, slightly off-kilter and keening, until the second half of the couplet leaned in and provided a corroboration, restoring balance. In the lowest register, the violin sounded like a dignified groan. Then, with only the barest running start, the notes raced up the musical slopes, shimmying and gyrating at the highest register, and they sounded so perilously improbable that Momo could not breathe, for fear that exhaling might dislodge them from the air.

He couldn't tell how long he stood there watching—Fifteen minutes? An hour?—but when the piece came to an end and the spell was finally broken, when she put the violin into its case and tucked it into a corner behind a row of chairs, Momo still didn't want to budge from where he was standing.

But because she was coming out of the room and he didn't yet know whether to speak to her, or how to explain that he'd been listening, he snuck around the corner of the corridor and watched her leave the building. Then he let himself inside the classroom.

He headed straight for the half-hidden violin case, slid it out, and opened its lid. He wanted to see what produced the music he'd heard, and how.

Inside, the violin was encased in purple, a color that made its wooden texture come alive. He lifted it out of the case with both hands, clutching it the way an archaeologist might hold a thousand-year-old stone carving.

In the violin's wood-and-string construction, Momo saw the fingerprint of science everywhere: the metal strings supported by a delicate wooden wafer, hollowed out in just the right places and set above the center of the belly, which was clearly the resonance chamber, designed for optimal acoustics. He tilted the violin's body to peer into its sound holes, a pair of curled-up slits shaped like the integral sign in calculus: it was closed but open at the same time.

Now emboldened, he pulled out the bow tucked into the lid of the case, tightened the bow hair the way he observed the violinist doing earlier. He hoisted the violin onto his left collarbone and leaned his chin toward it. He was just registering the scent of rosin on the strings when he heard the door to the room open.

"Who are you?" The violinist was glaring at him from the doorway. "That doesn't belong to you."

He felt heat rise to his face. He took his right hand off the violin and held his palm out in front of him like a shield. "I wanted—"

She now walked up to him, and in a blink of an eye, both the violin and bow were back in her hands, where, he saw now, they clearly *did* belong. She held the violin in the crook between her thumb and index finger, by its fiddlehead neck—as if it weighed nothing at all.

Oddly, now that his hands were empty, his mind was less clouded and he could speak.

"I heard you play last week," he said, "and wanted to hear

more. You were playing this—" and he hummed the snatch of melody that he caught.

She looked at him as if seeing him for the first time.

"That's close, but it's more like—" and she played the entire phrase to show him.

"Yes yes," he said, though he wasn't sure what he was referring to: the correct identity of the phrase recalled or the fact that she could play this as a way of finishing a sentence, as if she was able to reenter an elaborate dream, from any point, at any time.

It was a very different way of being alive.

"You must be in the school orchestra," he stammered. He had occasionally seen posters for concerts at the campus bulletin board.

She lowered her eyes. "Actually, I didn't pass the auditions."

"How can that be?"

"The conductor said the music I chose to play was wrong, that it was not the kind they were going to play for the masses," she said.

Momo nodded.

"I asked him, how could a piece of music be wrong, and he said I should reaudition when I have a better attitude."

"So this is what you're doing—practicing to reaudition?"

"No. I'm composing music." She pointed to the sheets of music on the makeshift music stand, all hand-copied in pencil. The glyphs on the five parallel lines were more of a foreign language to him than Russian.

"You wrote all this?" he asked, running his fingers over the sheet music, as if they could comprehend what his eyes could not.

"Not all this, no," she said, letting out a little laugh, "but simpler things like duets. I think of them as musical conversations I might have with my grandfather."

He felt a buzzing sensation being around her, from both nervousness and excitement, as if she was a newly discovered species of feral creature that no one could be sure would bite him or nuzzle him from one moment to the next.

As she talked and turned her head about, he noticed a reddish mark in the left hollow of her neck. "Does that hurt?" he blurted out, lowering his gaze to see it better. Before she could answer, he made the connection that this was the spot where the violin was clutched to her, the most persistent and also intimate point of contact between the instrument and its player.

She shook her head, probably at his apparent ignorance, and he felt a little embarrassed at having looked at her that way. Then she suddenly put her hand on his arm, startling him. "You have musical cells, as they say," she told him. "You know—sensibility."

This put Momo in such a tizzy that he didn't know what to say.

"I'm thinking maybe if I borrow a violin for you and teach you some basics, we can try out the duets together, and you can help me improve them."

"That's exactly what I wanted," Momo said, even though he didn't know this was true until now.

⚘

Dawn talked with her hands when she wasn't holding a violin. "The notes on the page are just notations," she told him. "This is not music yet. What the players do with them, that's the music."

He tried to absorb this.

"The greatest violinists of the past," she continued, "when you listen to their recordings—not a single one of them sounds the same."

"Even when they play the same piece?" he asked.

"*Especially* when they play the same piece," she said. "You have to listen," she told him, "I mean really listen, because music says only what you can bear to understand."

Sometimes she forgot that she was talking to a novice, and Momo had to interrupt to ask questions. She envied him, she said, because he was hearing all this music for the first time. What was it like?

Like wading in a too-fast river before learning how to swim, he thought.

Across university dormitories, electricity was promptly cut off at ten o'clock at night. But every now and then, in one of these dorm rooms, after the postcurfew banter died down among the roommates, a muted light would blink on under the duvets on a certain bunk bed, forming a cocoon of light around someone not yet ready to surrender to sleep.

Today Momo was in one of these cocoons in his upper bunk, copying music for elementary violin exercises. He held a flashlight in his left hand and a pencil in his right. He had a stack of paper on which he had earlier drawn in the five parallel lines with a ruler. The pages crinkled softly under the weight of his pencil. When he finished a line, he paused to admire what he'd done.

After a while, it was getting hot and close inside his duvet, so he lifted up a corner to let in some air. As he did, his fingers lost their grip on the flashlight, which rolled off his bunk, landed on the concrete floor with a crash, and went dark.

A plaintive wave of murmuring rose from the other bunks. One of his roommates farted in protest.

Momo had to climb down and grope around the floor to retrieve it.

Before he had time to get back to bed, Old Li, in charge of electricity and hot water and mail service in male dormitory number five, was standing in the doorway of their room.

"I know exactly what shenanigan you are up to," he barked. He did not bother whispering, as if the whole room was in cahoots together. "Time for bed!"

"I'm going, I'm going," Momo said.

Old Li watched Momo climb back up to his upper bunk, shook his finger at him, then left and shut the door. Momo lay on his back and crossed his hands under his head, waiting for Old Li to complete his nighttime patrol, so he could resume his copying.

Just what kind of shenanigan *was* he up to?

Momo tried to disentangle his feelings for the music from his feelings for Dawn. Both generated a small itch in his heart that he didn't know was good or bad. In fact, there was always something about his collaboration with Dawn that had a hint—however slight—of derailment and transgression. Like when he asked how she got into the classroom that was always locked. She grinned and extricated a bobby pin from her hair to show him. The pin was slightly bent out of shape, its lacquer finish abraded: a well-worn lockpick.

His eyes found their way to the dormitory ceiling, now illuminated by shadows from the courtyard. He squinted at the dappled pattern of the foliage and imagined it as notations. His left hand involuntarily slid out from under his head and assumed the posture of holding a violin's neck, the way Dawn had shown him on a violin she managed to borrow from someone, somehow. His fingers lifted and fell like pistons on the imaginary fingerboard. In his cordoned-off mind, he hummed the arpeggios he'd been practicing with Dawn.

In this position, he fell asleep.

⁂

It was Momo's idea to practice under the mulberry tree, in the sun and the open air.

When they met at the appointed noon hour, Momo leaned his bicycle against the tree and produced from his shoulder bag a length of twine, a piece of thin wooden board, and three pages of hand-copied sheet music. He set up the onionskin pages in sequence against the wooden board and bound them with the twine.

He'd been making good progress, and they could now play a short duet Dawn had written specifically for his skill level. He now leaned this makeshift music stand on the seat of his bicycle where it could stay upright. It gave him tremendous satisfaction to know that elsewhere on campus, hunched over desks or in their bunk beds, people were sinking into their midday oblivion.

"And here's my contribution," Dawn said, reaching inside a cloth sack she brought with her. Under Momo's eyes, she took out the bust of Beethoven, the one from the display case in the building, and set it on the ground in front of them.

He didn't need to ask how she had unlocked the display case.

"We need an audience member," she explained, "and only the most esteemed will do."

Momo gave the statue a salute. Dawn tossed her head back with a chuckle, then sobered her expression and cleared her throat. "We'll start with a slow tempo, and play all the way through to the end of the first section, for Teacher Beethoven."

They began the piece the way they always did: with the two of them looking at each other, and with Dawn drawing a small but precise breath in an upbeat before the first note, as if the very air between them was turned into a tether.

There were rough patches when Momo didn't manage to switch strings without bringing in an unwanted sound, or when his fingers didn't retract fast enough for the sixteenth notes, and they had to barrel through it, with Momo grimacing. But every now and then, when Momo did manage the exigencies of the techniques he had been learning, his countermelody came in at exactly the right moment to lift the melody up from below, and he heard the texture of the chords thicken and acquire a depth that was more than the sum of the notes. It was as if he'd parted a curtain and was allowed a glimpse of something intricate and inexplicable.

The moments were brief, yes, but he realized that they were making music together.

When they came to the end of the piece, they lowered their violins and Momo felt the dampness in his armpits from having concentrated so hard.

Around them, the wheat field was green and rippled with waves, an ocean where an ocean shouldn't have been.

An assertive breeze now reached them from somewhere beyond the field and ruffled the tree canopy above them. As if answering that susurration, Dawn held up a finger to tell him to wait, then bent down to bring her ear next to the bust of Beethoven.

"Teacher Beethoven said that wasn't bad," she told him, straightening up. "But you need to slouch less this time, and listen more carefully to our balance."

Momo stuck his tongue out at Dawn to acknowledge his failings. When the breeze swept over him, he felt as if his whole body was looking for a reason to spring into action.

As they forged on with the next section, Momo was more relaxed and rode with the melody as it was passed back and forth between the two violins. It felt, for the first time, like a real conversation.

Just then a more forceful gust of wind knocked their makeshift music stand to the ground. A knot on the twine loosened, and the sheets of music were swept up into the air.

Dawn yelped. In the time she was putting down her violin, Momo launched himself into the field, chasing after the airborne pages. For a second, he felt like a boy again, sprinting barefoot on the dirt paths next to Trout River.

Dawn ran into the field too, her long braids bouncing behind her. Momo managed to grab two sheets, but the last sheet was whisked higher and out of reach, as if it was a secret communiqué intended for the gods.

Momo had to gasp for air when his burst of energy ran out. He crouched down with his arms braced against his knees, cursing between breaths, his heart pounding. From the corner of his eye, he saw Dawn walking toward him. He didn't realize how fast he had been running: he was all the way across the field.

She laughed and sometimes doubled over as she made her erratic way toward him. He heard her shout something about a kangaroo.

"What?"

"Because of the way you were—leaping and punching the air," she said as she got closer, in between spasms of mirth.

She said other things too, but Momo had trouble catching it all. She was a sight against the undulating field of green, her braids draped over her shoulders, her upturned face lit by the noonday sun.

⚮

Years later, when he remembered this period of his life, Momo felt a pang. What he could recall wasn't a single thing he could put a name to, but more like shards of a mirror, each sharp but also gleaming, containing many reflections yet nothing in its entirety. Whatever else he felt about his younger self, he envied this self for his certainty—for having had no doubt about what was right, and what was right for him.

Among the gleaming shards, he could see that dissent was lurking between them from the start. He could sense the seeds of discord in how the two of them talked about music, even that time they went to the home of a friend—Teacher Zhou—who owned a gramophone. He had a rare recording of the Gadfly Violin Concerto, written based on the revolutionary novel and commissioned for a Czech violinist. When they listened with their chins resting on their hands, Momo felt he was being hurled around an orbit he could not control.

Momo said: "I hear advancing troops and the tide of pines. I think the composer has an upbeat outlook on the momentum of history."

Dawn said: "Whatever the name of the piece, at the end of the day music doesn't represent anything but itself."

He said: "Humans love music because we love pattern recognition. Given the chaos of the stars in the night sky, we mark out constellations called Grand Duke of Jiang Goes Fishing."

She said: "There are patterns, harmonies borne out by mathematics—yes to all that. But there are also the inklings of all the emotions we've never felt, and those we haven't dared to feel and might one day discover. In this way, music is also prophetic."

He wasn't willing to go that far. In physics, there were always boundary conditions, and you could understand a great deal about a problem by thinking of its two extremes. Music, it seemed to him, lacked such boundaries. One could go on and on in any one direction without ever coming back. It had a quality about it that resembled opium, the substance that nearly crippled China in the dusky years of decadence and excess.

He remembered her failed audition, the fact it had been her attitude and not her skill that hindered her. He asked her what kept her playing music. She said, after a long pause, "I can't bear to be alive without it. Because I *like* it."

She *liked* it.

There was something in this answer that troubled Momo.

He played the violin—he was sure—to bring music to the proletariat, to whom he could not remain debt free.

Beethoven from Beijing

ON AN EARLY-SUMMER DAY IN 1965, MOMO RETURNED TO HIS dormitory before lunch to find Old Li sitting on his wooden bench and smoking as he usually did, but the way he was looking askance at Momo from across the entranceway told him that he'd been waiting for him for some time.

Li stood up as Momo approached. "When it came to keeping curfew, I gave you slack," he began, shaking a finger at Momo as he did last time, "but now you really need to watch it with your *comportment*."

The word had a specific meaning and association, one Momo did not like.

"What do you mean by that?" he asked, more loudly than he liked, knowing that even this retort made him sound guilty. He tried to run through his mind all the possible transgressions he could have committed as of late, but he hadn't even been staying up past curfew to read.

"A *female* classmate came here to find you," Old Li said, looking at Momo in a way that rankled him further, "right up here, to the door of the male dormitory. A disgrace. I sent her away of course, but you need to submit to some serious self-criticism!"

Momo wolfed down his lunch and walked briskly to the building across from the mulberry tree. He found Dawn already sitting on the steps.

"I got carried away with a bit of news," she said by way of an apology, "and thought that you might be around outside."

"That Old Li—he—well," Momo said, looking at his feet and hoping that she wouldn't notice his blush. "But what is this about?" He had been annoyed at her rashness, but it was difficult to accuse her of that now.

"Remember Ivan Padushka, the Czech violinist? He's making an impromptu visit to Beijing."

Momo searched his memory for the violinist's name.

"The Gadfly Concerto? On Teacher Zhou's record?" Dawn reminded him.

That at last jolted Momo out of the awkwardness. He remembered the name now, and with it came the sonic memory of that scratchy record, on which something crystalline nonetheless came through.

"And," she continued without taking a breath, "I can get tickets to his open rehearsal, which will be just as good as the actual concert."

Momo was at a loss for words at first. "So we'll be able to catch this before we disband from Beijing," he said finally.

Disbanding—breaking up some kind of unit—was something everyone in their graduating class was thinking about, now that they had been assigned to their first jobs. Dawn was going to a factory in Baoding in adjacent Hebei Province, and Momo to a chemical plant in Silver Gourd Mountain, in the northeast. When he thought about the fact that their student days were numbered, he pictured himself at a desk in that northeastern factory and setting down Dawn's name neatly at the top of a sheet of letter stationery ("It's been a while since I last wrote"), and, in a corner of his mind more prone to sentiment than he'd like to admit, imagined filling that blank sheet with an inner world he'd never before entrusted to another person.

When the day of Padushka's rehearsal came, they took a long bicycle ride into the city center where the conservatory was.

Though they arrived early, the auditorium was already filled to the rafters with people young and old. The air had a palpable weight and thickness, from the June heat and all the bodies gathered in one place. Despite this, the audience was serene and calm. People fanned themselves with whatever they had on hand, but they waited without agitation and without speaking to each other, as if the performance had already begun.

Momo had never seen so many string players arrayed on one stage, a forest of bows in the air. Dawn pointed out each of the orchestra sections to him, and even though he understood how they functioned, the sheer scale of the ensemble amazed him. When Padushka walked onto the stage, he shook hands with the Chinese conductor and pulled him in for a hug, as if they had once been playmates as children. Applause rose up from around them, first a little tentatively, then with conviction.

The house lights dimmed and darkness fell around them. The timpani ushered in a series of notes, quiet but insistent. Then the woodwinds answered, and before long, Padushka lifted his bow and played his first note.

Momo knew this was what people called it—to "come in with his solo"—but what really happened was that a world of black and white, perfectly pleasant for the time being, became suddenly and irreversibly infused with color.

This was the concerto that had made Padushka famous. At first Momo admired the soloist's fluid movements in his wrist and elbow, the purity and heft of his tone, the way the galloping double-stops were balanced, as if he had all the time in the world to calibrate each note separately, then piled them up and sped up the whole thing tenfold. But all of a sudden—it was as if he stepped across some invisible membrane—he was inside that music. The rhythm of his breathing changed. He no longer thought about tone or bowing technique or even the violin. Momo was simply there, floating along a current but with the utmost clarity, moving with no effort whatsoever.

⚘

It was during the cadenza of the Gadfly Violin Concerto that Dawn felt Momo reach for her hand—or maybe he was reaching for the armrest between them to steady himself. In any case, her hand was already there, because she too needed something to steady herself, and so his hand now rested on hers, and they both held on for as long as the music made everything else trivial by comparison, even this touching of hands. After the final note died down, everyone in the auditorium breathed out and leaped to their feet, and Dawn and Momo had to retrieve their hands to clap. She clapped until her palms felt red and raw, and it was all she could do to keep herself from shouting.

After the rehearsal, because everyone seemed reluctant to leave, Padushka spoke to the audience in Russian, ad hoc fashion, through an interpreter they found at the last minute, who seemed discomfited by the task at hand.

The interpreter now stood next to Padushka and mumbled on his behalf, "My life is heavy—uh—and the notes necessarily undertake it."

It was likely that most of the audience didn't understand what this meant. They clapped regardless, still riding on the crest of a wave of enthusiasm generated from the first note of the performance.

But Dawn reconstructed the violinist's words through the botched translation job, separated the noise from the signal, and restored it to the impossible-to-ignore original.

Padushka had said: "When I play, I put the weight of my entire life into each note."

Dawn reached for these words in her head. *Entire life.*

And like a child who tried to comprehend objects of unfamiliar scale by putting them in relation to her own height and arm span, Dawn tried to counterpoise music with the prospect of her own working life ahead of her.

Onstage, persuaded by the audience's continued fervor, Padushka was now giving an impromptu master class of sorts.

"You can't play it like this," he said, then bowed one phrase from a well-known solo piece with exaggerated limpness. The orchestra laughed, and the audience followed suit.

Padushka waited for the laughter to die down. "You can't play it like that, because every note must be given its own life—"

He now sang out the notes as he demonstrated and swung his whole body like a pendulum to drive home the point: "Like this— pa pom pom pom pom pom!"

The audience burst into applause for the umpteenth time.

⚘

The two of them pedaled back to campus in silence, taking turns passing each other but never too far apart. When they reached campus, they dismounted and pushed their bicycles through the gate, the photogenic one with volutes.

The campus was poorly lit, but she knew that they were passing a pond, and that within its perimeter, lotus leaves and possibly furled blossoms were swaying, hidden in the darkness.

As they walked along, bicycle chains clicking, Momo carried within him a small field of illumination, a kind of electrified impatience. He was impatient for time to pass, so that in his life, there would be less yearning and more having, less becoming and more being.

They slowed down at the spot where their paths diverged,

one to his dormitory and one to hers. There were still forty-five minutes left before the curfew. Neither of them was in a hurry to move on. Now that it was so close to their graduation, Dawn didn't know how the two of them would eventually say good-bye, whether a door might be left ajar for something in the future. She was sure that neither of them wanted the door swung open, because they were not operating at the same frequency and didn't quite achieve resonance. At least not yet.

"I'd like to remember this evening, " she said, "exactly like this."

"So would I," he said. He felt in his chest that now-familiar itch.

"If you're serious, then—" She held out her hand to him at eye level, and it was her pinky that was extended toward him. "We must solemnly swear it."

"Swear to?"

"That no matter what we do and where we go in the future, we will take the feeling of this evening with us."

He took his hand out of his pocket and locked his pinky with hers. There was just barely enough light to see her face at this distance.

"I swear I will remember this," he now told her, "even when my teeth start falling out."

They tugged their entwined pinkies back and forth between them. This was the second time that evening they touched, and they did so now as children going through the ritual of oath.

For a moment, anything seemed possible between them.

When they took back their hands, there was a brief silence as they both tried to decide what to say next.

Her heart was aflutter over what she was about to confide. "Who knows," she began, "I might become a musician too."

The words hung suspended between them for a moment. "But you are playing music already," he said.

"I mean to plunge into it like it's the ocean," she said. She winced as she said this because it sounded quite alien, these words, but there was also no hiding her pleasure. She hadn't dared to tell this to anyone, not even her grandfather.

"But as an architect," Momo blurted out, "you can create things of importance." He thought about men in ages past who went mad just composing (his mind conjured up the bust of Beethoven), or performers who blithely followed the composer's map into madness. By now Momo knew enough about some of the more famous cases to say so.

"When I write music, I also make something, from inside myself," she said. She could already feel something slipping away from between them, something she knew she would miss.

"I come from a village where they still cook by burning cow dung," he said, "so I know that music doesn't feed people, not even for a Beethoven from Beijing."

That should have been the first cue for her to bow out of this while she still could, more or less graciously, but she could not stop arguing her case. "Music isn't useless—well, it's not for any of us to *use*, not like a screwdriver or a sickle," she said. "I mean, you heard the cadenza tonight too. Didn't it make you feel like waking from a dream?"

Yes, the cadenza, Momo thought. The orchestra had fallen silent around the virtuoso, and the rest of the world did too. Inside the invisible membrane Momo had stepped across, Padushka played for him alone, and Momo could see that the way the violinist gave himself over to the music left nothing in reserve. The incandescent cocoon of music was pure rapture, and it said to him: *Stay*. It was a powerful beckoning, to be held in thrall, to be consumed, annihilated even. Momo knew he had to make a decision, because if that happened, even every once in a while, he would forget himself and wouldn't be able to do what meant most to him: to offer up his service to people ready to slaughter their donkey to send off a university student from their village. It was at that moment that he reached for the armrest—something solid and outside the cocoon—in order to ground himself, so that he could remain free.

"For me, music inspires me to be a better engineer," he now said. "This, for me, is the state of being awake."

Dawn inhaled sharply. "Say what you will about your ambitions and the proletariat," she said, "but in the end you are just *afraid*."

"Afraid of what? " He wanted to tell her that she was about to derail her life for a hobby, when they were all on the cusp of making history in ways large and small. He now needed a word with sufficient gravity to convey what he needed to win this argument. "For you to say this, it's just so—"

"So what?"

"So *bourgeois*," he said.

He immediately saw, on her face, the effect of that word as it landed. At first it was a transient look of incomprehension, as if she could not recognize the word as issuing from his mouth. Then he saw hurt ripple across her face, but it was only the briefest flash of vulnerability, as her features immediately began to reconfigure into something more determined.

"Well, then," she said, already turning away from him, "that's exactly what I am."

Keeping her head lowered, she began pushing her bicycle away. He thought about chasing after her, thought about replacing that word with a more diplomatic substitute, but couldn't see how to apologize when he wasn't in the least wrong. He remembered, now, the way her slender wrist lay warmly beneath his hand when he had reached for the armrest during the concert, as if she wanted to shield him from the cold metal surface. He could have retracted his hand, but did not.

When her back receded into the darkness and he could see nothing more, he walked toward his dormitory through a campus that was again strung up with red banners.

BE NOT AFRAID TO CONFRONT ADVERSITY, one of the banners read. BE NOT AFRAID TO MAINTAIN A CLEAR POLITICAL STANCE, read another. BE NOT AFRAID TO CULTIVATE THE MOST BARREN OF LAND.

❦

When Momo left Beijing for his job in Silver Gourd Mountain, those who came to see him off, like the meteorologist and the oceanographer, clasped his shoulders so tightly that it hurt. It was as if his friends were trying to imprint a part of themselves onto him. They were saying good-bye not only to each other but to a youthful part of themselves they felt they had to relinquish in order to become men in full.

Even as he bade his close friends farewell, his eyes darted from one face to another among the crowd on the platform, the same way he had been shuttling back and forth between the mulberry tree and the abandoned building every day for the past few weeks, looking for Dawn. At first he did so nonchalantly, checking each place only once. But as their days on campus dwindled, his shuttling became more frantic, and he'd dash to the mulberry tree again and again, thinking she could have passed by outside while he was in the building. Dawn never showed up.

He didn't stop scanning the crowd until his train began to pull away from the station. With the first lurch of the train, it occurred to him for the first time that he might never see her again.

Years later, when he had his American visa in hand and as he hunted for the child-sized violin he would use to teach Junie scales before leaving China, Momo imagined how he'd tell her about the woman who once taught him how to play, the one who had braids that bounced up and down as she chased sheets of music among an ocean of wheat; a woman with whom he had shared an oath; a woman who was now middle-aged like himself and someone, he imagined, Junie would never meet.

He would tuck the violin under Junie's chin, position her hand on the fingerboard, and press her tiny fingers down on the string. And he would explain.

"She taught me the essentials of music," he would say to Junie, "but at that time the notes I played didn't have any weight to them. Because I didn't have you yet."

Insubordination

WHEN THE CULTURAL REVOLUTION BEGAN IN 1966, ITS ULTImate goal was a moving target always at the end of Chairman Mao's outstretched index finger. Young people converged from the outer provinces in every direction, having boarded trains now free for the taking, so that even the bathrooms were crammed full of riders, ready to spill their blood for the Revolution. When they talked among themselves about this fact, they sometimes burst into tears of passion.

Classes were canceled, and young people slept on the floor of the university gymnasium. In the classrooms, chalk dust ceased to collect in the gutters of blackboards. The regular kind of dust, though, slowly descended onto the desks and chairs, and settled. Sometimes the floor became spattered with blood belonging to members of the intelligentsia during what people called "struggle sessions," when an audience always packed the room. The chosen targets, bent over and sometimes with their heads shaved, submitted to denouncements: "counterrevolutionary," "former prostitute," "American spy." The most common weapons against these political enemies were fists, bricks, and spit—and, of course, words. Large placards hung from their necks, and on them their names were written and crossed out with a large red X.

In time, everything—dust, debris, traces of blood—was swept up by the newest janitors, who just a few months ago had been university professors.

Though Momo was no longer in Beijing to see it, consider what happened to the bust of Beethoven in the building where he and Dawn once practiced. Like the gymnasium, the building had been repurposed. In the winter of 1967, six young people wearing red armbands strode down its hallway, which echoed with their determined footsteps.

Among this group was a seventeen-year-old who carried a drainpipe. He had grown up in the countryside not far from Beijing, and all his life, when he wasn't listening to martial arts sagas spun out by storytellers, he dreamed of being a soldier in the People's Liberation Army.

The curvature of the pipe seemed tailored to his hand, and its heft was just right—slightly heavier than a brick but easier to grip. Of everyone in the group, only he carried hardware, and there was consensus among them that this was right. There was something about the way he walked, the way he always knew how to address the members of the intelligentsia, that made him the acknowledged leader. They called him First Brother.

Another young man of the group spotted the plaster bust at the end of the hallway. He pointed it out to First Brother and waited for him to notice it before they all approached the glass display case.

First Brother did not say anything at first.

"Bei-duo-fen," ventured a young woman in the group, reading the label on the plaster bust.

"The guy even has a perm," offered another young man.

"Disgusting," said a third. "Capitalist garbage like the rest—pollution to the mind of the masses."

"That's right," said First Brother. He did not let on that he could read the first two characters of Beethoven's name, but not the third.

He unlocked the glass display case with a key from a large ring of keys he carried and slid it open. "On behalf of the leadership of Chairman Mao, let me show you the right steps to take next."

He set down his pipe on the floor with a clack. With both hands he lifted the plaster bust from the display shelf. Beethoven's forehead confronted his, and he noticed that some dust had accumulated on the crown. Slowly, he lowered it to the ground and wiped off that dust with his sleeve.

He squatted down to be at eye level with the bust.

"Tanbai cong kuan; kangju cong yan," he said to the bust. Confession will get you leniency; resistance begets more punishment.

The others looked on gamely, almost waiting in earnest for Beethoven to act. First Brother waited a full minute.

"Now, don't say that I didn't give you a chance." He picked up his pipe, stood up, took half a step back, and in one smooth motion brought the pipe down on the crown of Beethoven's head.

Shards of white plaster flew apart, landing around the group. Cheering erupted.

When the detritus settled onto the floor, they saw that the composer's head was no longer there, but there was an oval hole in his neck that once led to a cul-de-sac.

"Now how about that?" First Brother mumbled. "I never would've thought that Bei-what's-his-name was hollow."

⁂

That evening Dawn's grandfather was in bed leaning against a pillow with his eyes closed—but not restfully, for he was constantly fighting back coughing.

"Spend as much time as you have with him," the doctor had told Dawn.

She understood that sometime in the near future, she would become an orphan all over again.

She had brought her violin back here from the factory in Baoding, and earlier in the day she tried to play him something upbeat, but it was a day when not even that could cheer him up.

Then she made the mistake of turning on the radio.

"Our much-revered helmsman Chairman Mao unequivocally
endorses the eradication of all roots of reactionary thinking," the
news reporter announced. Then the report mentioned the name
of someone Dawn recognized, a famous writer based in Beijing,
along with the name of a professor of physics.

"Two more enemies of the masses have terminated themselves
on behalf of the people," the report continued.

They both understood what it meant: *terminate oneself.* The
methods of suicide were as varied as those of public torture en-
acted in struggle sessions. Whenever possible, people chose quiet
and bloodless methods. By hanging. By poison. By drowning (that
was what the famous writer did). The desperate and more impatient among them jumped from buildings.

"Can't blame those two," her grandpa said, his eyes still closed.

She hastily turned the radio off.

"I don't know what this world is coming to," he said, "and it's
not going to affect me much longer—"

Dawn began shaking her head vigorously, but her grandpa put
a hand in the air like a conductor drawing forth a fermata. "I'm
worried about you, still fiddling with music, and all alone in the
world with that temperament of yours."

"This temperament of mine?" Dawn laughed, and was surprised that she still could.

"You always try to fight the prevailing wind," he said, "when
what you have to do is to avoid shipwrecks, to stay whole."

At this point he was interrupted by a loud knock on the door.
They both looked at the clock. Nine in the evening.

"Go see who it is," he said.

Dawn opened the door and saw six Red Guards. The one in front who spoke was a boy barely out of his teens.

"Our records indicate that this is the home of Li Yucong, who taught English and Russian," he said. "Is he at home?"

Without waiting for a response, the group crossed the threshold and poured into the cramped entryway. The ringleader was holding a metal pipe in his right hand, which dangled by his side.

What's this pip-squeak doing with a metal pipe? Dawn thought.

"My grandfather has already retired," she told him. "Plus, he's ill and shouldn't be disturbed."

"We are here to educate," said the ringleader, "not to make trouble. We just need a quick look around."

"To make sure your household is free from the evil influences of the capitalist West," another Red Guard piped up from behind him.

"Get out," Dawn said.

"Now, now," said the ringleader, shaking his head slowly and pointing to his red armband, "I wouldn't talk to us Red Guards with that tone if I were you."

There was the sound of an unsuppressed cough from behind her, and Dawn turned to see Grandpa on his feet, one hand on a cane and another flat against the wall, toddling toward the entryway where everyone stood.

She rushed over to redirect him back toward the bed, but he refused to be budged. He coughed again, this time to get the Red Guards' attention.

"I'm getting on in years and don't know what's up from down," he said, shuffling closer, "but you're referring to foreign books and such things, correct?"

"And anything else that poisons the masses," said the ringleader.

"Well, my granddaughter will bring them out," said Grandpa, and gestured for Dawn to go into the inside room.

"But you gave them all away when you retired from teaching," Dawn said. "Remember?"

"No, we still have some left," Grandpa said. "Go bring them out."

Slowly and deliberately, as if to show both Grandpa and the pip-squeak she was fully in control of herself, Dawn walked toward Grandpa's bookshelf. The six Red Guards followed her.

She didn't need to look at the titles on the shelf to know which ones to take out. As she reached for them, she discreetly nudged a few backward so that they fell into the crevice between the bookshelf and the wall.

She put the small stack on a chair.

The ringleader took a quick survey of the titles.

"Shred them," he said.

Dawn felt a pugnacious anger bubbling up within her, a lightness in her head. It was buoyant with its own energy. She picked up the first book in the pile and, resisting the urge to flip through it to see if there was anything tucked inside (Maybe a letter? An entrance ticket?), ripped it cleanly in half along its binding. What held the paperback together were rusty staples and old glue. It took no effort at all.

The young girl in the group cast a glance at their ringleader, then said to Dawn: "Do you think we are stupid? You need to do it for real."

Dawn picked up the flayed book and began tearing it across the pages so that it couldn't be glued back together. Again the paper surprised her with how easily it came apart along its fibers, and when she got into the momentum of it, something came unbound in her too, and the anger began to seep out and find its target in everything and everyone—her grandfather for making her comply, the ringleader whom she wanted to slap across the face, the female Red Guard who was poking her head into the bathroom. She was angry at the books for being inert and smelling of ink, and, most of all, angry at herself.

With this new energy she picked up the pace, and in no time reduced the books into a pile of paper rubble. She flung it all on the floor. "There," she told them, "no one was going to read these things anyway."

The ringleader waited a moment before turning to Grandpa, who was leaning against the doorframe.

"Now, is this everything, old man?"

Dawn cut in to answer for him: "You can see for yourself. It's all here."

"Wait—" Now the female Red Guard spoke up from the inside room where Grandpa's bed was, her voice shrill with discovery. "There's something else here—Western music."

The group immediately poured into the room. She was pointing to a sheet of music on the bedside stool. Just hours ago, when Dawn had finished playing to cheer him up, she had slid the violin under the bed.

And maybe, just maybe, she thought, *they won't notice.*

The ringleader now pushed past the others to examine the sheet music. Dawn snatched it away from him.

The ringleader turned to Grandpa and spoke calmly and slowly. "We thought you were the fuddy-duddy here," he said, "but it sure seems to be your granddaughter who is politically confused."

He said the words *politically confused* a tad louder, and as he did so, he turned the pipe in his right hand almost imperceptibly.

There was another spasm in Dawn's heart when she heard her grandfather laugh. It was hearty and natural, as if a child had just done something silly and charming in front of him.

"Can't blame her for missing that," he said. "The girl is tone-deaf, to say nothing of reading music."

"You have a musical instrument, then?" said the ringleader. "That's one of the things we need to cleanse."

"Well, it was an old souvenir from the old bourgeois days, just collecting dust here with the rest of my junk." Turning to Dawn, he said, "Take it out."

Dawn did not move.

Grandpa repeated his request.

Dawn looked at Grandpa to see if he was giving her a clue to take out something else instead, something more dispensable.

"Under the bed," he said.

Dawn squatted and reached under the bed. She pretended to grope around, then dragged out the violin case.

"Show them," Grandpa told her.

Dawn pried apart the latches on the case and swung the lid upward. She wondered if, even for a moment, the Red Guards might not be dazzled by it too, by the warm-hued varnish against the purple sheen of the velvet.

She extracted the violin from its nest, lifting it with both hands.

"Look at the dust on that thing," said Grandpa, pointing to the bridge where the four strings were held up and given their tension. "Taking up space."

He was pointing to the rosin dust Dawn produced just a few hours ago when she played for him.

"We can return this to the friend who gave it to us," Dawn volunteered brightly to everyone in the room, "to that Albanian friend who's a Party member?"

The Red Guards exchanged looks of incredulity. "And you want it to continue to spread spiritual venom, is it?"

The ringleader said, "You know what to do."

Dawn stood there. With every passing second, it was clear that she did not know what to do.

Now Grandpa took one step toward Dawn—a step that was tottering but without hesitation. He reached over and grabbed Dawn's hand, which was holding the violin's neck. Gripping both her hand and the instrument's neck, he lifted it up high in the air and hammered it down with all his strength onto the steel bedpost. There was a crunch as the wood in the violin's belly caved in and the neck snapped in half.

Dawn shrieked.

The shock wave of that impact traveled up her arm and torso and settled in her lungs, where it exerted a duller impact but one that was far more lasting. She let go the instant the wood met its fate, but Grandpa was still holding what was left of the violin's neck by the time it was all over. Slackened strings dangled from it.

Now he tossed that stub onto the floor too and grabbed onto the bedpost for balance.

"And that," he said, catching his breath, "that is everything. We have cleansed the evil roots of capitalism from under this roof. We have eradicated sprouts of spiritual pollution."

❧

For a long time that night, after the Red Guards left, Dawn could not look at her grandfather. There was something about the way he chose to let her feel the crunch of the wood in her own hands that made it hard to forgive him, even if he was trying to steer her away from disaster.

And when she cried, hovering over the carcass of the violin, *her* violin, he wouldn't even let her keep a piece of it as a memento. Not even the thin, elegant bridge, which was just a wafer of wood with intricate curlicues cut into it and could have easily fit inside her pocket.

"No," he ordered. "Put this thing into the trash—every piece of it."

"Why?" she said. It felt like another form of self-termination, and an unnecessary one at that.

He was slumped in his bed again. The commotion had taken a toll. "It's in our nature to give things value, and there are times," he said, "when we have to give these things up in order to stay whole, in order to keep going."

Dawn shook her head. She could not at that moment entertain what "keep going" meant.

"They're looking for tangible ways to incriminate. This is the easy part, you see? Now they'll never catch you playing music. Better having this thing broken, than you."

"But why do you call it 'this *thing*'?"

Now he shook his head as if she had uttered something infantile. "Make music if you have to, damn it—you will just have to do it without this thing."

Wisdom Tooth

IN ORDER FOR JUNIE TO EXIST, TWO PEOPLE HAD TO COME TO-
gether during the Cultural Revolution under circumstances that
one of them would later describe as inevitable, and the other, as
coincidental.

Cassia did not believe in coincidences. She had known this already in 1968, eight years before Junie was born, when she was a
nurse in Beijing and an opening came up for a spot in a factory
in Silver Gourd Mountain. She immediately volunteered, and since
nobody wanted to give up a position in Beijing for the remote
northeast, everything proceeded smoothly and she was able to
leave quickly. This perfect match of urgent need and opportunity,
she knew, meant that her mute and feverish invocations had been
answered—by a web of forces she was just beginning to understand.

Of course, there were no names for this kind of cosmic
weather, these invisible nets that entangle and catch. All around
her was the lexicon of revolution, verbs of conviction, targets, and
interventions. People said her generation would be the nuts and
bolts of the glorious socialist Motherland, as if everything was a
tangible assemblage of carefully calibrated matter. But because of
what happened to her the previous year in Beijing, Cassia understood that what set human events in motion were the most ethe-
real of tendrils, a kind of machinery no less powerful for its lack
of discernible shape.

It was only when she searched her memory for things older

folks said that she found expressions that got close to naming these intangible connections, the not-coincidences that she knew had inexorably channeled her life into the direction it was now taking. "Sometimes *zaohua* plays tricks on us," her mother had told her when she was dying, referring to the shapeless Artificer, the forces in the universe that create and transform. This word was so un-Marxist and fatalistic sounding that no one said it out loud anymore. Cassia didn't say it out loud either, but after the leap day in 1968 that changed the course of her life, she began to listen to ways that the universe was telling her things. She knew, of course, that everyone would call this benighted superstition: the vestiges of an antiquated worldview against the clarion calls of Science, a travesty to her solid education. But even unbeknownst to herself, she was cobbling together an improvised architecture of belief, an improvised system for solace, something that would allow her to make sense of things from a month ago, from a year ago, a decade ago, and centuries ago.

When Cassia arrived at Silver Gourd Mountain, the Revolution was sweeping through the northeastern provinces in its own fashion. Of the two white spherical polyethylene tanks in her factory, one was repainted red. When the red paint ran out on the second, a band of young workers suggested that they dye that tank with their own blood. They were dissuaded only when they found out that human blood turned brown after exposure to air.

Cassia, who had seen her share of bloodshed in Beijing, passed these tanks every day commuting from the female workers' dormitory to the factory clinic. And every day for the next five years, she did exactly what she had to do: she filled her hours with a sense of professionalism and duty, and befriended and conversed with those who had sunny dispositions, people who were movers and shakers and not merely dreamers. She even managed to gain back some of the weight she had lost that previous winter, even though the diet here was coarser and apples were the only fruit around.

But all the while, whatever happened, she stayed vigilant to the murmurings of the universe, and understood, in a corner of her being untouched by Science, that they were vital to existence—to *her* existence. And indeed, she was still thinking about these murmurings the day Momo walked into the clinic with a toothache.

⚘

Momo took pride in his robust constitution and the fact that having thrown himself into his job as an engineer, he kept his mind and body in tip-top shape. But it was in 1973, the year after the national ping-pong team traveled to America and back, that Momo's teeth began to torment him. This was something rooted in his makeup—bred in the bone, one might say—because Momo had inherited from his father a set of bad teeth.

The day the back of his mouth began to swell so much that even turning his head took great effort, Momo had no choice but to bicycle through the industrial landscape of Silver Gourd Mountain to the clinic, which had been a stable before the factory was built. He passed the pair of spherical polyethylene tanks, now painted white with red slogans. One of them read: FIRST, DO NOT BE AFRAID OF HARDSHIPS. The other one read: SECOND, DO NOT BE AFRAID TO DIE.

Momo was very much feeling the hardship of his tooth, his jaw, and, indeed, his entire person.

At the clinic, he was greeted by Dr. Fan, who was both the doctor and dentist. They already knew each other from their Marxism study sessions.

Momo pointed to the back of his jaw. Dr. Fan washed his hands in a basin, wiped them off on his coat, which looked more like a butcher's uniform, and pried open Momo's mouth.

Momo winced. Dr. Fan did too.

"I've never seen such severe misalignment," he said, as if he'd stumbled upon a new species of mushrooms in the woods.

Momo waited. Dr. Fan angled his head lower and squinted again into the recess of his mouth.

"Did you know," he said, taking a step back to rummage for something, "that the per capita toothpaste consumption in developed nations is seven tubes per year? In China—in China, it's one tube a year."

Momo tried to think about the numerator and denominator in this aggregate number and many other such numbers that needed to be raised. "It must have been pulled down by the rural population," he managed to say.

"It's a national disgrace," Dr. Fan mumbled. He had found a flashlight and directed its beam inside Momo's mouth.

"You're getting a wisdom tooth," Dr. Fan told him. "Given your misalignment, it's bound to hurt." He elaborated on this oddity of human evolution: how these vestigial molars creep up in people just when they think they are safely out of reach of all growing pains.

"Can you get rid of it?" Momo said.

"We will eradicate it," Dr. Fan said, "like we eradicate counter-revolutionaries against the proletarian people."

The pain from being handled was making Momo drool. This was also when he noticed Dr. Fan had an assistant with him, a woman who looked to be his age. She had on a white surgical mask and was fiddling with the bottles on the counter for minor maladies—alcohol for prepping, and a large bottle of mercuro-chrome for disinfecting cuts.

"We have a bit of anesthesia," Dr. Fan said, "but best if you close your eyes."

The assistant began to put out an enamel tray of tools and a set of pliers.

"Hold him still," Dr. Fan told her.

"Wait," Momo said, without knowing what he'd be waiting for.

Momo tried to look at the single light bulb suspended from the clinic ceiling, thought better of it, closed his eyes for a second, then opened them to take another look at her.

Dr. Fan injected Momo's gums with a syringe. "You're what, about thirty?" he said. "So this wisdom tooth of yours—it's coming in pretty late in life."

Momo was drooling again, his eyes watering.

"But these days you youngsters all want to 'marry later, postpone children,' right? Like our Party says to do? So this tooth is doing the same, you see. A most revolutionary tooth."

Although the assistant was wearing a surgical mask, Momo could tell that she smiled because of the slight narrowing of her eyes, which were lucid and large.

The pliers made sounds of bumping and grating when they went into Momo's mouth. He heard them not with his ears, but from the vibrations in the bones of his skull. Cranial reverberations.

"It's the job of a doctor to gently usher a person across different stages of life," Dr. Fan mumbled as he worked, "from birth, youth, maturity, into old age and, when the time comes, into death, collaborating with the patient's body, his environment, and all the limitations thereof."

Momo couldn't help but make a noise that sounded like "Wwhhrrbb?" What he wanted to convey was: *What a fatalistic thing to say! Doctors ought to save lives!*

"I need the bigger one," Dr. Fan muttered to the assistant under his breath. She did as she was told, then dabbed a towel over Momo's chin.

It was this small gesture of hers—her saving him from drooling when she did not have to—that moved him. He was aware of her fingers on his jaw; they were damp and cool, and surprisingly strong.

"The doctor's job isn't saving lives," Dr. Fan continued, as the pliers disappeared into Momo's mouth again. "This is a common misconception. A doctor in fact acts more like a midwife than a hero."

Momo noticed a lessening of pressure in the young woman's fingers.

"I wish someone had told me this earlier," she said. Her eyes had a different play of light in them, and she was looking at something outside the window. He instantly felt jealousy toward that unseen object, even if it was just a sparrow.

"Keep holding him still," Dr. Fan said, as Momo felt a pressure alarmingly close to pain. "There it is."

The pressure disappeared.

"Wwhhrrbb," he said again. He'd heard Dr. Fan use her name, Cassia, but that didn't dispel the mystery any. He made this noise because he wanted to make her turn toward him, and to ask her a question that currently nobody could answer: "Who *are* you?"

⚬

Cassia was a late child. Growing up in Beijing in the 1950s, she was the only girl in an all-boy household, unexpectedly born to a mother in her early forties, and even her youngest brother was fourteen years older. When she was nine, her brother took her to a temple fair just after the lunar new year, among streets crammed full of vendors of snacks and trinkets. There were acrobats and monkeys, and the snack sellers' operatic calls rose and fell against each other. Cassia should have been happy, but on this outing, her brother refused to carry her on his back, and she had to walk on her own. As they wove through the crowd, even standing on tiptoe, Cassia could see nothing but other people's shoulders. She pouted. She dragged her feet.

To keep her from sulking, her brother said he'd buy her something to eat, and turned away momentarily at a snack stand. What happened next took place in an instant: a middle-aged man swooped in out of nowhere, swept her up onto his arm in one fluid motion, and walked quickly away. By the time her brother turned around, it must have seemed as if she'd vanished into thin air.

There was no time for her to cry out.

"Hey, little girl," the stranger said to her after he carried her off. "How about we enjoy the fair together for a bit?"

There was no smell of alcohol or tobacco on his breath, smells she had come to dislike in men her father's age. Maybe because his face bore no sign of malice, or because she was still annoyed at her brother and wanted to exact a little revenge, or maybe because there were simply too many people and voices to be alarmed by any single person—Cassia was not frightened.

The man walked with nimble strides through the dense crowd; it seemed as if the sea of people parted before them. They whizzed through the best stalls, twirling about this way and that. Cassia got the best views of the acrobats and the monkeys. The man was humming a song the entire time, and she could not help but feel that she was the source of that glee. They passed an old man selling candied hawthorns, and he promptly bought her a skewer. It was a snack no child could resist: bright red berries lined up on a stick, a layer of caramel-colored sugar that glistened like glass. Cassia took it and crunched away the coating. The shards of sugar were still on her tongue when her next bite sank into the fleshy berries themselves, and her face puckered from the tartness.

She lifted her eyes to see him grinning at her.

Before she finished eating, the man bought another skewer, then carried her to an unused opera stage platform, one of the most visible places around. He sat her at the edge of the platform, then handed her the second skewer.

"I'm going to say good-bye now. If you stand on this stage and don't move, your family will come for you in no time," he told her. "Just wait for them to show up. Don't go with anyone you don't know."

"But I don't know you," she pointed out as she chewed.

"I'm different," he said. "The two of us have *yuanfen*."

She had never heard that word before.

"You remind me of my sister forty years ago, you see," he said. "It's uncanny. We both loved going to this kind of thing when we were kids. She must've wanted to keep me company today, and so you showed up."

Cassia turned around to look for the sister he was talking about.

"No, it's not like that," he said, and the brightness went out of his eyes a little.

"Why not?"

"She's been gone since we were kids."

Cassia knew that people said "gone" to mean someone was dead, and that confused her more, but she nodded anyway.

He began to walk away from her, gesturing with his hands to emphasize what he just told her: *Don't move, stay still.*

At first she could still make out his padded hat, but soon he was swallowed by the crowd.

Just as he predicted, her brother spotted her on the platform and made his panicked way toward her, before she even finished the second hawthorn skewer. When he got closer, she saw him wiping his face with his sleeves, as if trying to permanently rub away something from his skin.

Liumang—pervert, degenerate—this was what her family called this man, after she was safely ensconced at home. They asked her if he had tried to take her somewhere, if he did anything to her.

No and no, Cassia replied. She vaguely understood that both "somewhere" and "anything" had unpleasant meanings. Her parents eventually gave up their questions and had no choice but to believe, from their daughter's serenity and evident well-being, that it was someone whose behavior could not be explained by sexual deviance or the trafficking of girls to underworld brothels.

Cassia never mentioned what the stranger said about *yuanfen*, because she knew he meant it to be something good, like a kind of tether, and it didn't belong in the list of sins her family was trying to identify. From time to time, she remembered his mention of his sister. She wanted to ask someone about it: How could a person be gone and keep you company at the same time? She didn't know which adult to ask about this, and thought in any case that they'd probably all say the same thing, that is, he was just a lying, lowly, licentious *liumang*.

But even now, as an adult, after learning about the possible depravity of strangers, after knowing that when *zaohua* wants to toy with you, no one can save you, Cassia still could not get over the giddiness of being a child that day. It was the equivalent of being snatched onto a human merry-go-round, of having the great world spin below her and feeling, ironically, very safe.

❧

After Momo was dispatched from the clinic with a mouthful of cotton wads, he stood outside its door with a head full of questions that could not be quelled.

He pushed his bicycle and walked into the quivering, dazzling sunlight for forty, maybe fifty meters. Then he turned back.

The clinic was unusually quiet that day, and he had the rest of the afternoon off. These two factors, to Momo, were the coincidences that made everything possible.

When Cassia spotted him hovering at the threshold of the clinic, she walked over to him and asked, "Too much bleeding?"

Momo shook his head. The combination of pain's sudden disappearance and its replacement with a numbness, an undesirable emptiness—both were making him oddly confessional, the way he and his buddies became when they had too much sorghum liquor. And yet he was sorely aware of his sobriety.

"What Dr. Fan just said about being a midwife for the stages of life," he began to say to her with his mouth muffled by cotton but enunciating the best he could, "made it sound like—that we have to just brace ourselves for our fate."

"What?" Above the surgical mask, Cassia's brows were knitted in confusion.

Momo patted his pockets for a pen but found none. He glanced at the nearby counter, strewn with odds and ends, and saw a pad of paper there. In a flash of resourcefulness, he grabbed a bottle of mercurochrome, took out its dropper, and began to write with it on the paper pad.

The dropper was not fine-tipped, so he had to write big, and the sentence took up the entire page. He held it up to show her.

It read: "I think we always have control over our destinies."

Cassia unhooked one side of her surgical mask and let it dangle by her other ear, as if this would help her make sense of him. He saw on her face a riddle, and it was more striking to him for what it did not reveal, because he felt that he was on the verge of finding the key. It was as if she had recently arrived in this world, fully formed but foreign, and he—of all people—could be entrusted to make her feel at home here.

I can prove it, Momo wanted to say. *Let me prove it to you.* And it suddenly seemed very important that she understand him.

He reached for the mercurochrome bottle again, but in his haste, he knocked it over, and the red antiseptic spilled onto his hand.

With professional quickness, Cassia reached over, grabbed his hand, and tried to wipe the liquid off with a piece of gauze. Her ministering fingers brought heat to Momo's face.

"Wwwbbr," he managed.

But it was already too late. The liquid stained Momo's hand with an insistent redness and even a hint of shimmer, and it looked as if he had cut a vein open and it was bleeding.

❧

In much of the 1970s, courtships took place without ostentation. This was a time when couples announced their intention to marry by simply going to a movie together, because just being seen together in public was sufficient as a promise, a betrothal.

About half a year after Cassia helped Dr. Fan extract a gnarled and wayward-looking tooth from Momo's mouth, he asked her to go to a movie with him. Unlike that tooth of his, Momo was straightforward and full of good cheer, was never secretive or darkly aspiring. The changes he wanted to bring about in the world were robust, wholesome, and concerned with the collective. He was someone, Cassia felt, on whom the sun would always shine.

If she agreed, their next steps would be to register for a marriage license and apply for a couples' dormitory room. They would write to their respective families and enclose a photo of the two of them taken at a photo studio.

Neither of them was young: she was pushing thirty, and he already past that.

But all the same, Cassia stalled him. She stalled until she could get away discreetly to call on a fortune-teller deep in the countryside. That day, as Cassia politely lifted her foot across the wooden threshold of the fortune-teller's courtyard, the old woman eyed Cassia's neat, nonpeasant clothes and blurted out, "Ah! You're here to see about a *man!*"

The word jarred Cassia's ear, and her face burned. It had been a long time since she heard someone say the word *man* aloud; it was more correct to say "male comrade" or "male classmate." But Cassia nodded anyway.

The old woman ushered her inside her dank house and made the usual inquiries about her birthdate. Cassia did everything she was asked, despite her despair: she had come all this way to ask about a suitable man, but what she really wanted to ask was, *Can a person be gone and keep you company at the same time?*

The old woman looked into Cassia's face after the preliminaries. "Let's see now," she said, lightly gripping Cassia's wrist, as if feeling for her pulse. "There's some unsettled business from the past, and things are far from anchored."

Cassia was so hopeful and agitated at the same time that she could only continue to nod. She had so many questions to ask.

"But he's someone who will go far in the world, so very competent he is."

With a start, Cassia realized that the old woman was talking about Momo.

"I wouldn't cast him about, missus, if I were you," the woman cackled. "His heart is in the right place—that is to say, right in your palm, to do your bidding!"

Cassia composed herself enough to ask, "But what about others? Others I should think about?" She couldn't breathe out of fear that she would disturb the outcome of the soothsaying.

"What's past and gone is never worth holding on to," the old woman went on. "And among us living, good matches don't come around every day, you know."

Cassia glanced around the room, at the soot-covered walls that enclosed them and the greasy small stools they were sitting on, the mouse-friendly nooks and crannies. She saw that her message was clear: go toward the sunshine; take the smoother road.

The old woman's worldview had great resilience. If any Red Guards were to call her out on ideologies or principles, she'd swear up and down it was because she didn't know any better. She would then wait out the political storm, and when it blew over, she would return to her prognosticating. And in this way, the old woman would carry on and live to a ripe old age. She'd survive this revolution, and, after seasons upon seasons of struggle sessions, she would still come out toothlessly grinning.

"I suggest you snatch this man as quickly as you can," the old woman said.

⚭

On the first warm day of 1974, a year after they first met, Momo and Cassia went to the only photography studio in the area to have their portrait taken. The photo was black-and-white and from the chest up. Nonetheless, given the occasion, Cassia wrapped a lemon-yellow nylon scarf around her neck and tied it into a bow. It was a modest adornment, but even that was enough to set her off from the nonbrides wearing mostly shades of blue and gray. All day long, other women smiled at her as they crossed her path, as if a gleam of something was being rubbèd off on them.

The two of them sat on a wooden bench in front of a large canvas backdrop painted with alpine peaks and meadows. They folded their hands in their laps. The photographer leaned out from behind the camera to get them ready.

"This female comrade here," he said to Cassia, "tilt your head to the right—more—more—don't be shy now—you are newly- weds after all!"

When Cassia did as he directed, Momo caught a whiff of her scent, which he could only describe as soft and female. When the camera clicked and Momo's smile was captured, it was this soft scent that he was thinking about.

Outside the studio, Momo pushed his bicycle onto the small, unpaved road that led to their new double room in the couples' dormitory, a privilege for newlyweds. Cassia gave a small run- ning start and hopped on his back seat, sitting sideways. To steady herself, she wrapped her arm around the side of Momo's torso, outside his pocket where their marriage license was tucked. This pleased Momo immensely, not only because of the contact but also because it reminded him of the reality of that document and its official embossed stamp inside. All morning he'd been running his thumb and index finger over its red padded cover still smelling of vinyl.

When they arrived at their room, they saw that their friends had snuck in and decorated it with paper cutouts of the character for double happiness. There were gifts from them too, all of them in pairs. The hot water thermos was the most extravagant. Pro- duced at a time when raw materials were scarce, the outer shell of the thermos was a mesh made from sheets of metal after the shapes of bicycle chains had been cut out of them.

That night, friends and coworkers crowded into their double room and held an impromptu ceremony. They all pitched in with ration coupons to buy food and liquor, and though there wasn't a great variety of either, seeing it all spread out on one table created the illusion of plenitude.

This was as close to a wedding banquet as these things got. A worker nicknamed Stone Egg, known for his gift of the gab, began a rousing speech with, "Let the proletariat people bring on the revolutionariest bride and groom!" The rest of them burst forth with the most jubilant song they knew, beginning with "To Sail the Ocean We Need Our Helmsman," and moved on to other musical tributes to Chairman Mao.

Because no one wanted to leave even after the food was finished, they continued making toasts. Stone Egg stood with a glass held toward Momo. "Brother Mo," he said, "I salute you with—"

Momo stood up too quickly to accept the toast and tottered.

At this point, the light in the room went out. There was a brief silence before someone said to Stone Egg: "Your toast moved heaven and earth, so we have another power outage!"

Laughter erupted around the room. "I'll go grab a candle," Momo announced as he groped for the rim of the table, his head still spinning.

But the light flickered back on again before he took the next step, and Momo saw that during the interval of darkness, Cassia had stood up at the table too. There was a pink tint to her face, and the blush went all the way down her neck and into the opening of her collar. Her eyes met Momo's, and they said, *Let me get this one.*

"Why is it that you all toast him but not me?" she chided Stone

Egg with a festive tone. "Don't they say women shoulder half the sky?"

"Because I am an ill-mannered blockhead, that's why," Stone Egg replied, and immediately reoriented his glass toward her and raised it. An older coworker also piped up: "You have to go easy on Brother Mo," he said to Stone Egg. "This is one night he can't just collapse in a heap."

Laughter again erupted, and the bachelors, who laughed along with the married men, hid their complicated feelings behind their glasses.

∽

After the guests left, Momo and Cassia swept up the discarded shells of sunflower seeds from the floor and cleared away the cups and bowls. Finally there was nothing else to do except to sit together on the edge of their plank bed, which suddenly felt enormous.

Momo scooted closer to her and held out his hand, his heart having multiplied itself, it seemed, and pounding everywhere at once.

"Turn off the light first," she said.

"No," Momo said, suddenly defensive. "I just want to hold your hand for a bit." He knew that in many important ways, they were still strangers to each other.

"Turn it off just this once," she said, then added, almost as if to herself, "I promise: just this once."

Momo didn't know what to do. Cassia stood up to reach the string switch on the wall, but just as she was about to pull it, the light went out again.

Maybe because it was no longer filled with people and noises, the room seemed darker than it had been during the first power outage.

Cassia sat back down on the bed. He could feel her turn toward him.

"We will take this slowly," he said. "We will discover each other."

Cautiously, he reached over to unbutton her blouse, but was surprised to find that she had beaten him to it. Her hands were slow and deliberate in undressing, as if they were thinking. He helped her wiggle free of her sleeves, and she shivered as if she were cold. He lay down with her on the bed and put his chest against hers to warm her with his body. They drew three breaths together this way, and then, it seemed to Momo, a change came over her.

It was as if she somehow drew energy from the dark and blossomed into a person he didn't recognize. She unbuttoned him. Although their limbs were clumsy, blind, and often in each other's way, her movements were guided by a kind of single-minded recklessness that shocked and thrilled him. He buried his face in the base of her neck and took in the scent he had gotten a whiff of earlier.

When he was on the pinnacle of all the exultation in the world, her arms clamped around him as if she was keeping herself from drowning.

Afterward, he noticed her face was wet with tears.

"Did I hurt you?" he asked, sitting up quickly. He couldn't stand the thought that he might've been an unruly and recalcitrant beast and caused her pain.

"It hurt," she said, "but that's not why I'm crying."

He lay back down next to her. He knew there were happy tears, sad tears, and tears too complicated to explain. He assumed that she was feeling the same way he was. He assumed that he had all at once unlocked her happiness and desire—all the sweetness in life that was no longer off-limits to them. He was too distracted by the shifting chords inside him—both major and minor, both swelling and subsiding—to ask her to elaborate.

The outline of her face was beginning to emerge in his field of vision, now that his eyes had adjusted to the dark.

"I hope our child will have your eyes," he said before he drifted off to sleep, not knowing the nature of her tears, and therefore thinking himself brave.

The 29th of February

AS COUNTLESS UNBORN CHILDREN BEFORE HER, JUNIE—OR rather the idea of her—sent her parents headlong into hopefulness.

Of course there were no fetal ultrasounds available in 1975, and so they didn't know her sex yet. She was simply referred to as "the child" in conversation.

"Eat another apple for the child."

"I've already—well, all right."

For all that they didn't know about the child, there was room aplenty for fantasies, projections.

Momo came back to their couples' dormitory room one night and saw Cassia chatting with someone they called Grannie Lu, who was sitting in a chair in the posture of a matriarch. She was giving directions to Cassia as she took steps around the room.

"Be natural in your stride," Grannie Lu said. "There—stop. Now—start."

Cassia did as she was told and looked at Grannie Lu expectantly.

"Left foot too this time. That's two out of three now," she said. "You are very blessed!"

Cassia beamed a smile at them both.

"Left, boy, right, girl," Grannie explained for Momo's benefit. "It's in the way pregnant women walk. These things are very accurate."

Momo tried not to make a face about "these things." He was full of contempt for using superstition to predict the sex of unborn babies. Surely Grannie Lu knew Cassia wanted a boy and was playing into it. She was an avid matchmaker and amateur midwife, and seemed to have an endless amount of time to devote to the mergers and acquisitions of human beings.

"Boy or girl—I have no preference either way," he now said, with as much tact as he could muster.

After Momo first met Cassia in the dentist's office, it was Grannie who told him more about this intriguing young woman. No, she did not have a "prospective," as the word went. And no, she'd never had a boyfriend before as far as anyone could tell. Momo had been grateful to Grannie then for these pieces of intelligence, for giving him courage and ammunition for his next encounter.

He held back the harsher words for after Grannie Lu left—about the sway this woman had over Cassia, who really ought to know better, he emphasized.

"But there are things we have no way of knowing yet with science," Cassia said, "and until we do, what's wrong with investigating other means? Grannie Lu's predictive record is stellar."

"Record?" Momo said. "It's just a coincidence."

"Nothing is a coincidence," Cassia said with conviction. "And science is not the only form of knowledge. You don't want to believe that, but I know."

"How would you know?"

"From . . . life." Cassia's face darkened, and so Momo dropped the topic.

As Cassia and Momo constructed bridges into their imagined future, Junie floated about the aquatic confines of her mother's womb. Before she could breathe on her own, she drew out stories from her parents: they began to reach far back into their own

childhoods and grappled with memories that were barely distin-
guishable from wishes and longings. It was as if only by remembering their own beginnings could they hope to get parenthood
right.

It was during this time of hopefulness and storytelling that
Momo first told Cassia about his boyhood escapades, and in turn
heard about the time Cassia was briefly abducted by a stranger
during a temple festival.

"Did they ever catch this *liumang*?" Momo asked, imagining
Cassia as a small and portable bundle. "If I were your brother I'd
have tracked him down and beaten him to a pulp," he said. The
two of them were lying in bed on a Sunday morning, and he was
cradling Cassia from behind, the only comfortable way to do so in
her current state.

She turned around to look at him. "I've never heard you so hot-
tempered before," she said.

It was true. Momo felt high-strung, as if some kind of sympathetic paternal hormone was coursing through him, making him
ready to pounce against every possible threat. The tumult and
mayhem of the Cultural Revolution had mostly died down these
days. He'd been promoted to full engineer, and his application for
Communist Party membership was recently approved—a heady
milestone by anyone's standard.

And now he was enfolding, in the circumference of his arms,
all that pleased him about his life.

Momo sang to the unborn child. He wanted the child to hear
music, and he had no other instrument but his tenor voice. Sometimes Cassia grew impatient with him because he pressed his face
to her belly and insisted that he finish each song he began. "It's
important for the child to hear the development of a piece," he
told her. Momo had a seemingly inexhaustible repertoire of songs,

many of them Russian, like the love ballads that had been in fashion once but no one sang anymore.

"I wish I had a violin to play for her," he said in between songs.

Enclosed in her small amniotic sea, Junie gradually took on shape: here emerged her ordinary forearms, hands, and fingers; here her eyes and nose began to appear; here were the leg stubs that began but stopped developing and would unleash turmoil into the family in a few months' time. She probably heard the conversation between her parents, heard Momo's singing, and much more. As she approached full term, she may have also registered the new voices of her grandparents, who took a long train ride from Trout River and arrived at the snowy province in the dead of winter.

On New Year's Day 1976, two months before Junie was born, they all crowded around the unseen child in Cassia's belly, adding to the fray with their own stories of childhood. At that point in the year, nobody expected the string of calamities that would soon arrive in succession: the death of Premier Zhou Enlai within the month, followed in July by an enormous earthquake razing the town of Tangshan to the ground, followed in September by the death of Mao himself.

⁂

By the time the infant was bathed, swaddled, and presented, the wing of the delivery room was crackling with the awareness of something out of the ordinary, transmitted through the sotto voce snippets exchanged among nurses as they passed each other in the corridors.

Momo couldn't tell yet if the baby girl had Cassia's eyes, but there was something in her nose that resembled his own. Then the nurse unwrapped the blanket to show him her legs. As if the baby was recoiling from his gaze (which was confused and not affectionate), or simply from feeling the cold air (it was February after all), she began to cry. The outline of her ribs moved in and out, struggling with the new phenomenon of air.

Momo nodded as if he'd been shown a properly signed document, and the nurse covered the baby up.

"Will she—grow up?" Momo asked. His voice was tight, unnatural.

"She is healthy in every other way," the nurse said. "Nothing else is wrong with her."

"But will she . . . develop and become a grown person?"

"Of course."

What Momo had just expressed with his question was a wish—however fleeting—to start over with a different child. In the years to come, there would be long stretches of time when Momo forgot this moment, but he would never completely forgive himself for having asked that question.

He received the bundle from the nurse, who led him back into the delivery room. They told him it was important for the family to help break the news to the mother. Cassia had been injected with a sedative.

When she was shown the baby, first the face, then the body, Cassia asked Momo: "What's the date today?"

"February 29," he told her.

"We already told you this," the nurse said, more to Momo than to the patient.

"Are you sure it's not March 1?" Cassia asked, ignoring the nurse.

Something in this sequence of questions made Momo look over at the nurse, whose eyes said she was concerned for Cassia's state of mind.

"It's March 1, right?" Cassia asked again.

The nurse went over to feel Cassia's forehead. "She needs rest now," she said. "It's better if we let her rest."

Momo told Cassia no, it was a leap year, this being 1976, and at this point she cast a look toward Momo with an intensity he could not explain, and it gave him for the first time a feeling that he had failed at something without even knowing why.

"This was all my fault," she said. "I don't know how to explain it—"

"This is just life's way of testing us," he said.

"What is it supposed to test?" she snapped back. "And why do we of all people need to pass this test?"

After she and the baby were allowed to go home, Cassia drifted in and out of a long, hard fever. She could not breast-feed. Sometimes he changed the damp towel on her forehead and saw that she was wracked by nightmares. It was as if she was taunted by some persistent communiqué from a world that excluded him. She talked in her sleep now, trying in vain to fend off whatever it was in her dreams that made her miserable.

What worried him more than the fever, however, was the way Cassia lay in bed after it broke, when she could have gotten up if she'd wanted to. She was sleeping or not sleeping, but all the same she appeared to be thinking about something that only tangentially concerned him, or maybe not him at all. Sometimes Momo had the feeling that she was talking to someone not in this room and perhaps never would be. Could it have been her parents, both dead before she was twenty? Momo did not know how to ask, not in her current state.

As exhausted as he was, when he was alone with Junie, something different happened to him. He gradually began to find the words to placate himself, began to form notions about where to go from here. When he changed her diapers, when he fed her the bottle, and when he put her down to sleep, he could not avoid touching Junie's truncated legs. He held her stumps in his hand, and caressed and kneaded them between his fingers. It was then that his optimism, having buckled momentarily, returned like a tentative animal after the footfalls of a predator had just passed. He was surprised to discover how silky smooth the skin was, how soft and perfectly formed and brand new. Junie was already learning to flex her new body, already learning to smile appreciatively upward at the person—him—who had set her life into motion.

He found himself trying to anticipate her next move, her next expression, but always ended up surprised.

If it weren't for the rest of us, it suddenly dawned on Momo, all her life she'd never know anything was missing.

Orphans

IN SPRING 1976, THE SAME YEAR JUNIE WAS BORN, IN A SMALL town in the province surrounding Beijing, Dawn was approaching the last stage of courtship with someone whose land-tilling family was waiting to meet her. She was thirty-four, close to spinsterhood, even by the standards of the "Marry Later, Postpone Children" campaign. But Iron Monkey—his nickname because he was lean and dark—didn't seem to mind, and neither was he in a hurry. When he asked her questions about herself, he waited for the answer as if he could extricate one by one all the precious jewels buried in her past.

It was cleanup day in the textile factory where they worked, to celebrate Labor Day on May 1. Both of them had been sweeping and sweating. Sitting next to him on the building steps, Dawn noticed the deep bronze of his arms, a color that hadn't faded even though he was a cadre and no longer worked in the field. She always had the desire to touch those arms, to access that warm vigor, and even imagined them wrapped around her.

The first question he asked her today was, "Do you have any hobbies?"

Dawn froze, because it had been years since someone had asked her that question.

After the Red Guards had raided her grandfather's home, he told Dawn, "If you can't do what you love, then you must occupy yourself with something else—anything—in the meantime, because otherwise you'd become bitter and brittle, easy to break."

It was the closest he came to apologizing for what happened to her violin.

She had been doing everything else in the meantime: not playing, not composing. *Like a hedgehog that cannot unfurl itself, much less waltz*, she thought. But on this first day of May, the breeze was warm, and sitting next to Iron Monkey, Dawn felt more reckless than she had in a long time. So she said in a nonchalant voice that she liked music.

His thick eyebrows rose up, as if it was the first time in the history of the world that someone admitted this. Then, holding out his hands in front of him in a gesture for her to wait, he stood up, cleared his throat, and belted out the opening line of one of the eight model operas. These were sets of state-sanctioned melodies and choreography, a stable repertoire entrusted with carrying the message of the Revolution. On the best of days, these melodies were tedious earworms for Dawn. On the worst of days, she wondered if she'd ever be able to conjure up in her head her favorite musical passages, to say nothing of creating music.

Iron Monkey finished singing and looked at Dawn as if to say, *We can share this hobby of yours; we can enjoy this together.*

"That's it," she said, "though I also like other kinds of music too." She felt her heart clench a bit as she said this.

"What other kinds?" he asked.

She saw that he didn't know. How could he have known? There were no recordings to be heard, of course; they'd been smashed or, like the gramophone of her family friend Teacher Zhou, hidden away in root cellars so irretrievably that they became indistinguishable from the earth.

She jumped back on her feet with her broom so that she could face him with good cheer. "Sing another one," she said. "You have a good voice."

This was no lie; his voice was a clear, resonant bass. He had a perfect memory for lyrics but not the melody. In fact, Iron Monkey was tone-deaf. But she wanted to prolong his singing, if only for his enthusiasm and for the fact that his voice radiated the same vigor as he had in his slightly damp torso. She tried to focus on what was good and wholesome in his rendition, rather than what she was missing.

She had vowed to speak less after her grandfather died, because she knew she couldn't count on herself to say the right things, and because she knew that her ambition was the wrong tonality and color for the world. But the problem with speaking less was that she was forced to listen. At first she tried to fend off the ubiquitous strains of the model operas by rehearsing in her head musical compositions she loved. When no one was around, she hummed passages of the Gadfly Violin Concerto to herself. She hummed out separately the part for solo violin, then each of the string sections, and so on and so forth, to prove to herself that she could still remember the architectonics of music. But over the years, the model operas whittled away her memory, and she gave up on the mental rehearsals. Instead, her ear became attuned to a narrower spectrum of sounds: human voices from neighbors and colleagues, sometimes tentative, sometimes strident; gossip that led to conjectures, which became accusations and verdicts over time; information that could be bartered for favors, exemptions, tokens of power. To catch these pieces of intelligence, you had to calibrate your ear to pick up all manner of speaking, not just whispers but also the silences between words, which carried the most important meaning of all.

That was what Dawn thought about on winter evenings when she could watch the sky darken during the course of a meal, when she didn't see how life could change for her in this most important regard. It wasn't simply music that she craved, but the ability to generate something new, the way our bodies continuously shed old cells and replace them with new ones, because that was what it meant to be alive.

Marrying him would be one way life could change, Dawn thought. They could start a new life, even if the music in that life were model operas sung out of tune. And now, because she could see that he was trying to please her with his singing, she had never felt so grateful and forlorn at the same time.

⚘

At the end of July, Iron Monkey brought Dawn to his natal village to meet his family. They rode the last stretch of the trip on a donkey-drawn cart. He seemed to know by heart every ditch, every orchard, every stone in his village, and told her about them as they moved along: here's where he was attacked by a belligerent goose when he was three; here's where he got that scar on his temple, from a firecracker that exploded too close; here's where he tossed the first tooth he lost into a pond.

There are people who wear their childhood like a favorite coat, and Iron Monkey was one of them. In this way, he moved easily and gracefully in and out of his childhood, connected visibly and cheerfully to his past and his future.

But Dawn could not think about her own childhood without feeling a jagged and protracted mourning for the life she was unable to live. Her grandfather had told her to be patient, to bide her time and wait out the storm until she could return to music, but there still seemed to be no end to the waiting. So what if that day never came, and "in the meantime" was the rest of her life?

As she passed these places of significance, she repeated to herself, "Here's the pond of lost tooth." Then she tried out some imagined scenarios on herself. Large locust tree outside courtyard house: here's where Iron Monkey comes back with new bride to visit on lunar new year. Here's where his not-so-new bride brings their baby to show the family.

I'm worried about you being alone in the world with that temperament of yours, her grandfather had said.

The end for her grandfather, nine years ago, came without fanfare. That night she sang him Puccini, close to his ear. *O mio babbino caro*. She fell asleep sitting on a stool next to his bed, leaning against his banyan-like hands at the bedside. When she woke up again, his hand was turning cold against her forehead.

At least he could feel my skin all the way until the last moment, she thought in order to comfort herself. *At least he had that.*

It took her weeks to sort through his possessions—the piles of newspaper, the boxes of things that even she couldn't decide were trash or not. And when at last she left the empty apartment behind in Beijing, she could not help but feel like a small child who had been abandoned.

⚘

When they met her, Iron Monkey's mother and aunt gripped Dawn's hand with theirs and called her the "unfortunate child," because he had told them about her lack of parents.

"From now on all our kinfolk will be yours too," his mother told Dawn, and gestured to the uncles and cousins in the room. Iron Monkey smiled shyly but wholesomely from the sidelines. His cousins and brothers were dark and sinewy just like him, and yet he shone in their midst.

His mother, still gripping Dawn's hand, cried out to the rest of them, "Her wrist is so skinny. Look! It'd break in two if she tilled the field!"

There was some giggling among the women. The young men

in the room snuck sidelong glances toward her direction, but looked away quickly.

Iron Monkey piped up, "Look—there are different kinds of labor, and they're all equally glorious."

Dawn suddenly understood how he was able to become a Party member and rise through the factory's ranks so quickly: he never thought what he offered others was of limited supply and had to be rationed. His own peasant pedigree was unassailable, and he knew that by marrying into his family, she'd be elevated from the class of intelligentsia suspected of unsavory, unrevolutionary activities. He knew all this and still chose to believe that she was bestowing on him the gift of herself.

His aunt and mother seemed to be suddenly talking all at once, and faster than Dawn could follow. Near the wooden bench where she sat in the front hall of their home, a yellow dog crouched on the ground near her feet. As the chitchat resumed, the dog raised its head as if it got a whiff of something of interest and looked squarely at her. Among the chatter, she and the dog exchanged a pointed look that took her entirely out of herself.

She remembered thinking at that moment: *I cannot follow through with this.*

If she couldn't have music that was new and alive, then to stay unmarried was the only way she could still keep some element of the undetermined in her life.

The conclusion was so self-evident that she knew it couldn't be unthought. She also thought: *I will have to wait until we're back in town to tell him; it will not do to embarrass him in front of his family.* Then she thought, *After this, there will be no more prospects for me.*

It wasn't even as if she was holding out for something better. It was simply because she couldn't see beyond it: this day, and the one after, and the one after that.

꘎

They stayed overnight in the village. Dawn shared an earthen platform bed with Iron Monkey's aunt, and he slept with his youngest brother in a room across the courtyard.

Less than an hour after sundown, the lights were out in all the rooms of the family courtyard. Dawn lay awake inside the mosquito tent and heard his aunt snoring beside her. She felt a kind of lightness at the decision she had made earlier in the day, but was also wistful about the fact she'd never be cradled in Iron Monkey's lean and powerful arms, never be able to bury her face in his chest. Holding hands was as far as they had gotten, except one evening when she gave him a peck on the cheek as they parted. She ran away before she saw his reaction, and they never mentioned it afterward.

The July heat was oppressive. She managed to drift off for a while, and when she woke up again, she was lucid and restless. She slipped out of the mosquito net, skulked her way across the courtyard, and moved as quietly as possible toward the front gate of their house.

Before she could open the gate, she was startled to hear Iron Monkey whisper her name from behind.

"I can't sleep either," he said. "Let's go for a walk."

"How did you know I was here?" She was relieved more than anything that it was him instead of anyone else.

"I can see everything from my brother's window," he said, and eased the gate shut behind them. "Let's go somewhere breezier."

He took her hand in his, and it felt good there. She let him take her away from the village houses and toward the fields. They did not speak until he stopped at a patch of crops where there was a small opening.

"Here," he pointed to the opening.

It was a moment before she understood what he wanted, or what he thought they both wanted. The summer night was dense around them, and conspiratorial.

Her instinct was to say no, but it would've meant explaining why she couldn't marry him, and she didn't know how to do that yet.

Before he pressed his mouth against hers so tightly that it hurt, he muttered, "I will be good to you, I swear."

She was surprised by the jolt of electricity that swept through the lower half of her body. She breathed in the smell of sweat on him, which she'd always liked. She managed to push his mouth away long enough to say, "You have already been good to me."

And he had. Then the thought passed through her: If she wasn't going to marry him, then why not give herself to him, just this one night? And if she was going to be a spinster anyway, why not find out what this was like, once and for all?

He caressed her breasts and ribs awkwardly, as if he was mapping her shape and reprimanding her at the same time. But he knew just the right amount of weight to press down on her body. And if there had been some dread as she braced herself to be entered, he bit her neck at the exact moment so that she was distracted by the mingling of pain and pleasure.

She remembered seeing the night clouds part a little, revealing a fierce patch of stars. But she saw nothing in the sky of the ominous cloud shapes others said, later, presaged what was about to happen.

⚓

They'd been lying next to each other in the field for some time when the ambient noise of summer insects suddenly fell silent without any prior disturbance or footfall. The silence was so eerily complete that Dawn felt a chill. She reached over and grabbed Iron Monkey's shoulder.

Then she felt the tremors in the ground: muscular, undeniable, like the earth was intent on dusting off hangers-on from its surface. They looked at each other for an instant, before Iron Monkey leaped up and struggled to get on his feet. Tottering, he began running toward his house. Not knowing what else to do, Dawn followed.

Dogs had begun to whine and bark around the village. By the time they reached the family courtyard, everyone was awake. There was talk of this being a cursed year of the dragon. One piece of the mud wall in his parents' room fell onto the bed. They braced themselves for worse tremors, but nothing came.

Even amid all the commotion, nobody missed the fact that Iron Monkey and Dawn were missing from their respective beds that night. After the sun came up, Dawn noticed that the family looked at her differently. In their minds, the two of them had consummated their marriage, pure and simple, and the rest—like registering for a marriage license and applying for couples' housing—were details to be dispatched.

She was no longer someone to be wooed, but was now a given in their growing family. When Iron Monkey's father saw that the pigpen had a collapsed wall, he told his son that they might as well build a new addition to the house. "So that you two can use it when you come back from town," he explained. Female cousins Dawn hadn't seen before also appeared and fussed over her. They took measurements of her hips, her chest, her arms, and though she knew they were making clothes for her, she couldn't help but think they were also calculating the number of sons she could bring into the family.

To back out now would be to humiliate not only Iron Monkey but his whole clan.

❧

The full scale of what happened in the wee hours of July 28, 1976, emerged slowly in the next few days. The earthquake's epicenter lay under Tangshan, less than two hundred kilometers from Beijing, and it leveled the town in just thirty seconds. Out of the 300,000 people who died that day, some of them never woke up from sleep. Even in Dawn's own factory, three people died from the accidental fallout of the tremors: two from a collapsed balcony; a driver of an overnight truck veered off the road and overturned in a deep ravine.

The more Dawn understood what was happening at the epicenter while she and Iron Monkey lay in the crop field, the more she understood that her own recklessness had locked her into a life she had just decided to renounce. She didn't believe in omens, but it was hard to deny that, whether through omen or coincidence, she had been caught. She had thought that she could design her future the way an architect carefully plotted blueprints, when in fact the best she could do was to improvise each step.

At the end of August, Dawn and Iron Monkey went to receive their marriage license. On the photo taken of the two of them together, her face said that she was grateful given how things turned out. She was alive, while countless others in Tangshan were being dug out of the rubble—many of them in pieces—and cremated in a hurry.

Being alive and whole, after all, was what her grandfather wanted for her when he smashed her violin.

Later, when Dawn and Iron Monkey made love on the bed of their newly allocated couples' housing, she relished not only her aliveness but also her wholeness. She was glad of the still-new sensation of him on top of her, and even if she was not exactly young, her body was young enough for all they needed.

∾

That summer, thousands of children became orphans overnight in Tangshan. Of those, the children who were of school age were rounded up to be resettled in other cities, in an effort to keep them away from outbreaks of cholera and from piles of building rubble that seemed to house the wailing of ghosts. Some of them were sent to Tianjin and Beijing. Others were sent to places farther south, and trains full of orphans began to trundle through Dawn's city, Baoding, en route to Henan. Their route had a long layover in the station overnight, and the town recruited people to help keep up the orphans' spirits as they waited to board their connecting train.

Dawn volunteered at once. Someone from the factory who'd recently retired from the arts troupe had taught her a few songs on an accordion, and so she went to the station with his old accordion, intent on cheering up the children.

As the train from Tangshan pulled into the station around midnight, schoolchildren from ages seven to fifteen spilled out onto the station platform. They were dressed in clean, neat clothes and wore the red scarves of the Young Pioneers around their necks. Dawn noticed that one boy was wearing an adult-sized watch. It hung loose around his wrist like some misshapen bangle, the watch face having slid to the inside of his wrist. She knew it could only have belonged to the boy's father and was most likely taken from the father's body among the rubble.

Dawn's own parents hadn't seen death coming, and now she wondered what anguish had wracked the parents of these children in their last moments. She had feared seeing the orphans' faces in tears, but now that they were here, they were more impassive than frightened. Dawn sat on a folding canvas chair and found that the weight of the accordion in her lap anchored her somewhat. She played "East Is Red," and when she tried to get everyone to sing, the young ones gamely followed.

As she finished, Dawn lowered her head over the accordion to think of the next song to play. As she did so, a small girl from the group ran up to her and put her hand on Dawn's arm.

"Don't cry, teacher," the girl said, in a voice that was as steadfast as it was melodious.

Dawn looked up in astonishment. "But I'm not—" she began to say, then stopped. The girl was already highly skilled at comforting others, even preemptively. In a world where nothing was left standing, every gesture that involved turning the face away was interpreted as grief.

⚜

When a small group of these orphans settled into Baoding, Dawn volunteered to give them music lessons at their elementary school. She played every tune she knew on the accordion; she didn't avoid the model operas, arias from revolutionary ballets, and of course the standard schoolroom choral pieces. She played one song after another because she couldn't answer the questions some of the children asked her during breaks in between the songs, like why it was that the "army uncles" wouldn't let one boy see his father under the white sheet when they took him away.

After she ran out of songs, she began to improvise. She took one of the themes from *Scheherazade* and embedded it in a singable choral frame. She would have given anything to be able to hear the leitmotif as the undulating, tender violin solo it was meant to be, but if that wasn't possible, then she would do what she could. What she played on the accordion was a pastiche, true, and maybe even a touch ridiculous, but Dawn thought that if she couldn't have this music for herself, why not offer it to these children?

To her surprise, her improvised songs became an attraction at the school. Maybe it was the newness of the sound or the insouciance and energy of her playing. Children who weren't orphans came to sing too, along with other teachers. At first Dawn thought the teachers were going to demand that she return to a traditional repertoire, but instead they asked her for more, and sometimes they asked for the same improvised song two or three times.

She saw on the children's faces that while she played, they were able to forget themselves. They could flee from their landlocked memories and take refuge (whether they knew it or not) in the cadence of an enchantress recounting a sea voyage. She was surprised that she was the one to make this happen, after years of having been the opposite of a kindling.

A few days later as she played, two men who were obviously Party cadres came and stood at the outer edge of the circle of singers and listeners. Their postures spoke of their self-awareness that they could change lives with words of reprimand or approbation. One of them smoked purposefully as Dawn guided the young chorus through a second round of a song loosely based on the theme of the "Sea and Sinbad's Ship" in *Scheherazade*.

After the session ended, the older cadre put out his cigarette and came up to praise her for her selfless work.

"It seems to me that you must've had some professional musical training," he said.

Dawn paused a moment before answering, and in that moment, she thought again about the wrong tonality and color of her ambitions.

"No professional training," she said. "But when I was much younger, I dabbled in some classical music."

"We will surely keep this in mind," the cadre said.

This was just a week before September 9, 1976, when all music fell silent to show respect for the death of Mao Zedong.

Other Forms of Locomotion

IN 1978, JUNIE TURNED TWO. THIS WAS THE AGE WHEN OTHER children were running about and falling down. For Junie, this was the age when she discovered being taller than anyone else when she sat astride Momo's neck, her hands drumming the top of his head to make him speed up, or pulling on his ears to make him slow down. Junie's pant legs hung down along Momo's shoulders, and he gripped the ends of her legs, as if his hands had become their extensions.

When Momo took her to the zoo, Junie watched the animals as if she was on a stakeout, and they never got through more than three or four animals during each trip. She liked every creature: the ostrich, the forlorn-looking polar bear, the Siberian tiger. She looked at their every move. She looked at them even when they didn't make a move. Once they came to the paddock enclosing one of the most popular animals in the zoo, a species nicknamed "Quadruple Not-Look-Alike." The placard said that its formal name was *Elaphurus davidianus* or Père David's deer, and that the animal had the hooves of a cow, the neck of a camel, the antlers of a deer, and the tail of a donkey, but was none of those things. Momo wended his way through layers of parents and children waiting to see it.

"See? It's just like us." Momo turned his head around. "We are using two heads, four arms, and two legs."

"We are Quadruple Not-Look-Alike!" Junie squealed.

Shaking his shoulders up and down, Momo began a gallop, which made Junie squeal more.

To show Junie other forms of locomotion, Momo took her skating on a pond that stayed frozen throughout the winter. On her third birthday, there was no February 29 that year, so they went on February 28. Momo was a good skater (he'd learned on the frozen pond near the university), and with Junie on his shoulders, he glided around the empty white arena, twirling when he was able and yelping along with her when he was going very fast, until her cheeks were ruddy from the cold and exertion.

In the distance, he could see a chimney from their factory emitting a hazy column of smoke in the winter light.

"What do you call that color?" Junie asked him.

The color wanted to be apricot, blue, silver, and every shade in between.

"I don't have a name for it," he said. "But I think it's telling us that the sun is going down, and Mom is waiting for us to have noodles."

"I don't want the day to end," Junie said.

"Next year for your birthday we will do something just as amazing," he said, gliding to the edge of the pond to take off his skates.

But he forgot that Junie didn't understand yet what "next year" meant. As he lowered her from his shoulder and she began to kick her legs in protest, Momo tucked her under his left arm. This was his preferred mode for getting around more quickly, with or without her consent.

She opened her mouth; a whimper was lodged in her tiny throat, and it would be only a matter of seconds before it exploded into a full-on scream.

"Be careful!" Momo said in a suddenly conspiratorial, hushed voice. "Keep your mouth open!"

Junie froze, a little confused by the turn of events.

He reached his hand into her mouth and mimed pulling something out. He held the invisible thing at arm's length and high in the air, as if it was clawing at him.

Junie's mouth stayed open, but she didn't make any sound and her eyes were wide.

"That was very close," Momo said. "You almost got attacked by the hideous I-Don't-Want-to-Leave Monster. What should I do with it?"

"Toss it away!" she said after a brief ponder.

Grunting, Momo hurled the invisible monster away with both of his arms, then followed its trajectory to the far edge of the horizon.

"Is it really gone?" Junie asked, when Momo began dusting off his hands.

"Probably," he said. "But we have to get home pretty fast so it won't catch up with us."

Having just made a life-and-death decision, Junie did not protest. Momo put her on the back seat of his bicycle and began pedaling. "Going home," he chanted to her in a lilting voice, as if he were one of those itinerant vendors hawking kids' favorite hawthorn skewers.

The cloud behind them gave off a deeper glow now. Whatever that unnamable shade was, it inched closer to the color of dusk. Momo felt fatigue in his shins. He breathed in the winter air and could feel Junie's small arms around him. It was as if they had both become part of winter itself.

A Glass Heart

On a bright day in August 1979, twenty-seven delegates from Beijing disembarked from their plane and passed en masse toward the customs gate in San Francisco. Although there was no explicit order for them to form a line, they stood close to one another as if cordoned off from their surroundings. Before they left China, they had been briefed on Western manners and cultural taboos and how to use a fork and knife. Now, standing in the terminal's corridors, they marveled at the way their footsteps were muffled by the carpet, something none of them had experienced before, yet no one said a word. They were representatives of the Chinese nation and its arts, here to "exchange experiences" with musicians in America, and they were careful not to let on how material comforts like carpeting impressed them.

Dawn was among these delegates, shivering in the ambient chill of the San Francisco summer. What brought her here was a series of happenstances. She happened to have been playing an upbeat tune to earthquake orphans in 1976 when the two cadres in charge of cultural activities stopped by the school in Baoding. A year later, in the new atmosphere of reversal and renewal after the Cultural Revolution, when a classical music ensemble had a violinist brought down by hepatitis, one of those cadres, who also knew Iron Monkey, happened to remember Dawn's musical training. Because of the cadre's clout, her factory gave her leave for rehearsals and for the trip. And now she was abroad, part of a delegation that would perform in three American cities.

Walking among the other delegates, out in the absurdly hilly streets of San Francisco, she expected Americans to stare at them the same way she herself stared at the foreigners who had trickled into China over the past three years since Mao's death. But the Americans who crossed their paths nodded politely and moved on. It was still Dawn who stared: at their clothes with almost careless swaths of color, at the levity of their hair, and at the prospect of their unknown lives.

Dawn probably would have continued in this state of bemusement if it weren't for what happened the following afternoon. They were all crossing a downtown intersection at the base of a hill. A traffic light and crosswalk were placed there to keep cars from coasting down the steep slope. The placement didn't make sense: too much faith was given to brakes to counteract gravity. As Dawn and the others made their way through the intersection, a cable car sped down the slope toward them and there was so much momentum in that gliding that it seemed improbable that it could stop. The green light was theirs, so everyone continued walking ahead, and it was only Dawn who happened to look to her left and see the cable car bearing down on her.

She stood frozen in the intersection.

Back in China, even in the days when people jumped from open windows and tall buildings, the thought of her own death, however probable, had remained an abstraction. But the approaching cable car felt both tangible and powerful as something that could eradicate and destroy. And at that moment, on the crosswalk in a foreign city, it seemed to her that it was only her mortality that stood between her and what she could—or might—become.

The cable car stopped at the intersection. There was no sign of alarm from anyone. Her fellow delegates had already reached the other side of the intersection when they saw that Dawn hadn't followed. The group's interpreter had to go back and fetch her by the elbow, gently but firmly, from the middle of the intersection. They all teased her afterward, trying to hide their discomfort at seeing one of their own behave like a country bumpkin. The group leader said to her in a more relaxed moment, "Let's not give Americans reasons to laugh at us, because we are here representing our Motherland, after all."

Dawn nodded but was too distracted by a question to be embarrassed just then.

The question was: Just what *could* she become?

⚜

Later that same August, outside a Victorian house on a hillside neighborhood frequently shrouded in fog, a cellist named Edmund Hsu parked his car in the driveway and retrieved his cello case from the back of his station wagon. At the door, he hummed a passage from the symphony he just rehearsed with the Golden Gate Conservatory Orchestra.

As he inserted his key into the lock, he heard a rustling behind the bayberry shrub to the left of his door. A figure slid out from behind the shrub and intercepted him.

He jumped.

"I'm sorry to startle you," said the figure, a woman who spoke in Mandarin.

He recognized her. They had met two weeks ago when a mainland Chinese arts delegation arrived to perform. She was a first violinist, he remembered. When they played, he could see that her performance style, like that of everyone else in the group, had something drone-like about it that made him uneasy. Was he stereotyping them, he wondered, by attributing that rigidity to communism? The two of them hadn't talked. During one of the breaks in their program, he now remembered, she'd spoken to their conductor through an interpreter, in a way that was animated and determined.

She had no luggage with her, her clothes seemed colorless and misshapen, and she looked both weary and cold. She said she was here to ask him for a favor.

"I thought you were going to—" Edmund began, then stopped short. Having grown up in San Francisco as a second-generation Chinese American, he didn't know how to say "mug me" in Mandarin.

⚶

In Edmund's living room, Dawn surveyed the objects he'd amassed in his life as a touring musician: a beer stein from Germany; a cheerful but principled tile from Spain. From where they were sitting on the sofa, she could glimpse a pewter-colored body of water that was the ocean.

"So let me get this straight," he began in accented Mandarin. "The rest of the delegation—"

"Are on the flight back to Beijing," Dawn nodded. "Unless they missed the flight to look for me, but that's unlikely."

Edmund nodded and rubbed his hands together.

"I'm just a cellist," he said.

"I thought you would understand," she said, "because your parents must have fled China before Mao came to power."

This was a shot in the dark—a conjecture based solely on his apparent age. Edmund was slightly older than she was, but his face, although Chinese in every feature, had a smoothness about it that came from not having frowned much in his life.

To her surprise, Edmund didn't contradict her.

"Then you must have some idea"—Dawn touched his arm lightly—"why I want to stay."

"What you're doing is difficult even for famous artists," he said, "like Baryshnikov."

Dawn nodded. Neither of them had to use the word *defection*.

"And of course you know that if you have family," he continued, as if there was still time for her to go back on a plane and apologize, "they will pay a price."

A shaft of pain pierced her when she thought about Iron Monkey, who had insisted on seeing her off at the airport. It would have been kinder if she'd simply refused to marry him after the earthquake. In the last two years, despite the fact that she had started taking fertility-enhancing herbs as he urged her to do, each month she'd been secretly relieved when she found out she wasn't pregnant after all. This was another sign—she could see now—that she had continued to betray him in small and invisible ways.

And yet. She had spent the last umpteen years in a state of camouflage, waiting sheepishly for something to change on its own.

She pushed forward. "I'll wash dishes in a restaurant or clean the bathrooms in the conservatory," she told Edmund, "if you introduce me to the right people—that's all I ask."

"But you picked me—for some reason."

That she did. When members of the conservatory and the delegation went out to dinner, there was no moment for private conversation, of course. But amid the dinner chatter, when someone was talking about the San Francisco climate and the conversation drifted to home gardens, it had been Edmund, a proud amateur botanist, who described the plantings in the front yard of his house, along with its rough distance from the conservatory and the color of the garage door. Dawn had committed each detail to memory.

But she did not tell him this.

"I just felt certain you would understand," she said again.

Edmund continued rubbing his hands together. Dawn thought he probably wished there was something to fidget with, like a cello bow. Then the idea came to her.

"Let me show you something," she said, reaching into her pocket. The night before, she had put all her indispensable possessions on her person and into various pockets, so that at the right moment before their departure, she could leave her luggage in the van, then tell the others she had to go to the bathroom.

Now she took out one of these items—a thin piece of wood—and handed it to him.

Edmund rolled it slightly between his thumb and index finger and looked at it as only a string player could—with recognition for its function and appreciation for its artistry.

It was the bridge of a violin, the thing that gave tension to the strings, and which transferred their vibrations to the instrument's acoustic center, its resonance chamber.

"This violin seems to have some age on it," he said. "Was it yours?"

"The violin is gone. The Red Guards smashed it during the Cultural Revolution," she told him.

The story had to be simplified, she thought, for the sake of delivering the right message.

When she later thought about the violin splintering apart in her hands, when the ebony of the fingerboard was sundered from the front and ribs, she realized it'd been the first time she truly understood its architecture. From among the carcass of the instrument, she spotted the otherwise hidden sound post inside the instrument's belly, now laid bare; she felt the futile resistance of the quarter-cut maple wood that had once been glued together, with surgical precision, to make up each half of the violin's back.

"My grandfather wouldn't let me keep this last bit of it," she continued. "He didn't want me to get in trouble. But I fished it out of the trash and managed to hide it. I've kept it with me everywhere—for thirteen years now."

Edmund ran his fingers over the hollowed-out spaces of the bridge. At its base, there was a pair of apertures known as the kidneys, and above them, a void that resembled the shape of a heart.

For Dawn, the bridge had long ceased to be a structural component of an instrument and had become something known to her through its tactile texture inside her pocket. On its top edge, the curve was punctuated by four shallow notches where the strings once sat. Dawn spent many hours running the pad of her thumb across the notches and, imagining it was each of the open strings she caressed, heard each note resonate in her mind's ear as she did so. This was the first time since the house raid that Dawn had let anyone see the bridge, much less touch it.

"You've thought about doing this for a long time?" he asked.

"It's hard to explain," Dawn said.

⚜

Edmund offered Dawn his bedroom, but she insisted on sleeping on his living room sofa. To keep her warm in the autumn days, he lent her his UC Berkeley sweatshirt, which hung on her body loosely and made her feel like the preliberation street orphans depicted in comic books from her youth. During the day when he was out for rehearsals, she filled the birdfeeder in his backyard, washed dishes, and sampled his album collection, which ranged from Puccini to a band named Flame Nectarine.

From his living room, she watched the same wedge of ocean

change color throughout the day. Sometimes it turned the shade of blue she thought oceans were supposed to be; other times it took on the color of a bruise.

On the third day, when Edmund came back from rehearsal, she told him, "I think disco can be full of life."

Edmund laughed. "I think you just passed the entrance exam to America."

He played for her a new song, and lip-synched to it. Its effervescent lead-up to the vocals made her feel like she was being tickled on the inside of her skull.

"What do the lyrics say?" she asked him.

"A love with a glass heart," he told her.

She tried to imagine what that meant. That its conscience was unblemished?

"In America," he said, "it's the rockers who are proud to be outcasts."

"In China," she said, "to be shunned, you just have to mention you want to be Beethoven from Beijing."

On the sixth day, he came back with a borrowed violin so she could better pass the time during the day, and told her that one of his lawyer friends might know someone who could help her apply for asylum. Over the tomato and egg noodle she made for dinner, he described the work of American composers who looked to Zen Buddhism and the *Book of Changes* for inspiration. She was incredulous at first, then had so many questions that her own noodles turned cold by the time she was done asking them.

On the seventh day, she tried twice to write a letter to Iron Monkey, but gave up after only a paragraph, then sobbed on the sofa with her head buried in her hands. She did not know what her heart was made of: stone or glass.

On the eighth day, in the middle of the night, she tiptoed into

Edmund's bedroom and startled him a second time by slipping into his bed. She did it out of loneliness, yes, out of gratitude, yes, but more than anything else out of a sense of desperation, as when in the process of improvisation, a person suddenly finds herself out of ideas and must do something—anything—rather than nothing.

Edmund did not turn her away, as she feared he would. For this she was more grateful than for all the other things he'd already done. Perhaps he was lonely too. It was comforting to feel his arms and torso enfold her, the way his sweatshirt had done during the day. There was a civility to his lovemaking—less insistence, more waiting—that Dawn associated, rightly or wrongly, with the magnanimity and ease of being American. And afterward he held her in his arms briefly, something Iron Monkey never did, though Dawn knew it was not out of indifference.

Looking up at the ceiling, she thought about how one composer described music: a purposeless play.

Sleeping with Edmund was also her way of preventing herself from turning back to Iron Monkey, to betray him to a point beyond any hope for forgiveness, to cut herself off from that life of vacillation between determination one minute and losing her nerve the next. It was to make sure that, despite not being able to see beyond her next step, she would put one foot in front of another, then another, however tottering, however diffident, however unbearable.

Patient Seventeen

IN THE SAME YEAR THAT DAWN LANDED IN AMERICA, JUNIE WAS three and a half and Momo had his first nightmare about her:

The icy pond they'd been skating on melts without warning. The two of them are dropped into frigid water. Junie is only a few meters away from him, splashing. Momo wants to grab her, but he is tangled up in weeds and only his arms can move.

He yells at her to kick toward him as hard as she can.

"But I don't have feet." She points to where her legs end.

Momo watches as the pond yawns and stretches itself into a lagoon, then a lake. An iceberg drifts by. Then another.

Momo shouts and repeats his order for her to come closer, to kick her legs, all the while knowing that he is not addressing the problem.

Junie has other ideas. She ducks under the surface of the water and disappears for a moment. Then the current lifts her back up— but also away from him. He sees her stumps catch a glint of sunlight, before her small torso begins to recede into a vastness that is the color of shadow on snow.

Momo's eyes opened, and he breathed out. As soon as the room came into focus, he reached over to touch Junie nestled between him and Cassia. Her forehead was hot.

⚬

It was Momo's turn to take Junie to the children's hospital. He cradled her uncharacteristically placid body in the crowded waiting room and wondered what engine inside a child could generate so much heat.

As Momo and Junie were waiting to be seen, a father came in with a girl who was wailing so hard that even Junie, in her feverish state, looked over in sympathy. The girl seemed to be about five—just a bit older than Junie. She was clutching her ankle. Her father also clasped her ankle with one of his hands and was holding her with his other arm. People in the waiting room gave them a wide berth.

In a place like this, parents felt solidarity, but also took part in a self-juried competition called Who's Got It Worse? In just one or two glances, they sized up each other's misery in terms of degrees, durations, and intervention required.

"Her ankle got caught in your bicycle spokes?" one of the mothers asked. It was only at a certain age when a child's legs were long enough for this to happen.

"I'm worried that the bone is broken," the father said. They had been on the way to the zoo because it was his day off, the girl's father added, but now the day was ruined.

"Happened to my son once," said another parent, nodding. "Fortunately it was winter and he had thick socks on." Everyone was talking at once. The girl's wailing showed no sign of stopping.

Because of the commotion, the other father didn't notice Junie—not at first. But the human eye, it seems, is wired to eventually notice things out of the ordinary even amid chaos in a hospital. The father saw Junie, did a double-take, and asked Momo, "What happened to her?"

"High fever," Momo said coolly, pretending not to understand.

"No, I mean her legs," the man was forced to say.

Momo said nothing in response.

"You know that when you have a handicapped child, you can petition to have a second one, right?" the other father said. "It's a straightforward process."

Momo cast an icy glance at him.

Then the man added, "It will balance your family life, to have an able-bodied child."

Something boiled forth in Momo, and he wasn't able to control it: "Each of our children has faults—some we can see, some we can't. Who's to say that your kid won't grow up to be dimwitted, or turn into an ingrate or lout?"

Yes, he uttered those exact words: *ingrate or lout.*

The other father's face took on a genuine look of shock, as if a potted plant he was tending to on the windowsill suddenly leaped up and bit his nose.

Momo continued to glare at the man until he looked away.

For the next hour as he waited, he repeated in his mind the conversation he'd just had and imagined simply punching the other father in the face.

Over the next few weeks, a displaced anger periodically revisited Momo. *An able-bodied child.* Momo pictured a grown-up Junie in a wheelchair or with clunky wooden rods attached to her knees. This made him cringe. Momo had studied Russian in his university days, but now he started spending his spare time improving his English. He knew there were people who studied in America, got degrees, and then brought their whole family over.

After a few weeks, however, he began to allow himself to hope: What were wheelchairs and wooden legs but primitive machines? And who was to say how they would evolve in a few years' time? In a nation with higher per capita toothpaste consumption?

In his mind's eye, there was a great stage reserved for his

daughter. On it she would do something spectacular—he wasn't sure yet what exactly—and be the kind of performer who would stop people in their tracks.

⚘

There were nights when Momo could imagine Junie growing imperceptibly as she slept between him and Cassia. A new tooth sprouted today; another tenth of a millimeter added to her bones tomorrow. Neither of the adults would notice it, he thought, as the space between them widened cell by cell.

On days when Momo began to think that he and Cassia had made love for the last time, he missed the woman who held him on their wedding night, quivering in the dark. But it was more than that. Ever since the birth of Junie, there was sometimes a look of desolation that came over Cassia when she thought she was alone.

The few times they did make love, it was Cassia who insisted that they keep the light on.

"I have to see you," she said, when he worried about waking up Junie with the light on.

"Why? To make sure you have the right man?" he joked, and thought she'd laugh with him, but to his surprise, she froze.

"Let's have another child," she said, and to his surprise, she began sobbing. "Let's start over."

"She's not a mistake," he said. "Everyone treats her like she's a mistake."

"Who's going to take care of the three of us when we get old?"

"That's not a good reason to have another child."

"But the question still stands."

That presentiment of loss was the one major difference between the two of them, he thought. It was not in Cassia's character to stare down the gun barrel of fate and resolutely push it aside. Not that they were exactly young; even Momo conceded that.

Soon after, Cassia filled out an application to have a second child on the grounds that Junie was "severely handicapped" and—they were told to add this—showed "possible signs of arrested development." This lie, written in ink, distressed Momo more than anything else.

On the day their petition was approved, Cassia stir-fried some cabbage with more oil than usual.

"This is to celebrate," Cassia said when they sat down to dinner.

"Celebrate what?" Junie chimed in.

"Yes," Momo said to Cassia. "You need good nutrition."

"Don't I need good nutrition too?" Junie asked.

"Both of you do," he said, and felt the sting of guilt as he pinched Junie's cheek. He thought about that other father who'd told him he had to provide "balance" to their family life.

For over a week, Momo avoided Cassia at bedtime. At first he could find some pretext—needing to stay up to finish reading a document or because Junie had a cold that needed both of them to tend to. But by the following week, Momo knew that he was running out of excuses. He was being called upon. He took off his glasses, undressed for the night, and managed it. Or more accurately: they managed it—ingloriously, clumsily, under the fluorescent light from the ceiling, and with no pretense of this being anything other than a necessity.

Not that any of it mattered by the time Cassia's belly swelled up again.

In February 1981, with the baby kicking inside her, Cassia told Junie, "On your next birthday, you'll have a little brother or sister to celebrate with you."

"Why does everyone say 'brother or sister'?" Junie asked. "I know it's a brother!"

"How do you know that?" Momo asked.

"I just know," Junie said, as if it was the most ridiculous question.

Momo cocked his head at Junie, and his expression was full of amusement and affection. Cassia could tell that he did not believe Junie. But she did, and it pleased her.

Fortified by the thought that it now mattered less, Cassia considered telling Momo about the events of that leap day in 1968. She could begin, *There's something I never told you that happened before we met.*

Later that night, after they turned off the light, Cassia asked Momo what had been the most terrible thing he saw during the Cultural Revolution.

"It was during my first trip back to Beijing since starting this job," he said. "I hadn't met you yet."

"Yes," Cassia said, hopeful. She would listen to his story, and then tell him hers.

"I had to take care of some business for the factory," Momo continued, "and happened to pass Dongdan, where they lined up someone against a wall—someone I knew."

"From your university?" she said.

"A family friend connected to the classmate who taught me the violin," he said. "We called him Teacher Zhou, and we went to his house once to listen to his gramophone."

Cassia had heard about this classmate before, but not the family friend.

"They had him blindfolded and facing a wall," Momo told her. "They loaded a pistol, made sure he heard it. They told him to say his last words."

Cassia stiffened. "You watched this?"

"There was a small crowd. I squeezed into the front. I couldn't help him, and I couldn't walk away."

"So you saw him die."

"They pressed the pistol against his temple and pulled the trigger. But it only fired a blank."

Cassia sighed. This tactic was not unheard of, she knew.

"After that, they let him get up and go home, but you could smell it—he soiled himself. I found myself thinking it would have been kinder if they shot him."

When Cassia's hand touched his arm, Momo was shaking. She instantly regretted bringing this up. She had no words to comfort him, and what could they do about this, after all these years?

"I couldn't walk away," he repeated.

She considered again beginning with these words: *There's something important that happened before we met.*

But after what he'd told her, it now seemed as if she was one-upping him, as if this were an obscene contest to prove who had suffered more.

We will take this slowly—he had said to her on their wedding night—*we will discover each other.*

But once more, the words that needed to be strung together were there, yet, lacking buoyancy, failed to rise to her throat.

⁂

The room they put Cassia in was at the end of a long hallway in the maternity ward. A double door stood in between, and Momo pressed his ear against it for any possible noise—the groan of an adult, the cry of an infant. He heard nothing. Having left Junie at home with her grandparents who had come to help out, he arrived after pedaling his bicycle on what seemed to be an interminable street lit by sodium-yellow lamps.

He collapsed on a hallway bench and wiped the sweat off his brow. When did he become middle-aged? At thirty-seven, he was still fit, but his stamina was not what it used to be.

A nurse was walking toward him in the corridor, and he walked briskly to intercept her.

"Comrade," he said to her, "I just need to ask you one thing."

She begrudgingly stopped and raised an eyebrow.

"My wife—patient 17—this is her second time, and she . . . ."

She explained something to him about inducing labor and waiting, but Momo was so agitated by what he was about to ask that he couldn't fully make out what she was saying.

"I must know," he forged on. "If there is a chance, boy or girl, that this second child is—" and found himself unable to finish the question.

"It's too early to say," the nurse said. "The best way to help is to not burden our medical team. We're already understaffed as it is."

Momo watched her walk away, then returned to the bench and steadied his head with his hands. He made silent promises to himself. He would start over with this new life and new baby. He would hold Cassia's hand on Sunday walks (she would be embarrassed at first) and talk about current events, like they used to during their courtship. Maybe even music. He made a solemn promise to Junie that he would not let this new baby change his feelings about her.

He didn't know if he'd dozed off on the bench, only that after some time, the double doors opened, and he heard the sound of purposeful footsteps. Momo propped himself up from the bench and fumbled to put on his glasses.

Daylight was seeping into the corridor. A nurse was walking toward him in the hallway, and the way she was walking said that she had something important to tell him. He felt the pull of a future that now stretched out in front of him, and he could no more steer himself away from it than the earth could alter its orbit around the sun.

He searched her face for clues, but it was impassive, blank.

"You're the relation of patient 17, correct?" she asked him.

"I am, I am." Momo stood up straight, and for what seemed like the first time in his life, braced himself for his fate.

PART II

Deer Meat for the Soul

WHEN MOMO LEFT SILVER GOURD MOUNTAIN AND LANDED IN the small airport in the middle of the vast American plains in 1981, he was surprised to find that in Chimney Bluffs, there were no skyscrapers and neon signs. Instead, here the vast sky mirrored the land. Even with some one-story buildings clustered downtown, it resembled Inner Mongolia more than it did the capitalist nation he had imagined. This disappointed Momo more than he had expected. After all, he should have been grateful: college towns like this sprang into existence out of sheer optimism, and it didn't need the prospect of gold buried underfoot or nearby ports to launch oceangoing ships.

The first month after his arrival was filled with orientations and disorientation. On the university's campus, among impractically green lawns decorated by giant bronze paper clips that he learned were outdoor art, Momo sat down and met his PhD advisor in the engineering department and followed the program for International Student Day. September was hot and humid that year, and he learned to drink glasses of water with ice cubes floating in them.

The frozen cubes clattered around his lips as he raised the glass, and he felt momentary concern for his constitution. *Americans want everything ice cold*, he thought, *because they don't consider their blood as needing help with circulation*.

On a Sunday morning in his first semester, when he was walking on the side of a road without sidewalks, a gruff-looking American man, approaching in a pickup truck that reminded Momo of a tractor, slowed down and veered close to the curb to talk to him through the passenger window.

"Are you trying to get to that church?" The man pointed to one just down the street. His truck inched along on the road to keep pace with Momo.

"No, the university," Momo said, shaking his head. "I'm Chinese."

"So that explains why you're going to the university on a Sunday?"

"That explains no church."

The man narrowed his eyes to a sliver and leaned closer to the passenger window. "Say . . . you're not one of them damn *communists*, are you?"

Momo froze. There couldn't have been a way for the university to find out he'd been a member of the Party, he thought—not unless someone had tipped them off, and possibly not without cooperation from his former work unit in Silver Gourd Mountain. This was his first semester, and already the bounty hunter had caught up to him.

He stared at the man, and his mind churned with strategies and consequences. He could flat-out deny it—with dozens of Chinese students already in his department, couldn't mistakes be made? But when he opened his mouth to respond, what came out was a knee-jerk phrase he had learned from a cassette.

"I beg your pardon?"

The driver let out a belly laugh, as if he just heard the best punch line. It'd be another moment before Momo could be convinced of the sincerity—and levity—of that laugh.

"I'll give you a ride to campus," said the man, who introduced himself as Larry Winkler. "I work in the Physical Sciences building, myself. Occupational Safety."

This was how he began carpooling with Larry to campus on weekdays. Many of the Chinese students bought jalopies and drove themselves, but riding with Larry was so easy that Momo stopped considering that option altogether. On weekends, they shopped for groceries together at the local Hinkley Dinkley. Larry's pickup smelled of mud and tar. Occasionally it also hauled a dead deer, which Larry had shot with his rifle.

"Ever taste deer meat?" he asked Momo.

"No, but in Chinese medicine, the meat is special," he told Larry, "because it's good for, you know, the male thing."

"You've got to be kidding me," Larry guffawed.

From that point on, small packages of paper-wrapped venison found their way to Momo's freezer.

On the Saturday following Momo's first Thanksgiving, Larry accompanied Momo to Hunan Park, a restaurant that employed grumpy Chinese waiters who were also getting degrees at the university. On the menu were broccoli beef, moo goo gai pan, and canary-yellow egg drop soup, small incursions into the American diet made by generations of earlier immigrants.

Momo palpated his lacquer-shiny chicken slices with his chopsticks. This was the only place to get stir-fried or braised food if you did not want to cook it yourself, but now he was thinking that perhaps he should.

He noticed Larry looking at him.

"What?"

"During the winter," Larry said, "you're gonna need a hobby."

Momo thought about the frozen lake in Silver Gourd Mountain where he skated with Junie.

"I have plenty of research to do," he said. "And in a couple of years my wife and daughter will join me here."

"That's all well and good, but it's not what I'm talking about."

Larry shook his head, as if Momo had deliberately misunderstood him. "You need things to get your blood pumping when the winter gets here." He put a closed fist against his chest and thumped it rhythmically.

Maybe I was wrong about Americans and ice cubes, Momo thought.

Larry leaned in with his elbows on the table. "I'm talking about deer meat for the soul," he said.

⚬

Momo's first letters to Cassia and to his parents were cheerful and full of detail and local color, but increasingly, he began letters that he didn't know how to finish. His enthusiasm for reportage waned, and it was well into December before he understood the nature of his disquiet.

In China, collisions between people, desires, and trajectories were so constant that even jealousy of your neighbors resembled a kind of intimacy. There, simply by the changes in the smells of their cooking wafting in from down the hall in the cramped apartment buildings, you could tell which neighbor got a raise, was pregnant, or had digestive troubles.

In America, without having to jostle for elbow room, every person, idea, and object had its place to exist. Surely this spaciousness, this plenitude, was the most wondrous thing about America. But it was also its most terrifying, because at times, this wide-open, stake-your-own-claims space also resembled hollowness and oblivion: a vacuum. The air in America was pure and clean, to be sure. But it was also thin, the way the air of mountaintops made you gasp for breath. When Momo looked out from his lab window at the tail end of daylight, the sheer expansiveness of the unpeopled landscape exhilarated and tormented him in turn.

One evening before Christmas break when Momo worked late

at his lab, he tried to take a shortcut through an unfamiliar part of campus and ended up on an unlit athletic field. The night was moonless and clear, and he was so stunned by the stars overhead that he lay down on the grass, wrapped his coat tightly around him, and just looked. Though the grass was covered with frost, what he saw transported him to that sultry summer night just before he turned twelve, when his whole family slept on the low rooftop to avoid the heat.

He knew that his mother was frightened by what happened, but his own memory of it was scintillating with excitement. It was the first time he woke in the middle of the night and noticed how the span of the Milky Way above him had shifted. The stars seemed so fiercely close that he could feel them on his face: a cold kind of hot. The Weaver Girl Star, across the Sky River from the Herd Boy Star: these were the brightest ones. He was the only one awake. His older brother, next to him, splayed out his limbs, and Momo scooted farther toward the edge of the rooftop to get away from his brother's encroaching leg.

He remembered growing groggy again on that roof, and thinking that there was an eternity separating him and adulthood, and he could do nothing but wait. He dreamed that a meteor slashed open the darkness just above the horizon, blinking at him conspiratorially as if to say, *It's all right—you just wait.* He was so pleased that he rolled over to his side for a more comfortable position.

In the next moment, he was in the air. He had been dreaming at the edge of the roof, and now he'd tumbled over and was falling.

He remembered clearly the way time slowed down—way down. As he plummeted toward the ground, he recognized a shard of a blue bowl lodged in the dirt below: his father had broken it the month before when they ate dinner in the courtyard. Time slowed such that he could recount every single sparrow he managed to snare, every adventure he had with his older brothers, including the feel of the carapace of that turtle in the river when he held on to it for dear life.

When he tumbled onto the dirt ground below, he didn't break any bones from the fall but couldn't remember what happened after. Did he cry out? Who ran to his aid?

Afterward, he tried in vain to reproduce that eerie thrill of time slowing to a near standstill. He tried jumping from high ledges, holding his breath, and rousing himself from near-sleep. He never found that feeling again, but was sure something vital and mysterious had brushed against him.

⚘

It was during that first winter in Chimney Bluffs when Momo longed for a violin of his own. He particularly longed for its sound in the lower registers, the kind that came close to a groan from the bowels of the earth, but one that was also capable of rising into the clouds. He wanted this most when the sun had slunk low in the sky, when he could see darkness rising from the plangent plains. There was something about that hour that made him feel insignificant and stricken, and like the way hunger sharpens our sense of smell, he found that his ears were preternaturally receptive to rhythms and melodies, even sonic memories that verged on hallucinations. He could conjure up entire passages of Padushka's performance on Teacher Zhou's gramophone, back when he first learned to identify a certain look on Dawn's face that said she possessed some key to the music that he did not.

And at the end of each day when he returned to his apartment, he ate dinner next to the B-flat hum of the refrigerator in a kitchen that was too large for one person. He heard the way the building's outside stairs reverberated from people trudging to the upper floors—*tum, tum, tum, tum*—or when it was anyone under the age of twenty: *tum-ti-tum-tum, tum-ti-ti-tum-tum.*

Even without music, prosaic vibrations like these bore the signatures of lives. Before he left for America, their apartment in Silver Gourd Mountain was also suffused with small but significant noises. First, it was just him and Cassia as newlyweds. Then there was Junie. Then, after the second birth, it was briefly him, Junie, Cassia, and not-the-baby, who gave off noise too—just not within humans' normal range of hearing.

A Benign Form of Water

TWO YEARS AFTER MOMO HAD LEFT FOR AMERICA, WHEN JUNIE turned seven, Cassia's mother-in-law began to direct certain grim hints at her. These hints were oblique at first: "Young couples like you shouldn't be separated for too long, don't you think?"

And: "In America, students like Momo are all alone, without a proper structure of family and society to ground them."

And: "Americans are so permissive about things. No wonder they get divorced so much."

When Cassia didn't take up these hints, her in-laws finally suggested that "for Junie's sake," Cassia should go there to join Momo as soon as possible, to reunite the two of them.

And then Cassia finally got the drift. She asked her mother-in-law how long this affair of his had been going on. She answered that she didn't know for sure it was true, but that she got a funny feeling based on Momo's letters, about feeling "liberated in America" and about "getting reacquainted with youth."

"Wasn't there a classmate of his from university?" she asked Cassia.

"Yes, a violinist friend," Cassia said. "But they fell out of touch."

"Could they have met up abroad?" asked her mother-in-law.

Was that absurd? Cassia wondered. Momo's letters to Cassia came less frequently as of late. Whatever else Momo was, he was not deceitful. So maybe his reticence was another clue—though of what exactly, she didn't know.

Cassia's feelings were chameleon-like. She was puzzled at first. (He had always been loyal.) Then she felt sorry for herself. (Was this not the fate of all women approaching middle age?) But when the raw sting of the idea subsided, Cassia was surprised by an overwhelming sense of relief.

A mistress for Momo! This changed things. For once, she thought, Momo might finally understand what it was like to have a secret compartment in one's heart set aside for someone else. He might even come to know what it was like for Cassia to live with that kind of heart.

When Cassia applied for her American visa, she was driven by a sense of curiosity about The Other Woman. If she wasn't the former classmate, might she be a fellow Chinese student—someone who, like a dandelion seed, drifted away to the other side of the earth and found hospitable soil? Or might she be an American, who would take Momo to see the town where she grew up? Cassia imagined a picturesque place with red roofs and Christmas trees in the windows.

Something other than morbid curiosity also drove these speculations about the Other Woman. For it seemed to Cassia that this woman was a vision of who *she* might have been, had things turned out differently.

After her visa was approved and before leaving for America, Cassia took the southbound train to Trout River. She arrived to find both her in-laws fully occupied with giving Junie a bath in the kitchen.

It had been three years since she'd dropped her off in their care, and Cassia could see that Junie, who had just turned eight, had become a different child. It wasn't that she was a bigger version of herself, but that she had finally grown into her body just as it was—face, elbows, legs and all.

Junie was thriving *because* she was without her mother, Cassia reminded herself. Had she lived with Cassia, Junie would not have become the child she was now, easily delighted by life, unafraid to sleep and dream. Even a dull child, living with Cassia in a household of two, would have sensed her mother's afflictions from the past and sussed out her ever-present presentiment of loss. The two of them would have been wretched together, as Cassia went about fruitlessly rearranging their life this way and that.

In a tone that was meant to be firm and commanding, Cassia's mother-in-law told Junie, "Good child, say hello now to your mother."

This was about the proper form of address, but also about acknowledging the order of things as the adults would have liked them to be. But in the small bathtub in the middle of the kitchen, Junie ignored her grandmother's plea, and in doing so, made it clear once and for all that Cassia had succeeded in making herself the object of amnesia.

Junie had finally turned into a child of Trout River, slightly rough around the edges, spoiled but happy, and pouring out her heart in the lilting dialect of her grandparents. How many mothers in the world would feel honest-to-goodness relief about this? Not many.

Cassia cried, of course. But there are certain decisions that seem so right in retrospect that they irreversibly erase any thoughts that alternatives ever existed.

❧

In August 1984, Cassia's flight landed in San Francisco, where she was to change planes for Chimney Bluffs in the interior of the country. She had two large suitcases with her, filled to the brim with emblematic Chinese gifts—like silk handkerchiefs embroidered with pandas—to distribute to American friends she might meet later.

She carried her luggage to customs, where a uniformed man stood ready to ask her questions. The officer began with the usual easy ones—Where was she coming from? What was the purpose of her travels?—that she had rehearsed previously in her preparations.

Then he unzipped her first suitcase and began rummaging through it.

"Where's your toothbrush?" he asked.

She had to ask him to repeat the question.

"You're saying that you don't have a toothbrush?" he said.

Indeed, she had not thought to pack one.

"My husband," she said, "he will give me new one, when I see him."

And as she said this, she saw that it was the truth. Momo would give her anything she needed as long as she was with him.

"Did you bring any food with you?"

This was also a standard question, she knew. She'd heard the anecdotes. Chinese students arriving with a suitcase full of noodles or pickles or Sichuan peppercorns.

"No," she answered.

The officer took out a slightly worn Ovaltine can from her suitcase and put it in front of her. "And this," he said, "you're saying this is not food?"

She felt herself stiffen. "It is only," she said, "container for food."

The officer looked at her for a second.

"I need to look inside." He pried open the tin lid and peered into the can.

Cassia tried to keep her breathing regular so that she could search for the right word she needed when it became necessary— was the right word *souvenir*? How could she explain the can's contents?

The officer tapped on the side of the tin can a couple of times and tilted it toward him.

"Baby powder?"

"Yes," she said.

He put the can back into her suitcase and returned his attention to her passport with the F-2 visa.

After all these years, she should have already known this about herself: she never broke down at the critical moment itself, in real time. Her breakdown, if you could call it that, would come later, and only as a form of slow, delayed but inexorable disintegration.

"Welcome to America," the officer said, shutting her passport.

⚶

By the time she walked out of customs, the last connecting flight to Chimney Bluffs had already left.

"Don't worry. Dr. Wilder lives in San Francisco," Momo said, after she managed to reach him on the phone, "I'm going to call and ask him to come pick you up." It was the first time she had heard his voice since he left China, and it was startling how distinctly it came through the other end of the line. Right now he was using his problem-solving voice, for when they ran into glitches that were not big enough to be crises.

"He was Zhang Yue's professor, very hospitable to foreign students," he continued, "so I'm sure you can stay at his house for the night."

She didn't respond. The announcements over the PA system resounded through the airport interior, echoing with place names, numerals, and prohibitions, compounding her confusion.

"You remember Zhang Yue, right?" Momo said. "My meteorologist friend from college?"

Cassia saw in her mind's eye a motley crew of Momo's friends. The year they married, they often came over and had raucous, stormy debates about everything under the sun. She joined them at first, but it was more often a relief to her when they left. She could see even now their animated, linked-together faces. But she could not single out which one of them was Zhang Yue.

"You can catch tomorrow's flight," Momo said, "and you'll be here by dinnertime."

She suddenly had a sense of dreadful familiarity, as if she already knew everything she and Momo would say to each other the next day, and the day after.

"If my plane crashed—hypothetically speaking—what would you do?"

Momo chuckled. "What a question!" he said. "I better call Dr. Wilder now." Then he hung up.

You would cry a little, thought Cassia, *but then you would start over. Why wouldn't you?—I would.*

⚓

Dan Wilder showed up at the airport with a handwritten sign and a crown of explosive white hair. Next to him was his wife, Henrietta, a woman whose red blouse had a large sash bow tied in the front collar. Cassia couldn't stop staring at her lipstick, the same authoritative red, carefully gathered in a velvety pool into which the wrinkles around her mouth converged. How boldly the woman wore her primary colors!

"We've come to collect you," Dan Wilder said, in a crisp British accent that felt more familiar to Cassia than anything she'd encountered in America so far. The accent reminded her of the voices on radio programs they all listened to for learning English. It made him very easy to understand.

"To collect you," Cassia couldn't help but repeat after him, because that was what you did when listening to those programs.

"Not me, *you!*" Dan laughed, and put his hand on her shoulder. "You've probably had enough of this place. Let's get you out of here in a jiffy."

Cassia followed them. She had the feeling that in a different world—say, one in which her face matched the photograph of another passport—this couple could be her adoptive parents picking her up at the airport.

They loaded her luggage into their Jeep and let her sit in the front. They told her that Dan had spent most of his career in Kenya tracking cheetahs, and the vehicle was chosen out of years of ingrained occupational habit. He simply could not live without a Jeep.

"When Dan did research," Cassia asked Henrietta, "you went with him to Kenya?"

"Of course," Henrietta said.

To Cassia, such lives, in conjunction and each on their own, seemed impossible to understand, though she supposed no more so than her own.

"You must be so excited, my dear," Henrietta said to Cassia. "To be reunited with Momo after so many years."

"Yes," Cassia said. "Reunited."

"And to think," Henrietta continued, "here you can have as many children as you like."

Cassia turned to look out the window, not knowing what to say, until she remembered a tip from an etiquette guide. "Thank you for collecting me," she said to them. "It was so very kind."

The slopes of the hills on each side of the freeway were shrouded in fizzy white. When the Jeep drove closer, Cassia saw that what from far away resembled low-lying clouds were not clouds at all.

"Is that . . . ?"

"The fog rolling in, yes," Henrietta said. "It usually does, this time of the day."

To Cassia the fog had an inviting, tactile quality. Being in its midst must be like being embraced by the most benign form of water, because you could be immersed in it without drowning.

The Jeep maneuvered into the city and wended through streets that not only looped but also rose and fell on the surface of hills. Some of them even had palm trees flanking them, which seemed odd to Cassia, considering how chilly it was in the middle of August.

And then there was the rather improbable ocean itself. Dan took a detour on the Great Highway just so that Cassia could see it. It was not the tropical blue Cassia saw on postcards of Hainan Island, the southernmost point within China's boundaries. Rather, this ocean was a metallic gray. Confident in its greatness, it wasn't going out of its way to impress; it didn't need to woo anybody with its hospitality. It was simply what it was, and anyone who wanted to stroll on the beach would either have to bundle up or wait for a sunny day.

They pulled up to the Wilders' house at the end of a street. When they opened the front door and ushered her through it, it seemed that everything inside was made of glass. The outside world poured in; she could see the backyard from the living room sofa, for example, and beyond the backyard garden itself, more hills and more fog.

She stood there, orienting herself.

At dinner, Henrietta served them potato tart, which Dan ate with relish. Cassia, though, longed for food that had been stewed for a long time instead of merely browned in the oven. She badly craved a bowl of soup, cabbage soup even, but in order to be a good guest, she delivered forkfuls of the potato tart from her plate to her mouth. As she chewed, she watched the Wilders' hands wield their cutlery with fluidity.

"You know, we are newcomers to America too," Dan said to her. "Been here only five years, from England. Overall, we don't mind it really." Then he put his hand on Henrietta's. "Isn't that right?"

"Oh yes." Henrietta had a far-off look when she said this, as if the entire history of their courtship and marriage was being relived.

A feeling of envy bubbled up inside her. She knew that Momo would never say, *We don't mind this-or-that, do we?* and turn to her for confirmation. He would simply say it.

And she had been grateful for that, grateful for his certainty, for his energy and relentless cheer, which made so many things possible. In those days, declarations of love were all around them. We love Chairman Mao. We love socialist societies. We love the proletariat. Love, love, love. She believed that her quiet attachment to Momo was more solid than those declarations. Gratitude had been there all along, even when it didn't completely fill up the space where other things were supposed to be.

Later in the evening, in the Wilders' guest bedroom, Cassia lay on a strangely bouncy mattress and felt like it was swallowing her. She asked herself if she would be lonely on these shores if she were alone. The answer came to her quickly and just as clearly: she would not.

On the second day, the fog was still thick. This time Cassia's flight took off, but it circled in the air for half an hour before it was forced to return to the runway due to poor visibility. Chimney Bluffs had to be postponed for another day.

"I'm so sorry to cause trouble," Cassia said to Dan and Henrietta as they ate their second dinner of potato tart.

Later in the evening and again from the guest bedroom, Cassia watched the sky darken and house lights come on one by one on the hills. These lights shimmered as patches of fog skimmed over them. As she drifted in and out of sleep, she could even hear the low bellow of a horn far away. It was the kind of sound created by a resonant, wide, hollow space. She found it exhilarating that she couldn't be sure if she was on firm land or on a massive ship slicing through the sea.

She took out a map of the United States and spread it open on her bed. She found San Francisco on it, at the inward dent of an ocean of water. She kept one finger on the city by the bay, and then found Chimney Bluffs much farther inland, in what looked like the geometric middle of the continent. There was a lot of open space there, but not a lot of water.

What stood between China and San Francisco was the Pacific Ocean—vast, to be sure, but fluid and mobile. What stood between China and Chimney Bluffs, though, felt like an imaginary tunnel that went through the sheer bulk of the earth: crust, mantle, outer core, and inner core.

❧

On her third day in America, Cassia got up before dawn and walked out into Dan and Henrietta's garden. This was another thing about fog: it could hide you when you wanted it to, during times when motives for roving about a host's garden were too complicated to explain.

Cassia rolled up her sleeves and stood in the garden and welcomed the fog on her face and arms. She pretended to be one of those species of plants that, living on a parched plain, put out tendrils to catch precious moisture in the air. She drew the cool air into her lungs, held it, and breathed out.

How long would it take for all the molecules of water in her body to be replaced, one by one, by these new molecules of water on this side of the world?

A few years, perhaps.

Yes, a few years. And although that in itself wouldn't mean much except as a piece of trivia about human metabolism, Cassia couldn't help but feel that it would still be a milestone of some significance.

Standing in the fog, she realized that she was no longer curious about The Other Woman.

At breakfast with the Wilders, Cassia asked Henrietta, "In other American cities, is there this much fog?"

"Goodness, no! And I'm bloody thankful for it," Henrietta said. "I'm sorry about this rotten business with the fog. You must be anxious to get to Chimney Bluffs."

Cassia looked down to fiddle with her fork, but only briefly.

"I'm not going there," she said.

The couple looked at one another, then at her.

"You'd like to wait until you are better acclimatized?" said Dan.

Cassia shook her head.

"You'd like Momo to come here and meet you instead?" said Henrietta. Another look passed between husband and wife.

"My meaning is," Cassia said carefully, having anticipated some confusion on her listeners' part, "I would like to stay in San Francisco, and not go there."

And be The Other Woman.

She asked the Wilders if she could stay with them until she found a job. She would repay their kindness later, she said.

Although her words were clear and grammatically sound, her hosts took a while registering their meaning, as if it was they who were struggling with a language not their own.

"But . . . what about Momo?"

The way she saw it, she told them, even if she were to join Momo, she would either be a housewife taking English classes or work in Chinese restaurants to supplement Momo's stipend. There were more Chinese restaurants here in San Francisco, so it could be even easier for her to get a job here.

After a pause, they finally said again: "But what about Momo?"

The words were the same, but now they were asking a different question altogether. Couples who witnessed the dissolution of other relationships sometimes asked questions like this, full of bewilderment and also fear that this could happen to them too if they weren't careful.

They were really asking her: *What happened?*

It was a fair question, and Cassia wanted to answer that. She knew that words for such an explanation would come—one day. They would seep up from inside her like a tide. And although the words wouldn't be satisfactory in the end—nothing could be—those who deserved to hear them would still recognize the explanation as cogent and not without reason.

But today was not the day.

"Momo can come and visit when I find my own place to live," she said. "If he wants to."

⚓

Cassia was expected at a house in a neighborhood where the street dipped sharply. She looked around when she arrived and saw that every home here was higgledy-piggledy in some way, with their front doors cut at a slant in order to stay perpendicular to sea level.

An improbable construction, this house-on-a-hill business,

but it was no more improbable than her being snatched up as a full-time babysitter for a family, with a salary paid in cash that rivaled the amount of Momo's monthly stipend in his graduate program.

Now Melinda and Bernie greeted her at the door and brought out their baby, Cyrus.

They called this first meeting an interview, but it felt more like an orientation. Cassia learned that Bernie had been a computer whiz who went without his shoes in his office and who took a year off to hike in Patagonia before Melinda showed up in his life. Both of them were rising stars in their jobs.

"When Henrietta told us about you, we couldn't believe our luck," Melinda said to Cassia. "Without you here, I'd have to quit my job."

Baby Cyrus looked at Cassia curiously as his parents gave her a tour of the house. Melinda and Bernie each had a small office, and the rooms had shelves lined with books printed in colorful jackets.

She was astonished to find that Cyrus slept in his own room.

"All American babies sleep like this," Melinda said. Bernie chimed in and described experiments in which hatchling chicks were divided into two groups, and the ones that had to break out of the shell on their own ended up healthier adult chickens.

Cassia scarcely had time to digest this before they led her into the game room.

Melinda told her that Nintendo had been indispensable to her well-being while Cyrus took naps. "I started playing after I had Cyrus," she told her. "By now Bernie will never beat my score, ever."

Cassia gawped. It was as if in this household, adults lived like children, and the child like an adult.

"Some babies are brought up listening to Mozart in their sleep," Bernie said. "Cyrus gets the soundtrack of video games."

Cassia understood Mozart. Momo had talked to her about Western composers back when he still talked to her about those things.

And then the couple began to lay out her daily responsibilities. At one point, Cassia had to ask them to repeat themselves.

"Speak Chinese? To him?"

"Neither of us knows any foreign languages," Bernie explained, "and we figure we'll never learn Chinese at our age, but Cyrus has this incredibly elastic brain—all babies do, of course—and now he has you. He'll be a natural learner."

"But—what do I say to him?" Cassia asked. The idea seemed preposterous to her, to deploy her native tongue on this peaches-and-cream boy.

"You know—just anything you would say to a child naturally," Melinda said. "And he'll just soak it up like a sponge. We haven't even had the chance to ask you: You must have children?"

"Yes," Cassia said, and, out of desperation to avoid talking about her own history, she reached over to take Cyrus into her arms for the first time. It turned out to be a good move, because instantly all attention converged on the child. Cyrus saw the newcomer reach for him and showed no alarm. Even when he was firmly lodged in Cassia's arms, his good mood prevailed.

Melinda and Bernie watched the two of them peaceably regard each other and were visibly relieved.

Cyrus's hair smelled of a mixture of fruit, flowers, and milk.

⚭

On her first morning on the job, Cassia and Cyrus waved Bernie and Melinda good-bye from the slant-bottomed front door as they drove off to work one after the other. Now that she was alone,

Cassia held Cyrus and walked around every corner of the house. She could now take time to look at the jars of makeup in Melinda's bathroom, say. It was altogether a different feeling to be in a house without its owners.

Throughout the day, Cassia found that her English was adequate for conversing calmly with adults, but less so when Cyrus was grabbing toys off the floor to cram into his mouth.

"No! Not for eat!"

Her words were never as nimble as his actions, and she felt the futility of the situation. That is, until she remembered that she was supposed to speak to him in Chinese.

"We just had a nice lunch, didn't we? And the wooden block is not very tasty."

At this, Cyrus seemed to sense the new authority and fluency in her words. Pausing midgrasp, he gazed up at her with a calm, guileless scrutiny, as if he was trying to parse the new cadence of her speech.

Then he resumed putting the block into his mouth.

⚘

At the beginning of the second week, Melinda brought Cassia a spiral notebook and asked her to keep a detailed journal of Cyrus's day so they could "keep up" with what happened to him while they were gone. Cassia smiled when she took it, but she understood that it was a form of supervision.

If she had to keep such a journal when Junie was Cyrus's age, she thought, there'd be pages and pages blank.

She knew that the universe had a way of surprising you with its murkier logic. In this logic, you could give birth to one child and end up raising another. As atonement. Or remuneration. Or however that otherworldly accounting worked.

At first she wasn't used to recording everything as it happened. She would forget to write in it until late afternoon, then hurriedly filled in the details in the half hour before Melinda returned. She felt as if she was a first-grader getting used to the idea of homework.

A page from the notebook looked like this:

Tuesday

8:30: Breakfast. No poop.

10:00: Play in living room.

11:30: Poop. Pizza lunch.

12:30: Nap

1:15: Wake up; too much poop (Note: because yesterday ate pear; Chinese believe pear is "cold" and can cause ~~diaria diahreah~~ diarrhea)

1:30: Took bus to Fisherman's Wharf. Saw PELICAN (new word for Cassia!)

4:30: Drawing on kitchen floor. Try to eat crayon (favorite color for eating: "burnt sienna")

Often she had to look up words in a dictionary ("3:00: hiccups"). She carried a full-sized dictionary with her, the kind every learner of English in China had: black cover with embossed gold letters. Its onionskin pages easily ripped and tended to collect finger smudges. The day she forgot to keep the dictionary on the counter out of reach of Cyrus, it lost the pages between the letters *ch* and *cu*.

She used the dictionary with a new urgency. She carried a smaller notebook for herself to write down important vocabulary words for review later. The act of turning to reference books for the most prosaic words made her feel as if she was beginning something basic but important, perhaps years too late.

There were other resources besides the dictionary, of course. Once Cassia asked Bernie to tell her about the button people pushed before crossing the street.

"It's to make the traffic light turn green," he told her.

"Just because you push it?" she said.

"Yes, to keep pedestrians safe when they cross the street."

"But what if a . . . hooligan push it?"

"Hooligan?"

"People who . . . do bad things in public."

When Bernie cackled at this, Cassia explained that this word was in all the English textbooks in China, where the corresponding term was *liumang*, though it could also mean pervert, but not necessarily so. She explained to him the problem of hooligans in China, and later, she enjoyed knowing that Bernie repeated the story to Melinda as a charming example of cultural differences.

She was also realizing that there were Chinese words that, to convey accurately into English, required sustained examples and contexts that no dictionary could provide. She could fill a whole notebook with words that took a lot of trouble to explain. Her inability to properly convert them into English was the reason she couldn't explain to the Wilders, for example, her decision to stay here.

Vocabularies were simply impoverished when it came to obscure sorrows.

The Improviser's Guide to Untranslatable Words

1. *yuanfen* 缘分 (n.)

A condition two people are said to have between them, if they are brought together in ways large or small, for a few minutes or for decades. Lovers, of course, can be explained this way, but more often *yuanfen* is invoked to explain a stranger who brings a lost wallet to your door and ends up becoming your cousin's business partner, or an orphan child who grows up to have the same chin as his adopted father. Cassia could say she and Cyrus had *yuanfen*, for example.

Yuanfen acknowledges some unknowability in the workings of the universe, and implies there's an invisible mesh that loosely bound people and circumstances. It doesn't resort to the heavy-handedness of the English term *fate*, which is hardly equivalent. No deity of any kind operates any mechanism to deploy *yuanfen*: no looms, no spools, no thunderbolt. It exists more like ambient weather, and like weather, it may come and go and even disappear altogether on a whim. Sometimes people who want to permanently take leave of each other will say that their *yuanfen* has exhausted itself.

But most important of all, *yuanfen* presents itself in ways beyond human reckoning. To properly explain this, Cassia would have to begin with Junie's birth date, then go back eight years.

That Junie was born on the exact same day as when *that* young man died eight years previously could have been a coincidence, and many people would have said so. But Cassia knew that coincidences were merely the long-armed tendrils of *yuanfen*. Knowing what only she knew, the connection between the child's birth and the death of someone who had once meant everything to her— this was as unmistakable as a total solar eclipse.

She hadn't thought of any of this during her pregnancy, of course, because she had been the opposite of brooding, plus her due date was meant to be in mid-March. After she heard the newborn's first cries, the nurses whisked the baby away. She drifted off for she didn't know how long. When she woke up, there was a buzz, an extra quickness to the movement of the nurses and to their glances at each other. They told her it was a girl and that Momo was coming in to show her the baby. They gave her an injection that she only later realized was a sedative.

She didn't know what made her ask for the date. But when it came back that it was February 29, she knew something enormous had just happened. Then another nurse came in with Momo, who was already holding the baby.

"Are you quite sure about the date?" she asked.

"Quite," said one of them. There were more glances cast about, as if to tell Cassia that she was asking the wrong question.

"We must tell you some bad news," they said.

Cassia's immediate reaction at this point was to ask: "How did you know about February 29?"

It was only when the doctor came forward to speak with her and Momo both, and Cassia heard words like "missing tibia" and "congenital," that she began to realize that they knew nothing about the young man with the large eyes.

"This is all my fault," she said. And Momo mumbled something to her to contradict this. The professionals gave her sympathetic looks. They all understood her to mean the fact that her daughter was missing the bottom halves of her legs.

But for Cassia, a different realization was taking place. She saw very clearly the tugging of the net of *yuanfen*, and she was inside it, caught. She thought of all this even before she saw Junie's legs. Cassia lay there in disarray, her mind filled with both terror and unstoppable longing.

The universe was trying to tell her something, through him.

Because nothing was a coincidence.

⚭

Cassia met him in 1967 when she was twenty-three.

She was working as a nurse in a factory in Beijing. On Sundays, she and her girlfriends used to take out a rowboat in the imperial park behind the Forbidden City. The park had been built for the sixtieth birthday of the Empress Dowager. When they rowed on the lake surrounded by man-made hills and pagodas, she and her friends sometimes acted out scenes from the Dowager's life.

"What, shark fin soup with giraffe meat *again*?" Cassia intoned from one end of the boat where she was sitting, taking on what was meant to be a languid royal drawl. She pursed her lips in an effort to simulate wrinkles, and moved her fingers as if long nails were attached to them. "I want more of that tasty stuff—what's that thing called . . ."

"Tofu, your highness," said one of her friends from the other end of the boat, barely suppressing a giggle.

"Yes, *tofu*." Cassia flicked her fingers. "Now that's what I call a delicacy. Find that useless eunuch who ordered this shark fin garbage—and off with his head!"

And then suddenly no one had time for Sunday boat rides anymore. The Cultural Revolution was in full swing, and, as they did in other factories, her coworkers were all writing wall posters to pronounce the correctness and incorrectness of things. Blank wall spaces became rare, as the absence of words was itself a statement. The words and sentences were everywhere vying for Cassia's attention, even as she walked the short distance from her worker's dormitory to the canteen.

One of them read, CRIMINAL MINDS OF ANTI-MARXIST CONSPIRATORS LIKE SO-AND-SO MUST BE SMASHED TO SMITHEREENS!

There were frequently sounds of windows being broken. Glass, after all, was the easiest to smash into smithereens.

The first time she saw him, she was heading to the factory on her bicycle. From among the liquid stream of cyclists on the street, two men pedaled up from behind her. She heard one of them say to the other as they passed, "I'm going to go ask him how he did it," and he gestured toward someone in front of them.

She followed these two with her gaze. A few bicycle lengths ahead of her, the two men were approaching a third cyclist, a thin man wearing overalls. Carefully tied to his back seat was a porcelain pot of hyacinths. It was a strange time for it—deep autumn, much too early for the bulbs. And yet the flowers had opened. The colors of the petals were the usual frothy white, but what was unusual was that the flower petals were made up of luxuriant, crowded clusters. Cassia had never seen anything like it. They didn't just blossom, which would've been pleasant enough. That pot of hyacinths roared.

Without thinking about it, Cassia pedaled faster and edged closer. The two men had by now caught up to the transporter of the hyacinth.

"Comrade," said one of the two men, "what's your secret? To get them to grow so well?"

"I've tried everything with mine," his friend chimed in, "and they do all right, but nothing like what you have here."

"There's no secret," he said. He had turned around to glance at the inquisitors. This gave Cassia a glimpse of his young face, and she felt a jolt of recognition.

By now Cassia was riding side by side with the three of them, all of them traveling at a pace set by a pot of roaring hyacinths.

"I'm guessing you must use some kind of fertilizer," offered one of the inquisitors.

The owner shook his head.

"Are you a professional horticulturalist, then?" asked the other inquisitor.

He shook his head again.

"You have to share your secret," said the first inquisitor. "Look—even that female comrade to your right is waiting. You wouldn't want to disappoint her, right?"

Cassia smiled in spite of herself. She did indeed want to know. Perhaps involuntarily, the young man in overalls glanced at her as if to confirm her presence. When he saw that she was looking at him directly, he withdrew his gaze and blushed.

"There's no secret," he repeated to the pair flanking him, as if resenting the fact they tricked him into looking at her. Then he sped away.

It turned out the young man was a mechanic at the same factory as Cassia. After that day, she began to notice him at the canteen. At mealtime he sat with the same group of people, who talked and guffawed heartily while he hid his eyes from strangers. Every once in a while Cassia's friends sat with his friends in the canteen, and she found out more about him when their conversations mingled. He had worked in the factory since graduating from high school because he wasn't qualified to take the university entrance exam.

"This here is our boy genius," someone from his group said

about him as he came to sit down, "who's been studying on his own, mind you, to become an astronomer."

"To launch rockets?" someone from her group asked.

"No, no rockets," he said to his enamel bowl and chopsticks.

"Just stars and galaxies, then?" Cassia said.

"Yes," he said, still looking into his bowl, but in a voice that verged on tranquility. "Just stars and galaxies."

No one ever asked him to elaborate because everyone was more interested in rockets than in galaxies.

He was the first person she'd met whose dream wasn't driven by utility, and that dream seemed to be the only thing he was certain about. He was tentative about everything else, unable to form an opinion about whether the food that day was above or below average or about whether the chef's wife was getting fat from eating the canteen's leftovers.

She decided that she must have bumped into him in the canteen previously, without remembering. How else could she explain that jolt of recognition? Yet she couldn't shake off the idea she'd read in novels that are now outmoded: that people who were bound together in a previous existence can find each other in the subsequent one.

What she loved about him was the alertness in his large eyes that verged on fear. It was the kind of fear that nimble plant-eating animals showed toward the lurking movement of carnivores.

2. *zaohua* 造化 (n.)

The Maker and Transmuter, or, the makings and transmutations of the world. This isn't an anthropomorphic god of any kind, of course, but a shorthand for genesis, degeneration, and regeneration, encompassing the human and also the vastly nonhuman. And if in the making and unmaking of things, some of its transformations seem cruel, *zaohua* is indifferent to human pain, though this indifference is benign rather than punitive, a mere consequence of the fact that the human heart is but a small organ of an already minute component of this universe. It is merely up to the human heart to acknowledge its insignificance—if it ever does.

How many times had Cassia and the young man seen each other all in all? Five, maybe six, and she remembered them with clarity. On the second to last occasion, they were standing in line next to each other at the canteen, and he turned to her as if they had long been friends, and took something out of his pocket.

"If you have a good spot in your dormitory for it, well, you can put this in some water," he said.

Just then the PA system came on with announcements for that afternoon's denouncement session. She heard only the word *countcrrcvolutionary* as he opened his palm.

She saw that they were two bulbs—small, gnarled, and grimy, almost resembling cloves of garlic.

"I've been cultivating white hyacinths to improve their petals, and this is my favorite variety. You'll see why."

The PA system enunciated emphatically, "To shove the black elements of anti-Marxism into the garbage heaps of history . . ."

"I've never done this before," Cassia managed to say, in lieu of everything else that was on the tip of her tongue. "I may not get it to grow well."

"Then I'll give you another one," he said, and a smile crept up the corners of his mouth. "And another one. We have time. There's no secret to this."

No secret. So he remembered their first encounter on the bicycles.

"Before that time," she asked him, "had we ever seen each
other before?"

"I know we hadn't," he said.

"Then why did I think you looked familiar?"

"The same reason I thought you looked familiar," he said.

Her mind tried to absorb these words. *The same.* She felt as if
she'd been invisible all her life until now.

"And that's why I'm giving you this," he said.

She took out her hand and brought it near his, for the bulbs to
roll onto her cupped palm. That each of their hands had wrapped
around the same bulbs—this was the closest they came to physical
contact.

At the exact moment the bulb fell into her hand, when neither
of them even looked at each other, she understood that what he
offered her was a pact.

The pact was: *We will grow hyacinths together, for the rest of our
lives.*

When she closed her hand over the bulbs and put them in her
pocket, she knew that *he knew* this pact was accepted.

How did she know this, never having known any kind of courtship or known about the nature of promises and pacts?

Yet the knowledge of it-must-be-so filled her. It gave her days
texture and tension. At times both were excruciating. It changed
the way she slid into the grip of sleep, the way she felt waking up.
She was lit up by the thought of him, by everything she knew and
didn't yet know about him. It even changed the way she touched
herself, as if her hands were becoming his hands, and her body, her
skin, everything that it encased, now belonged not only to herself.
During the stretches of time when she didn't see him, the most

minuscule thing—the sound of an enamel bowl clanging, say—could set her off again, and she would be right back in the world that was filled with the idea of him.

Since they had never appeared together, no one suspected that there was anything between them. Cassia knew that if she had told her close friends about this, they would have thought it a foolish, one-sided infatuation. And she would've found nothing to reply with, except to say that she just *knew*.

The two of them shared an operating frequency, and if no one else noticed, it was because no one else was equipped with the right antenna.

Inside her was a constant tug-of-war between wanting to shout about it to the world and feeling that she had been caught.

She set the bulbs in a bowl filled with agate pebbles and water. She estimated that given the current life expectancy, the two of them might have forty or so years together; that seemed satisfactorily close to eternity. By the end of that eternity, she felt, their individual histories would become so intermingled as to be indistinguishable.

This was at the beginning of February.

⚭

His family history initially reached her as whispered tidbits, away from the canteen. She heard it first around the brick-made sink where factory workers came to wash their hands.

Already her ears were keenly attuned to any news about him, just as she was sure his were attuned to words about her.

"—American spy, his old man."

"At a foreign university—"

"You don't say!"

"The old man was weak and succumbed to the indoctrination

of the members of the Manhattan Project. He's been sent away for good."

Cassia turned off the faucet in order to catch the remainder of the words. "Who are you talking about?" she asked. To appear nonchalant and merely curious, she rubbed the towel over her palm a few times before she looked up.

"You know the son—the young man who looks shy, but it's usually the quiet ones who are up to no good."

Someone chimed in to say, "The naturally talkative ones could never be spies."

It was the first time Cassia had heard anything about his family. She listened mutely to his personal history as its details grew and included earlier generations.

"So who's the spy: the father or the son?" Cassia asked. It was a veiled comment. She wanted to use her apparent confusion to remind them that there were two different people they were talking about.

"If the old man was a spy, then the son is a future spy. You know how these things go."

A spy's son. Vice was hereditary in disposition, the voices around her insisted, and insurmountable besides.

Soon the whispers were no longer whispers. In just over a week, they became elaborate oral histories, collectively assembled and passed on.

Ever since he gave her the hyacinth bulbs, he had seeped so deeply into her mind and saturated her awareness that it was unnecessary to say his name aloud. She felt that to say anything in his defense would have exposed herself utterly, and everybody would know exactly how she felt about him. She wanted to keep the sanctity of her feelings intact, even if just for a while longer.

Besides, what could she have said to defend him once the collective verdict was set in motion?

In the end, what did him in was a foreign-language book. Cassia found out what happened through a combination of secondhand reports and conjectures. After she had asked as many questions as she could of the other witnesses, this was what she chose to believe as true.

It was a time when teams of revolutionary vanguards were going into the homes of Black Elements, collaborators with the West. They reluctantly let him come along on the raids in homes near the factory because he did, after all, labor in the workshops of the proletariat. During one of the raids, they went to the home of a member of the intelligentsia, a teacher in a university. He was already locked up; they were simply there to take inventory of contraband and dispose of it.

They took turns pulling apart the teacher's shelves. They helped liberate book pages from their binding, and the sheaves of paper began piling up on the floor.

"Dump them into the latrine," one of them said.

"Why waste all that paper?" said another. "Turn it all into pulp and make posters out of them."

"Or burn it for fuel," said a third, followed by a collective murmur of agreement.

Possibly it'd been a copy of Bertrand Russell. Or Ovid's *Metamorphoses*. Cassia had her guesses, but she knew she was only interested in the details in order to trick herself into believing that she had been present. To see the soft flicker on his face. Whatever that book was, instead of pulling it apart, the young man took a quick glance at its pages when he came upon it. Or maybe he didn't look at all. Maybe he knew what was written there already:

Mercury slays Argus of the hundred eyes, and they are now extinguished. Juno places his eyes on the feathers of her own bird, the peacock, and fills them with starry gems.

Right away someone saw the pause in his movements, or they saw the familiarity with which his fingers glided over the inadvertently parted pages.

Someone who wanted to prove to the others he was treading on the correct path walked up to the young man. "What, you want to read this stuff or something?"

There came a snicker from someone in the room who knew of the young man's family.

The team leader took another book off the shelf, opened it to a random page, and shoved it into his face. "If you want to ingest this poison, then, here, read it all you want," he said. "Read it out loud so that we can all hear the filth for ourselves."

The young man recoiled from the book, which had now become a formidable weapon. But his footsteps backward were closely matched by the other's steps forward: quick-quick-slow; quick-quick-slow. The more he retreated, the closer the book came to smothering his face. Now his nostrils were right up against the smell of paper and ink.

It was said that under the interrogation of the leader, the young man jerked away and bolted so hard that he stumbled into a casement window behind him. The glass panes in the window had been broken long before, during the first raid on the teacher's house. The unlatched, glassless frame easily swung open against the weight of his body when it was flung onto it.

From that window, he fell five stories onto the pavement below. When he hit the ground, people below began to shout, "Someone jumped from the building!"

He must have hit the pavement headfirst, judging from the evidence. Cassia happened to be on the ground floor of the building when this happened—another coincidence she could not properly explain. She saw it all quite clearly and reacted before some of the male coworkers tried to block female colleagues from coming closer. She ran to him.

His head was bent at an angle, and his left leg was twitching. The color of his face was a blush that had gone wrong. His eyes insisted on staring at the sun.

And, yes, the day was lucid and sunny. Everything laid bare on the sidewalk was daring her to scrutinize it, as if to say, *You wanted to see? Here's what's left to see.*

Her nurse's instinct made her reach for a pulse, then her lover's instinct took over, so it was as a lover and not a nurse that she touched him, for the first and only time, on the inside of his wrist.

His eyes let go of the sun, roved all about, and eventually found her face. There was recognition, then anguish—the kind in which life mingled and jostled with death, the former resentful and panicked, the latter steadfast and gloating.

He was far gone already, and yet, as clearly as anything, she heard him speak.

I thought we had time.

Then she saw it—the change that came over him. It wasn't anything she could put her finger on. Not the eyes. No, it was nothing as obvious as that. But in an instant, she knew she was alone.

More people approached the scene, but her feeling of being utterly alone remained. Someone hoisted her up by her elbow so she could stand up and step away. After four or five paces, she turned and looked over her shoulder one more time.

She was struck by the fact that the body on the sidewalk was just a placeholder—it was just a *thing*. He was gone in the most straightforward sense. Like those Taoist magicians in stories from centuries ago, he had flitted away, leaving behind a cicada's shell.

In the panicked mishmash of voices in that aftermath, no one noticed the laugh that escaped from Cassia.

But that was exactly what she did: she laughed.

All her life she had been taught to believe in Reason. She knew that everything Reason created was of use: it built things, maintained things, set boundaries around things. Now she saw how much of life was without mass, invisible and immaterial. She had not previously believed in ghosts, spirits, reincarnation—they were all forms of superstition.

But this all changed that sunny day, the 29th of February.

Cassia didn't know it then, but standing there, she came to a realization that would change her life inexorably eight years later in the delivery room. Death was not a void, and a person no longer alive could keep you company—maybe indefinitely.

Come and find me if you are out there.

Someone brought a cup of hot water to sooth her nerves. They said it was selfless of her to tend to the wounded as a young nurse in training, when she must not be used to all this blood yet. All around her, people whispered about the young man being the son of a spy. Some said he jumped, so this was clearly a case of "self-termination on behalf of the people," they reasoned, which proved his guilty conscience.

She could have defended him: *No, it's not like that.* She could have declared their connection: *We had a pact.* But the truth felt like fog, whereas the story other people told was solid and could be easily picked up and passed along. So she said nothing and obediently drank the hot water they offered her, and accepted their compliments on her professionalism. They didn't suspect she had a different story because she never once cried.

That March, indifferent to the plight of their human caretaker, the hyacinth bulbs burst into bloom, their petals lush and white, but also emitting a tinge of blue such that when the light failed in the room, she could almost be convinced—almost—that they were glowing.

∿

Cassia pounced on the first opportunity to leave. When she transferred to Silver Gourd Mountain, she found that although thoughts of the young man followed her to the northeast where the winters were more brutal and snowstorms more urgent, the change to a more mountainous landscape still helped. Not having to ride her bicycle on the same street where she first glimpsed him helped. She also found that the more time she spent talking to other people in a calm, public voice, the less she carried on conversations with the young man in her head and the less she mulled over the shadowy workings of this and other worlds.

On their wedding night, Cassia asked Momo to turn off the light so that they could make love in the dark. She did it because she wanted to know—just this once—what it would have been like to be embraced by someone who had been the first and only object of longing in her adult life. She wanted to imagine the young man she had loved in bed with her, just this once, so that the two of them would have a memory instead of a dream.

She promised herself: after that night, she would forget him and be a good spouse to Momo.

So maybe it was the perverse tendrils of *yuanfen* at work, but what happened that night in the dark—the inchoate pleasure of it—surprised Cassia. In the coming days, when they continued to make love in the dark, she tried to live up to her promise. But more often than not, it was still the young man's face she saw in her mind's eye, and try as she did, she could not separate that face from the heat of Momo's skin, his mouth, breath, and his weight on her body.

This continued until she became pregnant with Junie.

3. *ciji* 刺激 (n.)

In its most neutral, neurological sense, *ciji* means "stimulus," as in "neural stimuli"; in its more cheerful sense, "thrills," as in what daredevils seek out on the racetrack or alpine slopes. In its most widely used colloquial sense, it refers to acute psychological trauma that may drive someone to behave erratically. When someone says, "So-and-so has been subject to some *ciji*," it is a way to explain her behavior in the wake of some unexpected tragedy.

Such is the nature of *ciji* that people cut you a wide berth, like after Cassia gave birth to a stillborn boy. She never saw the baby. She stayed in the hospital long enough for them to cremate him and show her the ashes instead. They were in an urn for adult-sized ashes, much too large for what was there. She remembered the urn sitting in her lap for an afternoon—long enough for the light to change in the room. Then someone came and tried to take it away. She remembered the effort of that tug-of-war in the muscles of her forearms and fingers, and because she wasn't at her strongest, she tried to cradle the urn with the rest of her body, to become a cocoon with it at the center.

The person who finally wrested it away from her was Momo. He didn't say a single word to her through the tussle, something that even then struck Cassia as odd, since Momo always managed to find upbeat aphorisms at times like this—the most admirable quality about him, yes, but also the most maddening.

But this time, he simply used his strength to pry it out of her arms, because, she supposed, he—even he!—could not find the words to say.

Notes to a Prodigy

WHEN CASSIA CALLED MOMO FROM SAN FRANCISCO TO SAY SHE wasn't going any farther to join him, he had been tidying up the apartment and humming a waltz-scherzo. When he finally understood what Cassia was telling him, he allowed himself a few seconds of panic, then resorted to a schoolboy's trick: he stalled.

"Stay with the Wilders," he told her, "even for a while longer. You don't have to decide yet. Get used to things."

But what Cassia was telling him from the other end of the line didn't sound panicked or impulsive, not like the first phone call when she asked what would have happened if her plane had crashed. And as much as he tried to make sense of her motivation, it was only hours later—after he'd set down the receiver—that Momo understood Cassia wasn't calling to tell him she needed time to get used to things. She was saying she had already begun something. Without him.

When did this happen? It couldn't have been during the short span of time she spent in San Francisco.

Throughout their life together, he had taken pride in the fact that against whatever troubles they had faced, he'd been pulling not only his own weight but hers too. He had assumed that even when the weight was at its heaviest, there had been a rope that tethered them to each other, such that pulling was possible.

Now, for the first time, he suspected that whatever connected them was not in fact a rope, and pulling was no longer an option.

After Cassia left the Wilders' house and he was no longer able to reach her, Momo tried to distract himself from this fact of his life. He went to football games with Larry and found temporary solace in the tidal roar of the fans. But since it was at home where he needed the most distractions, he began to leave the TV on at all waking hours. He could see the mouths of news broadcasters move and hear sounds coming from them, but he was glad to not have to make sense of them beyond the fact they were noise.

It was during this period of lassitude and listlessness that he first saw the young violinist on an evening program. She was wearing a green gown and playing Vivaldi standing atop a soaring vault among the ruins of some Gothic cathedral—in Italy? Spain? He found himself worried about her safety right away: the vault was at a height equivalent to three stories or more, and she could easily lose her balance and dash herself and her violin to pieces.

She was young, maybe barely twenty. He turned up the volume on the TV and sat down. The Vivaldi was a jazzed-up version, impatient with polite society, waiting for an opportunity to cut loose even during its more pensive moments.

His first response was indignation: this young person was violating classical music—through gimmickry and image mongering. Did she have no faith in what Vivaldi had to say?

He got so worked up about this that he had to turn the TV off. He sat in place and fumed. He wished someone—some conscientious audience member—would write to her and point this out. "You are misusing your considerable talent," the letter ought to begin. He continued to phrase declarations of this kind in his mind, translated them into English, wrote them down on a piece of paper, and ended up with a long and complex one: "You deprive

Mr. Vivaldi of his noble intent by imposing on his work your own ardor."

Thus liberated from his indignation, he was able to turn the TV on again in time to catch the last movement. The light hitting the cathedral vault seemed to have changed. Almost in spite of himself, he wished he hadn't missed the previous portion of her performance.

In the following days, he sometimes thought of her version of Vivaldi as he walked up the stairs to his office, as he put on his shoes, or as he chopped up vegetables for dinner. He found that he missed the urgency of her playing and the way it willfully dislodged what was familiar. Whatever gimmick this might have been, whatever audience she was pandering to, he could see that she tried to take some carefully made thing apart and put it back together again with her own conviction. Even if it meant that the end product looked wobbly, it would be more alive for its crookedness than for its perfection.

Now, it seemed, he saw traces of her everywhere. In the Discover Classical Music section of the university bookstore, he spotted her latest cassette displayed on the shelf. In the cover photo, she was sitting in a stuffed chair in a drawing room suffused with golden light, her head tilted back slightly with a languid air, violin dangling from her outstretched hand like it was the cane carried by a dandy. The photo showed her looking directly at the camera, as if to ask: *How would you know what Vivaldi would have wanted?*

Before he knew it, he was standing in the checkout line with the cassette in his hand. He knew that it would cut into the money he was putting aside each month, money that was eventually going toward buying a refrigerator for his parents. As he reached for his wallet, he imagined his gangly father cycling to the market in the morning, with Junie sitting on the back seat, and his chest felt tight. And yet he could not bring himself to put the cassette back on the shelf.

At home and at the end of his day, he took out the cassette liner notes. On the inside was the violinist's bio:

Viridiana Bae-Virag was a child prodigy before she became an international sensation. She took up the violin when she was five. Her first album, *Iridescence*, was released to international acclaim, and she has performed in celebrated venues across the world. A champion of new music, she has collaborated with composers from many countries, some of whom have written compositions expressly for her.

He read the paragraph one more time, registering her age and the fact that she was, possibly, still looking for a way to grow up. Perhaps what she really wanted was to make new music, but short of doing that, she was trying to strain the classical repertoire to its limit, maybe even toward its breaking point.

At times during Viridiana's playing, he could hear her push a certain note so that it almost—but not quite—got out of tune. He knew that some people would say this is not tasteful, but he knew she would have had to fight for such choices, and he admired that about her. He would rewind the cassette back to those passages to relish them, to feel as if he as a listener were a willing accomplice to these almost-transgressions full of color.

It was a splurge upon a splurge, but in order to listen better, he also bought a set of headphones. They enveloped his ears with cushiony leather that smelled like the interior of a new car and fended off the noisy intrusions of the outside world—the ho-hum noise of the refrigerator, the whir of car engines from the parking lot. The headphones shut out everything except the music that was piped into his ears, and his alone. The privacy of the music from the headphones transformed everything taking place in front of him. From his window, Momo could be watching a pedestrian bend down to pick up a bag of potato chips that fell from a grocery bag, but when this happened at the precise moment when a cadenza began to break free and soar, he felt as if he was looking at a film montage from the future vantage point of omniscience. He now heard the counterpoint with great clarity, the way the cellos made a piece three-dimensional. It was as if the music was speaking directly to him.

And he wanted to speak back.

⅃

September 1984

Miss Bae-Virag:

My friend Larry is helping me write this letter to you in grammatical English. I have never done this before, but I hope you don't mind.

About twenty years ago Ivan Padushka visited Beijing and I watched him perform onstage. My friend who brought me to the concert had opened a skylight for me into the world of music, although I didn't fully understand that at the time. She said that an artist draws from his audience as he performs. That seemed selfish to me, at the time. But now, seeing you play, I believe this is true, and that it is a good thing.

They say "each and every family has a Buddhist sutra that is a pain in the ass to read through." (This is my friend Larry's translation.) I have been sad lately, and listening to your album takes me out of myself and away from my family troubles.

I want to ask you what it is like to be a prodigy, even though I know it is a silly question. To ordinary people like me, you must represent a kind of dream, or maybe a fast track toward destiny. A music critic wrote that you were a child prodigy who is "facing the threshold of becoming a mature artist with impact."

When did you cross that threshold?

Do you ever feel lost?

I just wrote "ordinary people like me" but it's only recently that I began to accept I am ordinary. This too is a threshold. But maybe as an ordinary person, it will be easier to start over.

Sincerely,
Momo

⚘

The second time he saw her on TV, Momo was watching a foot-ball game with Larry. At halftime, Larry was channel-surfing, and Viridiana flicked into view.

"Stop," Momo said to Larry, his eyes fixed on the screen.

A rugged-looking pop music star with muscular arms was hosting the show. He introduced Viridiana and, as she walked on-stage, gave her an affectionate kiss. That set off even more fanatic cheering from the crowd. It wasn't clear to Momo whether the crowd was excited because he was the kisser or because she was the kissee.

She was playing an electric violin, a chimerical wonder: a trans-lucent fingerboard attached to a crescent-shaped body made from acrylic—maybe crystal, for all he knew. Yes: a crystal violin. Here was the preposterous, impossibly sleek shape of an instrument that needed no resonance chamber, its shape devoted to beauty alone.

She began a rendition of "The Star-Spangled Banner" with a folksy intensity that sounded more like a tricked-out guitar solo. She let the last note reverberate in the air briefly before she lowered the violin from under her chin to take a bow with her arms outstretched. As she did so, the crystal violin traced out a luminous arc in the air before it came to rest by the side of her body.

"So this is the gal you've been writing letters to?" Larry said, handing him a beer. "She's kind of pretty, but music like this sounds all the same to me, if I can be straight with you."

"Well," said Momo.

When the cheering died down, she walked up to the microphone, and as the stage lights dimmed, said in a manner found only in those who were accustomed to being watched by multitudes: "Now I have for you something written by a living composer."

She switched to a traditional violin. It didn't make sense for her to do so after the electrified crowd-pleaser, but there she was, having worked up the audience to a fever pitch only to subdue their quickened pulse, and, with her opening phrase, coax them to begin again, to start from silence.

She played much of the melody on the lower strings and made the violin sound like—was he hearing it right?—a Mongolian fiddle with a throaty, keening sound. Whoever wrote this piece must have been familiar with vast empty spaces, he thought—if not the American prairies, then maybe the desert. One minute, he felt as if the piece was ancient, as if it had been discovered by an archaeologist and transcribed, but the next minute it also sounded shiny and brand new.

Who could have thought of this? Momo wondered. The prodigy had found new music after all.

"You look like you just spotted a tornado touch down," Larry said to him. "No, seriously, are you okay?"

⚘

March 1985

Dear Miss Bae-Virag:

I apologize but I have to write this letter in Chinese, because my friend resigned as my letter-writing helper. This is probably for the best, because the things I want to confide in you I can only articulate them in my native tongue. So I can only hope that when you receive this, you will find someone to translate it for you, somehow.

When I heard you play that composition by the living composer as you said, many memories flooded back into me. Allow me to tell you one of them.

In 1981, before I left China, I tracked down the only person in our province who might have a child-sized violin. It took me a long time to find him. He was a lowly worker in charge of the local irrigation pump motor. I had to find him during his night shift, and he was dozing in his chair. You have to understand that he was sleeping in a room with about 80 decibels of noise because the pump motor was running. I didn't know how to wake him up, and yet when I walked close to him without saying anything, he jumped up from his chair. He shouted at me as if I was a hooligan about to attack him! I was amazed and asked him how he heard me coming in. He said it was simple:

*whenever anything gets between him and the motor, the noise
gets quieter, and so he instantly wakes up.*

*So finally I told him I wanted to borrow a violin for my
daughter, because I heard that before the Cultural Revolution
he was one of the best makers of violins for children in a
conservatory.*

*He looked annoyed, and said, "Who still has a child-sized
violin these days? You know very well they have terminated
themselves on behalf of the people—years ago."*

*Now, he could have simply said "go home" or "no way."
But only someone who cared about musical instruments
would take the trouble to say all that, so it gave me hope
and I told him, "That's all in the past now. This is for my
daughter, who was born after all that. She's still little, but
I'd like to teach her something about music while I still can,
because I'm leaving for America soon and won't be back for
years." His face was blank. He said that ashes cannot be
turned back into wood. But I said I wouldn't ask to borrow
a cello or harp, but a violin is small enough to tuck away in
an attic. Doesn't he know someone? Or someone who might
know someone?*

*The man finally stood up and began to walk away without
saying anything. I followed him into a small storage room
in another building. He reached for a key to unlock the
rusty chains. Inside it was piled up with planks of wood,
old banners, placards with red X's on them. They made
you wear these on your neck if you were accused of being a
counterrevolutionary. Then in one corner, there were stacks
of leather and fabrics, and buckets that held what looked like
glue.*

My heart was beating fast at this point, because I understood what this meant: this was a storage closet for contraband from the Cultural Revolution. I said to him, "I knew there are people like you in the world." He moved aside a pile of fabrics, and in the pile was a bundle wrapped in layers of old newspapers— from 1966! Inside the newspaper, there was another layer of wax paper. And finally in the middle, wrapped up like an infant, was a quarter-sized violin with very scratched-up varnish.

I felt like I was about to rewind the clock and relive the moment I first touched the violin. I felt young again.

"Now does your child have musical cells?" the old man asked. By that he meant whether she had musical predisposition, or if this was going to be a case of "playing the zither to the ox" (another Chinese phrase). I said, "I'm very sure she does," and I could tell he was getting a little excited by the idea that a child would use this again. I couldn't believe my good fortune.

(I should add that my daughter was born without her lower legs. I add this not because it changes my story—to me, it doesn't at all—but to not mention this to you would also feel dishonest somehow.)

Now, because there were so many things to do before my departure, I wasn't able to get the violin fixed up until the last evening before my flight to America. By then, it was late at night, and Junie was already asleep.

When I took out the violin and woke up Junie, my wife asked why I had to do this, right at this moment. But I insisted, because I wanted to show Junie the instrument and just teach her a few basics before I left, and maybe other teachers could teach her the rest. It would be better than nothing, I thought. I said I wanted her to see something amazing and I put the chin

rest under her left cheek and her left hand at the end of the
fingerboard.

The violin was just a little too long for her because she was
just five at the time (as it turns out, the same age as when you
began playing), so I had to place my hand on hers to keep her
from dropping it. I tried to get her to play "do-re-me" by moving
her fingers for her. But by the third time we were through, I
knew it was getting nowhere. She was gradually slouching until
I told her not to, but after a while, she would start slouching
again. I tried to press her head down on the chin rest to keep
the violin from sliding away. She complained, but I wouldn't
give up.

I was of course familiar with the disposition of my daughter,
but I was in too much of a hurry to be persuasive in the right
way. I should have told her why it was worth the trouble, about
my friend who first taught me how to play. But there was no
time. So instead I said, "You can't sleep until you play at least
one full scale."

That was when it happened. She flung the violin away from
her. She was aiming for the other side of the bed, I believe, but
her force launched the violin all the way across the bed, and it
landed on the concrete floor.

I still remember the sound it made, the wooden ribs crashing
on the concrete. The neck broke off cleanly, probably because
of all those years of being in that closet, with no vibrations to
keep alive the fibers of its wood, only dampness and cold. It had
survived all of the Cultural Revolution but not my daughter's
tantrum.

I slapped her. I like to think it was my muscles that made the
decision, because my brain would never have allowed it. But who
is to say which is more our true self, our brain or our muscles?

I have never hit her before. Ever. But now, this is how Junie will remember me before I left for the other side of the world for years—the equivalent of a lifetime for her. This was all that I could think of for a long time. It was the only thing on my mind when I was flying above the Pacific Ocean.

Sincerely,
Momo

The Wayward Knife

EVEN AFTER TWO MONTHS WITH CYRUS, ON DAYS WHEN CASSIA found herself alone in the house with a toddler, she sometimes forgot that she didn't always live in a foreign city so perpetually shrouded in fog. The fog made it hard for her to tell the difference between outer weather and inner mood. It wasn't that she didn't understand her status as an employee paid in cash. Rather, it was the fact that seeing a child totter, fall down, and get back up on his own was new to her. She stared as Cyrus clambered about in the driftwood-laden sand on Ocean Beach. She watched him stomp on bloated stalks of kelp and poke at sand dollars.

She would teach him how to talk, teach him the proper names for things, starting from scratch. She found it a remarkable thing that he wore socks that got dirty, that his feet and ankles could be held, pinched, and tickled.

Even now, in San Francisco, when her connection to Junie was tenuous, Cassia still believed that leaving Junie with Momo's parents, thereby making herself dispensable as a parent, was the best thing she could've done for her daughter.

When Cassia came home from the maternity ward for the second time and after her in-laws returned to Trout River, she and Momo took up the question of his acceptance letter from the American university, which had arrived when she was pregnant.

"I can't leave you and Junie alone here," Momo now said. "Not after—"

"Your parents will help with Junie," she said, and knew immediately that this would be true. "You'd regret it if you didn't go."

In the lives of families all over China, decisions like this were made every day. The reshuffling of bodies to accommodate housing shortages or parental absence. Aspirations were either pounced on or postponed, and were sometimes subject to the whims of the consular officials granting student visas on any given day.

"I'll bring you both to America," Momo said, "after you're ready. Then Junie will have the best prosthetic legs in the world and learn to play the violin and . . ." His voice broke.

How strange was the ebb and flow of resilience in the space between two people! She felt oddly upbeat at the precise moment when he appeared more depleted than she'd ever seen him.

But by the time she received Momo's first letter from Chimney Bluffs, telling her that he had arrived safely and everything was in place, her resilience was no longer there. It'd been edged out by a question that finally had time to unfurl and formulate itself in her brain.

How did an umbilical cord turn into a noose?

At night, lying next to Junie's curled-up body, the answer came to her. In the womb, in *her* womb, the neck of the fetus was the perfect spool, and the umbilical cord, a skein. In most cases, floating against the skein, the fetus prevailed. But in her case, the skein prevailed. The baby took a shortcut through life and moved on, heedless of everyone else's plans about his destiny.

They only told her it was a boy and that he had well-formed legs. What message the universe was trying to send her this time, she could not say.

Alone with Junie, she became overwhelmed by the simple fact of gravity. It became a Herculean task to get up in the morning, to brush Junie's teeth, then her own. The baby had been alive inside her, then died. She couldn't help feeling that other parts of her would follow suit, one by one, and that maybe this process had already begun. She was afraid that one day, in the middle of a mundane task, the scale would finally tip, and she would be unable to function once and for all.

There had already been one close call. It was an evening when Junie wanted an apple, and wanted it quickly.

With a folding knife, she began to peel the apple slowly (her hands were so heavy, her left thumb on the apple could hardly budge). She began with one incision at the base of its stem.

Junie fidgeted on the bed. "Is it done?" she asked.

Cassia wanted to hush her, but found that she could only concentrate on the knife. The knife in her right hand confronted the exposed thumb of her left hand. She pushed the tip of the knife under the skin of the apple.

"But is it done yet?" said Junie.

Despite her deliberate movement or maybe because it was deliberate and therefore not fluid, the knife sensed weakness in its victim. It skidded over the apple's skin and plunged into Cassia's thumb.

She cried out in alarm and dropped the knife as blood gushed out of her thumb. Junie stopped fidgeting and became quiet. Cassia grabbed the nearest towel to wrap around her thumb, but the towel happened to be a warm one, so it only exacerbated her bleeding.

She didn't need stitches, in the end. This was fortunate, because she didn't want to return to the same hospital and have to walk past the maternity ward she'd left earlier that year. She went to her neighbors for some gauze to bandage the wound. They dissolved spoonfuls of sugar in hot water and made Cassia drink it, to get color to return to her face. But it wasn't the sight of her own blood that had made Cassia faint. It was the thought of other places in her body where the wily knife could have sliced. Like across her left wrist with its throbbing veins, in a seemingly accidental way.

When the feelings surrounding such an image came into sharper focus, she found that she *wanted* to succumb to the will of an inanimate, sharp object. She *wanted* the knife to slash across her veins, because it might bring oblivion, and with oblivion, relief from the feelings of weight on her chest, in her eyelids, in her feet.

In the coming days, her thumb healed, first throbbing, then not, before settling down to an occasional itch. But after that day, she could not banish the thought of a wayward knife. It was now always winking at her, beckoning, with fatal consequences disguised as random mishap.

Her battle became one to banish this *idea* of mishap, because she could not stop imagining over and over again Junie seeing her in a pool of a blood and calling out to her in a quaking voice. These visions were so powerful that it became hard to separate them from reality, as a prophecy of what was to come.

Cassia decided that to win that battle, she had to turn Junie over to her in-laws as soon as possible. After that, when she was finally alone, she could let the knife slip whichever way. She could let the skein of the universe tighten around her own neck—if it hadn't already.

She set about immediately to make this happen. With a renewed vigor, she wrote to her in-laws and began planning the trip south.

"You will have a great time there, with your grandparents," Cassia said to Junie on their long train ride, as she revisited Momo's childhood anecdotes. She had to press her mouth close to Junie's ear, to fight against the clanking sound of the swaying train, and also to keep at bay the encroaching looks of pity from the other passengers, disguised as curiosity and concern.

"Will you have a good time there too?" Junie asked.

You will soon forget me, Cassia thought.

"I will come and visit often," she lied.

To her surprise, Junie did not protest and did not appear to feel abandoned. Cassia always knew that Junie preferred Momo to her.

On the morning Cassia was due to leave, Grandma was holding Junie in her arms, and all three of them were seeing her off by the well in the front courtyard. Junie did not make a fuss. As Grandpa lifted up Junie's arm to wave good-bye, Cassia suddenly remembered that she'd forgotten to pack Junie's favorite pair of knitted gloves. Junie especially liked them because they were a vibrant shade of coral, something rarely found in stores. She would certainly miss them.

I cannot go through with this, Cassia suddenly thought with panic. *How could I let her down like this, when I may never see her again?*

It was then that a small boy, only slightly older than Junie, charged up the road. He was running at full tilt and pulling along a small wooden trolley, the kind people used to transport vegetables and coal. He was pulling it so fast it seemed as if at any moment, the wheels would break off and fly into the air. Behind the speeding boy was an angry middle-aged woman, probably his grandmother. She was brandishing a bamboo pole in her hand, apparently to be used on the boy after catching up to him.

"Get back here, you dirty scoundrel!" the woman hollered, panting. The odds appeared good for the boy and the trolley.

The boy indeed looked dirty. His feet were barely covered by what was left of his shoes. At the same time he left his footprints on the muddy ground, the same ground, made of the detritus of everyone and everything that lived in Trout River, was clinging to him and making its imprint on him. Fed by food cooked over fires kindled from dried dung, substances that passed through life and to life returned, the boy looked unbreakable.

In that instant, in the span of a breath, Cassia felt the weight lift from her chest. Her limbs felt light again, like those of the boy. She turned and, as casually as possible, tucked in Junie's collar. "Look at that trolley," she said to Junie. "Maybe Grandpa can make you one just like it. Wouldn't that be great?"

Then, before anyone said anything more, Cassia turned and walked away.

The Invention of Floating

In August 1986, after June ventured into the crop fields and left her horse wagon there, a new energy crept into the home she shared with her grandparents. It was as if the adults knew that more ingenuity and resolve would be needed to get through whatever was coming. In this state of wariness and hope, there was often the gong-like sound of pots being dropped onto the kitchen floor, or the dull thuds of Grandpa's bony knees banging into stools. Grandma walked more upright than before despite her arthritis, and even seemed to regain the two centimeters she had lost to osteoporosis over the decade.

Junie was a year and a half away from her twelfth birthday. She asked her grandparents if they would take her to the river to learn to swim.

"You can watch me," she said, "to make sure."

Her request was at first met by silence. She could tell that her grandparents were trying to refuse but couldn't yet reach a consensus as to how.

"You said that during the summer, the current is always the slowest," Junie reminded them.

It was Grandpa who came up with the idea of a harness. He wound a thick nylon rope around each of Junie's shoulders, then around her waist, then gathered the strands together to converge at the center of her back, where a knot anchored a long stretch of the rope that was to be a tether to the shore.

Junie giggled as she was being outfitted this way: she felt like the leaf-wrapped *zongzi* that people ate during the fifth lunar month.

All three of them walked to the river together. Grandpa pushed his bicycle with Junie sitting on the back seat, and Grandma walked alongside. From the edge of the road to the river, Junie rode on Grandpa's back, her arms wrapped around his neck, her heart pounding. The rope strands between her torso and Grandpa's back felt like the rib cage of another creature.

With Grandma holding the extra stretch of the rope behind them, Grandpa waded into the knee-deep shallows, bent down, and lowered Junie into the soft current. The river was no more than three meters wide there, but his face said it might as well have been the roaring gorges of the Yangtze.

With her grandfather's hands still underneath and supporting her neck and the small of her back, Junie lay on the surface of the water. She let the gurgling current tug at her clothes, and felt them get soaked up and expand.

Something else expanded in her too. Without hesitation, she rolled off her grandfather's hands and paddled into the middle of the river where the water was deeper.

She had dreamed about this, of course, but nothing had prepared her for the actuality of buoyancy, for the lightness with no known analog on earth. In the unobstructed liquidness around her, while other children might have cried out in alarm with nothing to hold on to, she felt an invitation to unfold her limbs. She laughed out loud, almost in spite of herself. Then she began to swing her thighs, backward and forward, as if using them for the first time.

"I'm floating!" Junie shouted to her grandparents as she stared at the sky, even though she knew perfectly well they were both looking at her.

Grandpa stood rooted at the spot where he'd released Junie into the water. He squinted at her in the river, as though the fact of his gaze would ensure that Junie did not disappear. Grandma wound the end of the harness rope around her wrist, expecting a tug-of-war with the river.

Passersby crossing the narrow stone bridge over the river also looked on. They watched the child move in the water, tethered to her grandparents standing on the shore. The rope between them was long but slack, almost as if the elderly couple were flying a kite. Every one of them who stopped to watch stayed longer than they intended to, because what Junie did in the water—the way her arms turned her about—looked uncannily like dancing. Not one of them noticed anything different about her legs.

Going home that afternoon, Junie sat on the same bicycle seat as she always did, but now she saw her town differently. The dirt roads, the slopes extending up from the riverbanks—all the topography of Trout River made more sense, now that she'd seen it from the water's level.

After that first swim, Junie's dreams changed too. In them, she moved up the river against its gentle current to find that the channel widened and became flooded with sunlight. It was filled with aquatic creatures with large foreheads and eyes full of curiosity. The swarm of creatures, with their silvery bodies, stretched as far as she could see, shimmering at the boundary between water and air.

※

When summer turned into autumn, Grandpa came home from the market one day with a polyhedron cage the size of his palm. It was woven together from thin bamboo strips and jewel-like in its geometry.

"What is it?" Junie asked.

"We call it a goo-goo—or cricket," Grandpa told her, "if you want to go by the scientific name."

Junie peeked through the crevices to look for the shape of the critter inside. "I can't really see it."

"If we wait quietly for a while, it'll start chirping."

The cage had a length of string attached to it, and Grandpa hung it on a nail on the balcony. After a few minutes, a chirping emerged from the cage.

"Will it stay inside?" she asked.

"Until late autumn," Grandpa said. "Crickets only live until then."

"Then it will die?"

"Then it will die."

Now that it wasn't so hot, the three of them moved back to sleeping on their plank bed. At night, Junie listened for the cricket on the balcony, and under the cover of darkness thought of the open field where the cricket might have come from.

"I feel bad for it because it can't go anywhere," Junie told Grandpa in a whisper, "but I don't want to let it go either."

Grandpa was facing away from her, pretending to be asleep.

The next day, he scrambled up the creaky bamboo ladder into the open attic above them. He stayed there for about an hour, turning over piles and opening boxes. Dust from the attic rained down and floated about in the sunlight.

When he came down from the ladder, he brought another sack of carpentry tools with him and arrayed them on the floor.

Junie scooted over to touch them. He showed her what they were—the plane, the chisel, the chalk line. "They are from back when I made lots of things," he told her.

Grandma looked at the tools too. "What made you take them out all of a sudden?" she asked.

"I've been thinking," he said.

"Of what?"

In the small pocket of silence between the question and an-swer, the cricket in the bamboo cage chirped on.

"About her," he said. "Walking."

⚬⚬

When Junie still had the horse wagon, getting around was a whimsical diversion. But Grandpa saw now that they could no longer go back to that old life. He remembered what Junie said about turning into a fish and swimming back from America. That pronouncement always landed in his gut with a percussive force. What would she really turn into, say, in a couple of years or in ten, and after they were no longer around to see these transforma-tions?

Having been a carpenter all his life, he was accustomed to de-signing cabinets, chairs, and desks. He made them with a practi-cal simplicity he was proud of, but they had all been immobile, designed to stay put.

Grandpa began by watching Grandma walk. He sent her cross-ing slowly from one end of the room to another, as he crouched down to scrutinize her legs midstride. He made her walk while he clasped his hand on her calf, to find out which parts of her leg flexed and which parts stayed rigid.

"No, no, slower than that," he ordered.

"Let's see if you could walk any slower and not fall down," Grandma said.

It was like asking someone to hold their breath in order to understand respiration. He found that she was more helpful as a model for walking on days when the arthritis in her knees flared up because she unthinkingly compensated for movements that were more painful, and he could compare those to her ordinary way of walking.

We learn so much more about things when they are broken or unmade, he thought.

He wracked his brain over how to make joints that might flex like the human ankle. He contemplated how to attach the wooden leg to Junie's stump without chafing her skin, and about how often the legs would have to be replaced as she grew. He thought about Junie's knees—the fact that she had them—and how much more difficult it'd be if he also had to fashion knees out of wood.

Grandpa didn't know it, of course, but in designing his latest contraption, he was pushed by necessity and common sense to produce inventions that paralleled the emerging science of modern prosthetics. He tried to capture the movements in Grandma's stride, for example, without having heard of concepts like "gait analysis" or "range of motion." He made a plaster mold of the ends of Junie's legs so that he could carve something to be easily strapped onto them, without having heard of the concept of "residuum."

He also didn't know that in agonizing over these things, he was already duplicating the evolving biomechanics work going on in the West (Pitkin and Kogler 1983, Kistenberg 1980), and from the North American Society of Orthotists and Prosthetists.

Before making a single-axis foot that could pivot, he knew that the legs should be as light as possible without sacrificing strength, so he drilled tunnels into components of the wooden calves to reduce their weight. The result was a lotus root: rigid, but with empty spaces inside its walls.

In fashioning Junie's legs, Grandpa cared about making them resemble actual human legs—the same way that the first designers of electric light bulbs made them look like the wax candles they replaced. It would be another decade before a revolution in prosthetics led to more radical designs: alloy blades to sprint on, propelled by cheetah-like flexion.

Grandpa did not know any of this, nor did he know that what he was about to make would one day garner attention as an artifact of Junie's celebrated personal history.

For weeks, he took up all available surfaces of their room for his prototypes. On every table and chair, he spread out parts, alternative parts, and eventually failed parts. The floor became covered with wood shavings. During the day, squares of sunlight moved across these surfaces, illuminating one by one each wooden part strewn about. He always tried to envision the finished product, to fend off paroxysms of frustration and doubt.

He worked with his eyebrows furrowed, but there were also times when he sang to himself. Like his son, he had a good singing voice.

⚶

For weeks Junie watched as Grandpa moved among chisels, saw, gougers, and planes. She watched him turn over pieces of wood this way and that for a better carving angle. It was as if Grandpa already knew which parts didn't belong, as if he could see in the wood something she was not yet able to. She liked the sawdust that settled down on the ground, and the smell of wood in the air.

It must be the smell of a forest, she thought. Then she thought: *I would like to take a walk through a real forest someday*.

When the legs were finally shaped the way he wanted and the ankles were pivoting with the right amount of play, Grandpa asked Junie to try them on. He helped her strap them to her stumps with leather fasteners converted from belts. First the left, then the right. When all was in order, he propped her up.

"I'm so tall," she said.

It wasn't that she'd never seen the world from that height be-fore; but when she did, she'd always been on someone's shoulders, on a bicycle seat, or sitting on a cabinet.

"I can make you even taller than that," boasted Grandpa, un-able to resist. He was, by this time, able to imagine a second set of legs, maybe even a third. He thought he might even design ones that could withstand being in water—a pair of swimming legs.

She took her first steps, hanging on to Grandpa's arm. Her stride was jerky and unafraid.

Grandpa retracted his arm slowly but his fists were tightly clenched at his sides. Her footfalls made thudding sounds on the floor. She repeated, "I'm really tall—"

And in the next instant her left leg snapped out of the fastener from underneath her, and she was in a heap on the floor.

Junie's face was a contortion of hurt and puzzlement. The whole situation was so new that its shock delayed the tears.

Grandpa had to keep himself from rushing over to her, the way someone would toward a toddler. He needed her to get used to this: there would be many more tumbles.

She had been walking with her feet too wide apart, he deter-mined; there was not enough traction in the feet. *Even after all the time I spent on them,* Grandpa thought as he returned to the bench, *these damned things are hardly better than stilts.*

"The taller you are, the more it hurts when you fall down," Junie said eventually, through her sniffles.

⚘

Junie liked returning to the routine rhythms of her days, like when she could ride on the back of Grandpa's bicycle without her new legs. This was to give them a break, Grandpa told her, because of the way the fasteners scratched up her thighs. They still rode to the post office, asking after letters from afar. Or they rode into the market, asking after the prices of eels and vegetables.

Grandpa and Grandma seldom mentioned America to Junie again, but they told her that if she absolutely must, she could write Momo a letter about why she didn't want to go.

They showed her how to address the envelope. The stamp they had to use was ten times the cost of a domestic letter and was so lovely she hated to send it away. But she learned how to spread glue on the back of it and pressed it down on the corner of the envelope herself. On it, Grandma wrote with careful, neat English letters: CHIMNEY BLUFFS.

They explained to Junie what these words meant. This explanation conjured up in her mind a town that was a forest of smokestacks.

What Momo and Cassia could be doing there in a smokestack forest—this she could not imagine at all.

A Village Full of Fish

AT THE BEGINNING OF THE FALL SEMESTER IN 1986, A NEW PIZ-
zeria opened on campus, across from the building where Momo
worked. It gave off an unfamiliar yet not unappetizing smell of
baked bread and animal fat that seemed bent on infiltrating his office. On a day when he forgot to bring his usual lunch of rice and
stir-fried vegetable medley, Momo decided to investigate.

The eatery was empty because it was not yet lunchtime. A
young woman was stationed behind the cash register, wearing a
paper hat with the word CIAO on it. When she saw Momo come
in, she affixed her beam upon him and gave him a smile. The smile
was so hopeful and trusting, it was as if he was the first and only
person to walk through the business.

It said: The world is lovely. Do not be afraid.

It also said: It is possible to start over in life, don't you think?

He didn't know how to flash that smile back at her, so instead
he asked for pizza, even though it was much too early for lunch.

"Which topping would you like?" she asked him. "We have
five."

Momo pretended to squint at the display menu to hide his
frown. It seemed that here in America, he was constantly being
asked to choose from a spread of seemingly endless yet identical
items. Momo was about to mutter an excuse to leave, when the
young woman leaned forward and said, "You know, when I don't
know what to choose, I always ask for the special."

"What's special about—"

"Absolutely nothing," she said, already sliding the slice toward him. "It's just a shortcut, to make people feel that it's their own decision."

Momo touched the edges of the pepperoni pieces with his finger as if to ascertain their material properties. They looked like floating islands on a sea of cheese, which to Momo was a form of grease with more tensile strength.

He asked her for a takeout box, because he thought he needed some privacy in order to bite into it.

"If you come back tomorrow," she said conspiratorially as she handed him the box, "there's a chance the special will feature vegetables—but I can't promise anything."

Over the next few days, he went back and, freed from the task of choosing toppings, chatted with this young woman—Nina—about everything else. Her bright teeth and her improbably red hair made her seem as if she'd sprung from a land of sun-drenched prairie grass. But what kept him going back was more than that. It was the way she accepted him as part of a harmlessly varied world enriched by his alien nature—his accent, his apathy for football, his ignorance about cheese. It was the way she said it was "cool" that he lived through the Cultural Revolution, that it was "cool" that he knew Russian, as if these were choices Momo actively considered, then espoused to assert his individuality.

When he was with her, Momo glimpsed the world the way she did—without antipathy and foreboding. He learned to say "I'll try" when asked to do something, because only here in America, he reasoned, did earnest intentions count as much as the results. And when he was with her, he became temporarily convinced that good intentions were all that was needed.

Sometimes he was afraid she'd utter something to break the

spell, so that he'd come to recognize her for what she was: an American girl half his age getting a master's degree in psychology—someone who had nothing in common with him.

Between serving customers, she sometimes quoted passages from her textbooks to him.

"Do you know," she said to him once, closing her book, "the first thing that men notice about women, according to a recent survey?"

Porcelain skin like yours, he wanted to suggest, but he said he had no idea.

"Her clothes," she said, and paused for effect.

"Okay."

"Now, guess," she said, "what women first notice about men."

"His voice?" Momo ventured. He had been thinking about how nice it would be to sing to her. In fact, he even felt foolish enough to try.

"Wrong! It's still clothes."

This came close to breaking the spell. But not quite.

"Your textbook's author never lived in China, then," he told her, "because men and women wear the same clothes."

She considered this for a moment. "If that's true," she said, "then what do Chinese men notice first about Chinese women?"

There were so many ways to answer this question that Momo found himself briefly unable to. But when he spoke, it was his stomach and its new dissatisfaction with a pizza-heavy diet that took initiative.

"I'm making dinner for some friends next week, for Mid-Autumn Festival," he said. "You can come and ask them for yourself."

༺

At least once a month, the Chinese students living in Chimney Bluffs carpooled fifty miles each way in order to procure essential grocery items from the nearest Asian market: scallions, sesame oil, and fish that hadn't been deboned and hacked to pieces. These markets were often run by Asian families from countries that still had border skirmishes with China or had once invaded China. When they shopped, however, these student sojourners overlooked geopolitical boundaries, because they understood that true patriotism deferred first of all to the stomach.

Right now, Momo was one of these people practicing patriotism-by-the-gut. The amount of pizza he'd eaten lately had a way of imperialistically taking over his stomach and sometimes waging war there. Tonight, to celebrate the full harvest moon and to help everyone forget how far away their families were, he wanted to make something that would be an antidote to pizza. He wanted to prove to himself that the old country had not receded from him after four years of being abroad, that a part of himself that once ate differently could still be recovered.

Now these friends sat in his living room bantering and cracking open sunflower seeds with their teeth. They would have preferred to speak in Chinese, but for the benefit of Larry, who drove them to and from the store, they conversed awkwardly in English for a few sentences every now and then, before slipping back into Mandarin.

Momo was in the kitchen cutting up pressed tofu for the appetizers when Nina arrived. Seeing her in the kitchen, *his* kitchen, made his heart constrict a little.

"That sure smells good," she said, pointing to a pot of soup simmering on the stove behind him.

"Thank you, thank you," Momo said. The soup's aroma was promising.

Nina walked around him to the stove, causing another small constriction in Momo's heart as she brushed past him. She lifted the lid off the pot.

"But it's white," she said.

"Yes—white," Momo agreed happily. The color was the result of his having coaxed a whole fish into yielding all its fat and flavor. Nina's observation was the greatest compliment, now that the alchemy was close to complete. Momo only had to turn off the burner when he finished cutting, and the whole pot could be welcomed at the table.

It didn't occur to Momo that the white color signaled something else to Nina: a blank, a lack. Namely, it lacked resemblance to the Chinese food she'd eaten in buffets like Hunan Park, where each entree dish was vivid and glistening.

"It needs some color," Nina said, and began to rummage around Momo's pantry with its arsenal of jars and bottles. "It'll be better with soy sauce."

"Wait—" Momo looked up from the cutting board.

By now Nina's hand was already wrapped around a bottle of soy sauce, which she correctly identified because of its panda logo. She twisted off the cap and brought it over to the pot of soup. The dark-brown liquid in the bottle was about to flow out and merge with the creamy white in the pot.

"No!" Momo tossed his knife aside on the cutting board with a loud clang that startled both of them.

"No?"

"No—" Momo walked over to her and, with the authority of a veteran cop disarming a juvenile delinquent, removed the bottle from her hand and placed it back in the pantry. "The soup should be clean, to capture the taste of fish. It's the opposite of soy sauce."

"But won't it be bland? It looks bland."

"No," Momo said again. He pointed at the pot using his middle finger, because he had yet to learn the special meaning that finger had in the language of gestures. "One drop of soy sauce in there— soup will be ruined," he said.

Nina looked nonplussed. "Oh."

"I grew up in a village full of fish, where even poor people could eat fish," he said lamely, to explain his vehemence.

He was surprised by the sentiment of nostalgia in what he just uttered. All his life he'd been leaving Trout River again and again, with the confident determination of an aerialist who puts one foot in front of another without blinking. All his life he saw clinging to one's roots as a weakness, a form of wanting to be coddled at the expense of reaching for ambition.

Yet here he was, in his middle age, succumbing to just that kind of weakness.

⚯

Momo presented the soup to the diners around the table. He told both Larry and Nina not to bother with the fish with its encased bones and to just drink the broth. Larry declared that this was the only "fishy" thing he would ever eat. Nina let the steam rise into her face before she sipped. "I've never been to the sea," she said, "but this sure tastes like it."

The fish was a freshwater catch, but Momo did not correct her.

For a moment, while everyone's head was bent over the bowls and nobody spoke, his kitchen didn't feel too large as it often did.

After the meal, the conviviality continued in the living room. Momo's Chinese friends laughed at Larry for his frustration with the sunflower seeds. ("Seems a hell of a lot of trouble for a little piece of food, no?")

For days prior, Momo had been looking forward to seeing Nina sitting on his living room sofa. And not just sitting on the sofa, of course. Also lying on it, and with him on top of her if that could be arranged. Yes; he admitted his lustfulness. He wanted to touch her hair and neck and find out the temperature of her skin.

But he knew too that these urges were not the same romance he felt in his youth. He could not look at Nina's wide, toothy smile without wondering if he'd ever been that young himself, that green and unsullied. In college, maybe, in an age of certainty and conviction, though he knew even less than Nina knew now about the world beyond the campus wall, to say nothing of his own heart.

When it came time for the guests to disperse, he made sure to not keep Nina later than the others.

What he missed about romance was the feeling that, whatever was about to happen, its course could be easily nudged into a different orbit by the choice of a different word, by a decision to turn your head this way and not that, or by letting your hand touch another hand on an armrest in a concert hall.

It was in those moments when the potentiality of love made it the sweetest, because the possibilities seemed limitless.

The next day, his daughter's letter arrived.

⚭

Junie wrote in a hand that was poised for a ten-year-old. She must have done so sitting on the high stool in front of her grandpa's workbench. Some of the reasons she gave for not going to America could be easily dismissed by adult logic, but others made Momo wonder if he'd forgotten what it was like to be a child—or if he ever knew what it was like to be *his* child.

She wrote: "I am happy here because it is home. Ever since Grandpa brought home the cricket in a bamboo cage, I hear crickets everywhere. Grandma said that they've been here for as long as she can remember, and that you played with them too when you were little. I asked her why I didn't hear them last year, and she said that it's because each year, as I grow, my eyes and ears learn to take in more and more things around me, even if they've always been here. Maybe next year a blue mushroom will grow by the river! I want to be here to see that too."

The content of her letter was calm and reasoned, and because of that, reading it produced in Momo the opposite effect: he felt agitated and impatient, not unlike when Cassia called him from San Francisco to tell him she was not coming.

Momo stood up and paced back and forth in the room when he came to this line. *No*—he almost said this out loud—*home is where you can achieve your full potential, and you don't know yet where that is until you've seen more of the world.*

Junie wrote: "Grandpa and Grandma say that in time, they will get old. I think it means that they will start to get forgetful. I want to be here to remind them of things when they forget. Like about the cricket, or the name of the eel seller, or the time everyone thought you were tiger food but you were only getting flowers. I will help them remember everything."

Momo knew that his parents were using the long-established euphemism for death. They were trying to prepare Junie, in the least alarming way possible, for the fact that they were only her temporary guardians. He stared at the ceiling in his bed, where just a week before he had been fantasizing about Nina.

I will bring my parents here too, Momo thought, *and we will fill up a two-story house with a three-generation family.*

The staircase outside the apartment again resonated with footfalls. *Tum-ti-tum-tum, tum-ti-ti-tum-tum.*

Now these sounded more like a marching beat to him, a call to action.

He leaped up from the chair and dialed Larry's number. When

he picked up, Momo asked, "How long does it take to learn to drive a car?"

"Well, it depends—" Larry began.

"Can you teach me?" Momo said. "I need to drive to San Francisco."

A Joint Act of Mischief

ABOUT THE SAME TIME MOMO RECEIVED THE LETTER FROM Junie, Dawn was living in San Francisco and starting a job as the conductor of the newly formed Peninsula Philharmonic. The years after her training at the conservatory were exhilarating, extroverted, and full of jet lag. She juggled odd jobs and boyfriends, saying yes to any opportunity that seemed reasonable. When she rehearsed with musicians or talked with composers and an outrageous idea surfaced, they said, "Yes, because this is the eighties," to mean now anything is possible, the same way people said, "The Cultural Revolution is over and the Gang of Four toppled," to mean that there is nothing to be afraid of now.

But Dawn was still afraid of many things. Lately one such thing was being interviewed by journalists who wanted to photograph her in the Japanese Tea Garden and to subtitle the interview "An Ambassador of Eastern Music." More Chinese musicians were arriving in the United States these days, through invitations and exchange programs, and she knew that the ease with which she slipped into a music career in America could not be separated from the fact that she was an émigré from communism, and was trading on the history of her country, willingly or not. Yet under the pretense of curiosity, the journalists reminded her of her otherness, of the fact that she had been trained by the enemy, and of her cultural analog, the relatable panda. They wanted her to sign off on a biography they had already cobbled together on her behalf.

Just the previous night, at a reception for his quartet, the cellist Edmund Hsu, in a fit of gin-infused pique, let it slip that he thought her composition, "that Gobi piece," was prone to nostalgia and did nothing to call out the atrocities of communism.

"My music isn't about regimes and borders," she said, also in a fit of pique, "and you know that."

"But America sheltered you," he said, "when you had only the clothes on your back."

Edmund was now a husband and father of twin boys, and this was the first time he said anything to her that reminded her of the days she spent in his Victorian house.

"You mean *you* sheltered me," she said. "Of course I haven't forgotten."

"Maybe you haven't," he said, a bit louder than was needed, "but you and I both know that I'm just a streetlamp—on your road of life headed to god-knows-where."

She opened her mouth but could not arrive at anything to say in response. Then Edmund began to apologize, explaining that child-rearing was depriving him of sleep and therefore good judgment. He even hugged her to prove his sincerity. They leaned against each other briefly like that, two people who had no established vocabulary for the intermittent feelings of disquiet that bubbled up.

But something about the subdued rancor of that exchange stayed and gnawed at her. Edmund had unleashed a powerful metaphor. Of not knowing her way somehow. Of abandonment. Of damage to others. For the following day and into Dawn's rehearsal run with the orchestra, the metaphor of the streetlamp saturated her thoughts. It sapped her strength.

The orchestra had gone through a recent strike and change of management, and the rehearsal, although productive, did not have the creative dynamism Dawn had hoped to ignite. When the session ended, she drove back toward her home in San Francisco across a bridge aglow in the rare afternoon sun. She could see the city shrouded in a fog that was still making up its mind whether to stay, and as she exited the bridge, the sunlight impelled her to turn and head toward Fisherman's Wharf. She parked and leaned on the door of her car to take in the controlled chaos there, animated by shellfish vendors, panhandlers, and portrait artists looking to stop pedestrians to sit down and pose for them.

The thought suddenly occurred to her: *I want to be one of them, these beseechers of attention from passersby.*

Out toward the water, the sky and the bay periodically gave off glimmers of blue where the fog tore open, then repaired itself.

She opened her car trunk and took out a spare violin she stashed there for work but rarely used these days. She tuned it and carried it with her to the convergence of two sidewalks that seemed well situated for street performance, and stood for a moment with the violin tucked under her arm, surrounded by gaiety and motion.

What she felt now was stage fright, but a different kind from what she'd always known. It wasn't the fear of making mistakes or even not delivering the best of oneself, but rather, of the indifference of the wider world.

She took a breath and began with a standard repertoire piece she could perform from memory. She played, a little rusty with her techniques, but with vigor. Still, she was surprised at how frail the violin sounded outdoors. A young couple drifted into the circumference of her music and tossed two quarters into her case as they walked past, having heard at most a few bars of music.

When the final note evaporated into thin air, she put her arms down and surveyed her surroundings. For the first time in a long time, she felt alone. She reoriented herself to the ambient soundscape—the scraping of milk crates against the sidewalk; conversation churned up by wind; high-pitched beeps emitted by a truck as it backed up. On the other side of the sidewalk, an old woman doling out bread was holding court with half a dozen cooing pigeons and a maverick seagull.

This, after all, was why she stopped here: to unleash music where there was no presumed interest in it, where the day would go on as usual in the absence of music.

Dawn decided to move forward with more of a crowd-pleaser, a tarantella. It was when she launched into its animated spirit that her first serious listener arrived. The curly-haired toddler, who seemed to have only recently mastered running, shot out from somewhere beyond her peripheral vision and stopped a few feet away. He planted his feet shoulder-width apart, in the most stable of martial arts stances, a stance designed to endure. And he probably could have done just that, if his nanny hadn't caught up to him and tried to steer him in the opposite direction.

The child shook his head: *NoNoNoNoNo.* He rotated his torso and squirmed out of her grip.

His nanny glanced at Dawn, then at the stray coins glistening in her violin case. Her look held both embarrassment and sympathy that someone her own age, gender, and ethnicity was panhandling for a living. But Dawn wasn't about to give up her young audience. She made a point of looking down directly at him, catching his eyes and nodding in rhythm. She now arrived at the liveliest part of the tarantella, a part played with spiccato, and she greatly exaggerated the motions and made the violin bow ricochet on the strings. The child broke into a grin and began flapping his arms, as if she had done this expressly to impress him. (She had.)

When she got to the end of the piece, Dawn tossed her head back and laughed. The child let out a squeal of delight and reached his chubby arm up toward her. It was as if the two of them had completed a joint act of mischief.

Dawn squatted down to say hello. What would happen, she thought, if in a few years' time someone put a child-sized violin into his little hands?

Released from the music's thrall, the boy was suddenly shy. He now staggered away, again setting his nanny in motion after him. Having dashed around in a large circle, he eventually ran back toward Dawn, flapped his arms again, and said to her in a fit of glee, "Moooore!"

Dawn obeyed him. How could she not? She began to improvise, trying to capture the rhythm of horse hooves. She tried to make the resulting medley as effervescent as possible for the boy. Now a kind of tug-of-war began for the attention of the child who could vote with his feet: His familiar nanny here, or this stranger there? Dawn was so intent on winning that she didn't even get a chance to speak to the nanny, who throughout the performance was trying to tell the boy—in Mandarin, incredibly—that his parents were waiting for them to go home, and that they were already late.

ℒ

Two evenings after Dawn played on the wharf, her phone rang. At first she thought it was a prank call: the voice at the other end sounded like that of a teenager.

"You don't know me," the caller said, "but I saw you play on the street the other day and I was too shy to say hello. Hope you don't mind me calling out of the blue."

She gave Dawn her name. It was a young violinist who'd gotten some press lately for merging pop music into her repertoire. Opinions varied as to whether this was boundary pushing or a form of selling out.

"But I didn't see anyone like you out there," Dawn said, "and believe me, there wasn't exactly a crowd."

"I hid from your line of sight," she said. "I've never done anything like this before."

Dawn wasn't sure what she was referring to—the busking, watching someone busk, or calling someone out of the blue. She waited for the caller to clarify, but she didn't, and it seemed that it was again Dawn's turn to make conversation. *This is an interesting turn of events,* Dawn thought, *especially for a performer who should've been more comfortable with the limelight.*

"In case you're wondering," Dawn said, "I didn't get enough money to even pay for parking."

"I could see you were just trying to, I don't know, return to music in some basic way."

"Yes," Dawn said. She couldn't imagine how it might have been obvious to anyone.

"I was moved by it because I can relate," the caller said, as if reading her mind. Then she added, "I also feel stuck, like in a rut."

Dawn almost laughed but stopped herself, not wanting to sound dismissive. "You're too young to be in a rut."

"That's what I was hoping to talk to you about," she said. "I've been experimenting with pop music, but really I think what I want to play is *new* classical music, if that makes sense."

That made a lot of sense, Dawn told her. But she remained confused about how this came about, even though she knew their community was small.

"I've played one of your pieces before, 'From the Gobi's Shore,' and I love it that it made me think a desert is also an ocean. So I picked up phrases from that piece in your improvisation as I was walking by, plus I could connect your face to that profile of you in *Orchestra Digest.* I'm kind of excited to have bumped into you like that, though I'd probably bump into you eventually some other way."

"Still, I'm glad it was at my big debut," Dawn said.

It was now that the caller laughed for the first time, and hearing that gave Dawn a buoyant feeling.

"I hope you don't mind," the caller said, "I would like to meet you."

A week later, when the young woman showed up on her doorstep with her violin, Dawn was still surprised at the ways in which the TV cameras and album covers failed to capture Viridiana's personality. When she wasn't holding the violin, when she was simply walking around the living room, or leaning against a music stand and nodding to something, she was both awkward and reckless. It seemed as if her limbs were still looking for ways to arrange and express themselves. She told Dawn that she'd never met her Korean father, but that sometimes members of the audience, often Asian men, would meet her backstage after a concert and claim her as one of their country's own.

Later, between the brainstorming sessions, they took a lunch break sitting on the stone steps in her backyard. They basked like a pair of lizards in another day of fog-free warmth.

"So what is it like," Dawn asked, chewing and glancing sideways at her, "to be a recovering child prodigy?"

Her young companion's eyes were shining, as if she'd been waiting for this very question. "For the most part, it was pretty lonely. And I think I was always angry at something." She squinted into the sunlight. "But things are definitely looking up, now that I'm collaborating with a recovering ambassador of Oriental music!"

Hue

CASSIA HAD TO BE EXTRA VIGILANT NOW THAT CYRUS COULD run around Fisherman's Wharf, his default playground. She could never tell what would catch his fancy on any particular day. Today it seemed to be artists offering on-the-spot portraits, who clustered on sidewalks and oriented their easels such that passersby could see what they were working on. They displayed sample sketches of Michael Jackson or Marilyn Monroe on poster boards. Some were realistic portraits in charcoal; others were cartoons done with markers.

As Cassia followed Cyrus through the rows of easels, she heard a male voice call out to her from behind.

"Hallo! I draw picture for your son," the voice said. "Only three dollar."

When she turned around to face that voice, she saw a Chinese man next to the easel. Normally these artists never talked to her because it was obvious that she was the nanny.

With her facing him, this man seemed to realize this too.

"See—I'm not the mother," she said to him in Chinese.

"Yes, your job is much harder than his mother's," he replied without missing a beat, "because you cannot make mistakes."

He was dark and compact, and although he was bony, he looked as if he was also used to labors of strength. A quick glance at his sample display showed that he belonged to the cartoonist school.

"Let me sketch both of you for free, then," he said. "If his parents like what they see, they can come find me here for a group portrait on the weekend."

This was a promotional model Cassia hadn't encountered before. Usually the artists competed with each other by lowering their prices. Three dollars was desperately low.

"What do you say, Cyrus?" Cassia said, trying to buy some time. "Do you want this uncle to draw you?"

Cyrus looked at the artist and nodded thoughtfully. Then he reached into his pocket, found a brown crayon, and handed it to the man. The man broke into a grin that stretched across his entire face. This exposed his crooked teeth, the kind Cassia was used to seeing before she came to this country.

He took the crayon from Cyrus and said, "That's exactly what I was looking for," and to her surprise, Cyrus smiled too.

Now it was harder to refuse him. *Fine*, she thought. *All in a day's work.* She sat down on the stool with Cyrus on her lap.

"This won't take long," the artist said to Cassia as he began to put the brown crayon to paper, "but if you're tired of running around with him all day, I will slow things down so you can take a load off your feet."

There was sun on their faces, and it was nice to sit like that, so Cassia thanked him and asked him to take his time.

It took talent to sketch a boy who seldom stopped moving. His eyes darted between Cyrus's face and the easel, between Cassia's face and the easel. When he looked at them his gaze was light-hearted but respectful. Then after a point, he only looked at the paper, with a knowing, though not unkind, smirk.

"Is this your only job?" she asked him, then immediately regretted the implication of the question.

"I also deliver Chinese food," he said. "Then for what's left of the night I paint, though for that, no one pays me anything."

He must have been an artist in China, Cassia thought. Perhaps he came with one of those visiting art delegations and just stayed, as people sometimes did.

"From my high school years on, I spent five years in Yunnan," he told her, perhaps sensing her curiosity. "Getting eaten alive by mosquitoes, breaking my back doing farmwork, getting rusticated by the Revolution."

A sent-down youth. Cassia did a quick calculation: he'd be just over thirty years old right now. He had belonged to that marked generation that had been made to feel preternaturally important, then turned into instruments of political insurrection.

"One of my closest friends drowned there," he said. "A girl. After that I thought: I have to get out of here while I still know my cardinal directions; I didn't want to get swallowed by the jungle."

She wondered if he'd loved her. If he had been there to see the body—if they found the body at all.

"When I was finally able to return home and get a city job, I couldn't stop thinking about the damn place. The light there was different. It made you feel like you could never get old. Aren't we humans perverse?"

Just as Cyrus was beginning to fidget in Cassia's lap, the artist turned the easel around to show them the portrait.

He had used Cyrus's brown crayon well: he switched to a realistic style, not the cartoon version, and there was an unplanned quality to the portrait that wouldn't have been possible if done in black marker. He didn't flatter her by making her eyes bigger, and there was just the barest hint of a smile on her face. Cyrus, of course, was the main feature of the portrait, and what emerged on the paper was a more impish version of the boy. It looked like this version of Cyrus would be capable of even more mischief, and yet you'd be more likely to forgive him for it.

"Remember to show it to his parents," he told her as he rolled up the portrait. "They can always find me in this spot on the weekends. And if not, my contact info is here."

He handed her a business card that featured a small image of an oil painting. It gave a studio address in a part of the city she didn't recognize. Under his name, it said "Hue Sheng."

"Hue?" she couldn't help but ask. The spelling didn't correspond to any Chinese characters. "Don't you mean *Hu*, with no *e*?"

"No. *Hue* means color," he said, grinning. "You get to name yourself anything you want in America. So that's my name now. And this is my color-infused life."

⚓

She didn't know what compelled her to go to his studio unannounced. It wasn't as if he'd said, *Come and visit.* She wanted to see what sustained him, this person who was clearly without legal status in this country. Cassia's mind couldn't help but return to his mention of his friend's drowning.

She set out before it got dark. The bus that stopped closest to his studio had a circuitous route, the kind that would be the first to get canceled if the city had a budget crunch. It took her past warehouses and abandoned lots, parts of the city nannies never went to. The stark industrial landscape the bus passed through made it impossible for her to change her mind and hop off halfway. For the last twenty minutes of the ride, she was the only passenger.

When she eventually found his building and took the empty staircase up to the second floor, she stood outside the studio door for five minutes, trying to think of reasons to justify her visit.

I have always loved art, she might have said. Or, even more disingenuously: *It's always nice for a sojourner to see landscapes of her native country.*

She heard a chair scraping the floor from behind the closed door. She imagined nude models, in the flesh and in plaster casts, and her urge to leave resurfaced. But the prospect of taking the empty bus back so soon seemed even more unthinkable.

And so she knocked.

He came to the door and showed no surprise that she was there. If he was glad she came, there was no trace of any smugness. Instead, he invited her in, courteously and with patience. He made her feel that it was the most natural thing in the world for her to be there.

She had been wrong about the models. The studio was cluttered, as she imagined these places to be, but in a much more prosaic way—receipts, cardboard pieces, twine. He seemed to know exactly where everything was. When the only other chair he produced for her sake proved to be wobbly, he reached straight into a plastic tub to fish out a piece of cork just the right thickness to stabilize its legs.

There were pieces of paper strewn about that were cartoons of families or kids—perhaps portraits he offered for free that remained unwanted. It occurred to Cassia that it cost him next to nothing to draw a portrait for someone—really anyone, and that he'd come out ahead if one in ten of them paid for a drawing.

He did not ask about Cyrus, the boy's parents, or even how she got there. When he moved between the paper drawings from the day to the canvases he painted at night and told her about them, he did not act as if this was an undue struggle or the world owed him anything.

On his canvases, one could make out delicate-waisted girls in long skirts. The subtropical landscape in the paintings was not a familiar one, though Cassia recognized it from descriptions of Yunnan out of geography books that extolled the vastness of the country.

In her imagination, it was a land where, if you parted large plantain leaves, you might see young people splashing each other in a river.

"I'm not ashamed to tell you this," he said to her, "but there are days on the wharf when I wonder if I wouldn't be better off not having left Yunnan at all."

There was a small cot in one corner, a one-ring stove in another. It had never occurred to her that he slept here. In her jittery state, she somehow missed the fact that as he talked, he was putting the kettle on the stove to make tea. Now she saw, too late, that he was pouring her some.

It was only when she sipped her tea, and thus had her eyes lowered for a moment, that she caught him looking at her.

All through this, he never leaned in too close, never uttered a suggestive word, and never asked for anything beyond what she would have gladly offered. So seamless was the eruption of desire, in fact, that she could not say for sure who—or even what—initiated the sex.

He did not smell of paint or turpentine, as she expected him to. Just dust and a hint of woodsmoke. In the frenzy of it all, they threw themselves against the wall of the studio. She repeatedly cried out in a voice she hardly recognized, as much from surprise as from pleasure. When they caught their breath, his hands were gripping her temples, his damp forehead on hers.

And even though she knew that on the spot on the wall where his body had repeatedly pounded against hers, there was no dent or smudge on the plaster, the idea of an impression, or mark, persisted. It could be picked out the next time, she thought, and you would be able to point to it and say, *There—right there—that's where it happened.* Long afterward and in her own bed, the knot in her stomach still writhing, it was all Cassia could think about: the inevitability of it all.

He did not avoid looking at her when they pulled their clothes back on. His eyes were bright and reflective, though not from anything so simple as hope or happiness. "I'm going to paint for the rest of the night," he told her. "You can sleep on the cot. But if you stay long enough, I will want you again, so be warned."

⁂

One night she came to him and found him with a black eye. He told her he had a row with another street artist over their territories. The other guy took a swing at him, but at the end of the day, they parted as friends. It was while touching his bruised face to survey the damage—perhaps with her erstwhile nurse's instinct— that she found that she wanted him intensely, right then and there, as if he had just fought over her and emerged triumphant.

"What, you want me to pick a fight every day now?" he asked her afterward.

Before this, lovemaking always reminded her who she was; now it allowed her to forget.

She told him about stumbling upon *Playboy* magazine in her employers' bedroom that they used as a "marital aid," told him her reaction to the buxom nudes. Practicing artists see so much naked flesh, he said as if to reassure her, that the sight of *Playboy* or *Penthouse* failed to excite him. Sure, he said, the occasional parted thighs can be nice, but it was always something else that drove him crazy. Like an unexpected glimpse of an ankle.

She had beautifully shaped ankles, he told her, and added, "I bet I'm the first man to tell you this."

He was.

Some nights they took his beat-up van out for a ride, and sometimes he switched places with her in the parking lot and let her drive, just for the hell of it, and she'd arrive back at the studio with sweat-soaked armpits but invigorated—it was the good kind of *ciji*.

One night, she missed a turn on the road, but instead of turning around, he told her to keep driving until they ended up at a beach near the Presidio.

"Let's park here and take a walk," he said. "There's something you have to see."

Once they reached the wet, compacted sand, he seemed to know exactly where he was going in the secluded section of the beach. There was a partial moon overhead, though anything could be lurking among the shadows of the jagged cliffs. Her senses were sharper than they'd ever been in daylight.

They walked farther on, and she began to notice an oddly familiar stink in the air.

She tried to keep up with his stride, walking between the flatness of the sandy beach and the jagged rocks near the cliffs. To stabilize herself, she sometimes grabbed on to the rocks, and was surprised to find they came apart by the fistful, that they were soft and claylike.

"What are you trying to show me?" she asked. "Why can't you just tell me?"

"Wait just a little bit and you'll see," he said, walking on. She was annoyed at this, but had to swat the annoyance away because she wanted to find out what the odor was and where she'd smelled it before.

It was the scent of decay—organic decay.

Hue stopped moving ahead, finally, when they were nearly at a cove carved into the jagged cliffs. "There it is," Hue said, turning around.

In front of them was what was left of a large animal. A good deal of its flesh had rotted away; its head was pointed away from the ocean. It was in a halfway state, no longer a carcass but not yet a skeleton. One could easily make out its mammalian rib cage against the blackness of the cliffs.

"I came here the day after it washed ashore," he said. "I've been watching its slow transformation."

It was a small whale. She stood, immobile, against the crashing of the surf.

He said, "I know it smells bad. We can go soon if you—"

She shook her head vigorously. Hue cast a quick look at her to ascertain her mood, then sat down on the sand. He looked at the whale while she looked at a point past the whale, offshore.

She took in one breath, then another, before it finally came to her. This was the smell of public latrines in the tiny alleys of Beijing, brick-made outhouses shared by families living in courtyard-style houses, before people moved to high-rises with indoor plumbing. For three years, she had lived in one of those houses with her brothers after her parents died and before she started working for the factory. Unexpectedly, she was thinking about the days when she was twenty, twenty-one, then twenty-two. On winter mornings, the scent of latrines mingled with the slightly acrid-smelling soot from coal stoves. On those mornings, you got out of bed reluctantly, wrapped a padded coat around your shoulders, and you had to run to and from the outhouses, because to relieve yourself you had to put up with the cold.

It was absurd—her youth, her golden years, captured in the volatile molecules from the decaying flesh of an accidental messenger, one that had followed some ocean current to end up here like this.

"Do you think it was already dead when it washed ashore?" she asked.

"I hope so. I'd hate for its last moments to be in a world it didn't recognize."

She was grateful for his presence even though she could not

find the words to tell him that or describe what was happening to her.

He turned to her. "Makes you want to push it back into the ocean, doesn't it?"

Yes, how infinite the sea is, she thought, *and how accommodating.*

"The ocean is a good place to let the dead go," she said.

Despite its relatively small size, the decaying whale was not easy to move without tools or advanced planning. Its bottom was partially sunk into the beach, after weeks of surf washing over it and depositing sand around it. They shoved at it, kicked it to try to dislodge its bones, telling themselves that the first steps were the hardest. They finally gave up after what felt like half an hour of grunting and heaving and wiping their hands on the sand. They stayed on the putrid beach until the partial moon began to set, and only because Hue feared that it'd be hard to find their way back without the moonlight.

They stumbled back across the sand, dirty, cold, parsing both dreams and nightmares from an elsewhere they could not share with each other.

✗

Their days kept them separate, but their nights merged this way, uneasily. In the evening, Cassia would say good-bye to Cyrus and hop on the bus for the long ride to Hue's studio. There were nights when the bus suddenly filled up with women in miniskirts and feather boas, with no jacket to fend off the chill. Cassia could not help staring at these women, these girls; it was impossible to tell their age. They talked loudly and laughed shrilly. Under ordinary circumstances, Cassia would have preferred no company to their company, but these weren't ordinary circumstances.

There were nights when she deliberately stayed away. She did it to test the limit of their endurance, to see how much he wanted her, or to punish herself, to reassert control, or for the thrill of it, or to eliminate the need for talking—there were always new reasons, and the permutations were endless. Then, as soon as she stepped in front of his studio door she felt light-headed. She could never fully predict how she would feel the moment he opened the door. Would they be a little cruel to each other tonight? What memory from their past would they dredge up and share with the other person? How long would they talk before they would tumble onto the cot? And she suspected that it was the sureness of being surprised—by pain or pleasure, it didn't even matter—that kept her coming back.

She never brought up Momo, and Hue never asked questions, not even the times he fingered the scar on her belly left by the C-section. He did so as if it was just another small contour of her body, like her ankles, there to be discovered by him. She let him come to his own conclusions about her, and that too was a thrill. When they made love, she imagined there were moments when he held back the urge to say, *Can he do this for you? Does he?* In those moments she gave in to his vanity, and told him—truthfully—how much she liked fucking. (She learned to say *fuck* without wincing.) She'd read somewhere that in certain cultures, young men were sexually initiated by older women. Their situation was, absurdly, the opposite.

Back when she had a younger, firmer body, she hadn't known just how much more slowly sensations left the body as it got older. She hadn't known that she could carry all the tactile memories of a night with him all throughout the next day. Yet she did.

She never remembered what the bus ride back was like.

Relative Speed

THE WHITE ROAD DIVIDER IN FRONT OF HIM, CHECK. THE REAR-view mirror showing a safe distance between him and the next car, check. Staying out of other cars' blind spots, check.

Momo did not expect driving could be so—and here the English word declared itself loudly—*fun*. He felt for the first time that he could control a vehicle with the grace and agility that he once thought was possible only on a bicycle.

They were on an open country road with dusk coming on. It was November, when daylight and wind directions were both changing, but not so completely as to make people forget what it was like to barbecue on the lawn, with arms and legs bare. They could still keep the windows open.

"Now you're ready to floor it," Larry said, pressing one palm down onto the back of his other hand to show Momo what he meant. "Pedal to the metal."

"Really?"

"You know I don't joke about safety."

Momo floored it. Larry poked his head out of the window.

"Woo-o hoo—oo . . . !"

The sound of Larry's voice trailed behind them, or at least Momo thought it did, because he felt he really was going that fast.

A month later, Momo bought a used car. Before the snow began falling in Chimney Bluffs and while he was still learning to distinguish the different kinds of hums and whirs in his Subaru,

Momo took some additional safety lessons from Larry, which involved a series of imaginary scenarios.

"Let's say that a crazy guy suddenly walked into the middle of the road in front of you," Larry began. "What would you do?"

"Brake. Hard," Momo said. "What else can I do?"

"Works only if you were going slow enough," Larry said, "but let's say you're already going pretty fast. Let's say you're going fifty, sixty on a city road, which, given your predilections, will happen eventually."

Momo got a little lost in the words. "What?"

"Point is," Larry said, "you may not to be able to stop in time. So what do you do?"

"Okay, then—go around."

"To the left or right?"

Momo looked at Larry to make sure he was serious. "Well, if I'm on the left lane, then it's probably better to steer to the right," Momo said slowly, "because I will either hit another car going in the same direction or a mailbox, maybe. Compared to on my left, it may be a car coming toward me—so, not so good."

"Correct," Larry said. "You choose the collision with the lower relative speed. Excellent. Most right-handed people will swerve to the left, because if you have only one hand on the wheel—your right hand—then that's a more natural rotation for your right hand, see? A lot of driving is anticipating these decisions, because if you don't anticipate them, the decisions will result from habit, and be made for—you—"

The last two words were squeezed out of Larry's clenched teeth, because during this interval, Momo was accelerating toward a telephone pole in the parking lot and swerved twice—first a sharp left, then a sharp right—to end up on the other side of the pole.

"Amazing!" Momo said after the car stopped and their bodies

bounced back from the tug of the seat belts. "It really feels very different!"

He knew this had been reckless, but couldn't help it—something about driving made him so. This shenanigan of his marked the end of his lessons and their joint grocery trips ("Um, I think you're good now," Larry said). They still carpooled to work, out of loyalty to each other, but from this point on, Momo drove for hours on the weekends by himself, to clear his head.

During those drives, he found that he was addicted to seeing the landscape move backward past him. To speed. Some days, even without any destination, he could fall into a peculiar rhythm in which the road in front of him seemed to stretch invitingly forever.

The lunar new year in 1987 fell at the end of January, and on that night, since he knew there'd be no interference from the moon, he returned to the campus athletic field where he'd first seen the night sky in America. The viewing conditions were again excellent, and he could even make out the smudge of light that was the Andromeda Galaxy.

He remembered that a year ago this time, the news had been abuzz with the *Challenger* disaster and there was talk about the poor viewing conditions for Halley's Comet.

Junie would be eleven soon. She was in fact eleven already, by Chinese reckoning. He thought to himself: *The next time Halley's Comet comes close to the sun, Junie will be eighty-six years old.*

Vapor condensed in front of his mouth. The repeated motions of craning upward were making him dizzy—or maybe it was the absurd insistence to look so far into the future. He knew he was sometimes driven to hopes that were the wrong size for the world.

Still, he had to wait until late spring, for the semester break, before he could leave for San Francisco.

A Toast

BECAUSE DAWN FOUND HERSELF TRAVELING LESS THAN USUAL for a few months, she held a party at home to usher in the 1987 lunar new year. Her living room filled up with people piling dumplings on their plates, and the room gradually acquired the smell of soy sauce and chives and savory steam. Edmund brought a large sheet cake that said "Happy Year of the Wabbit!" at the insistence of his five-year-old twins. A waltz was playing, and the twins were both shrieking with laughter as Viridiana whirled them around the room, one on each arm.

At some point during the impromptu dancing, Viridiana swung an elbow out too far and brushed a vase off a shelf. When the sound of the crash stopped the waltzing trio in its tracks, the boys watched in stunned silence as Viridiana, without a moment's hesitation, squatted down to pick up the shards of glass.

"No, stop, let me." Dawn swooped in with a broom and lifted her up by the elbows. "You're a violinist! You need your fingers."

"I will replace it for you, of course," Viridiana said, looking up at her, seemingly not concerned at all about her hands' other uses.

"Oh, it's time Peter's vase moved on, like he did," Dawn told her. "Let me sweep the remnant of my last boyfriend into the dustbin."

Viridiana stood up and curtseyed to the small mound of shards gathered in the dustpan. "It's been swell, Peter," she said. "Goodbye and good luck."

"Good-bye and good luck," echoed the twins, who had been kept a few steps away and watching.

When even the late-arriving guests had had something to eat and the hubbub reached a saturation point, a kind of consensus emerged among the guests. Dawn's former conservatory mentor, a Hungarian with a voluminous silver mane, began tapping on a glass.

"We want a speech from the latest winner of the Orfeo Prize," he said, looking toward their hostess, "and we want it more than dessert."

Dawn tucked a strand of hair behind her ear. She hadn't wanted to make this a career celebration of any kind. But by now, she was used to giving statements about the prize, sometimes several times a week. There had already been press about it, about her being the first Chinese-born composer to win it. She knew that with this accolade, it would be possible for her to return to China now, reforged as an accomplished sojourner abroad rather than a defector.

By now she'd learned that the way to handle these requests was to be cheerful and succinct. She lifted a glass and surveyed the room. "You know that I washed up on these shores like a beached whale, and all of you"—she gestured with her arms—"helped me grow my first pair of feet, and then helped me learn to stand on them. You made my career possible. So here's to all of you, dear to my heart!"

There were festive whoops erupting in the room, and in between she could hear a percussive winter rain against the living room window.

She felt a touch of light-headedness. Had she lost track of how many glasses she had had? She knew she'd hit the right notes and should just stop here. But maybe because everyone seemed to be enjoying themselves and her mentor was still looking at her waiting for more, she broke her own rule for brevity.

"For a long period in my life, the only form of music took place on large stages and with a dominant chorus of voices," she went on. "And what I missed then wasn't the solo rendition exactly, but small, honest dialogues, say, between two musical voices, three at the most. This is why I'm drawn to writing music for small ensembles."

Her eyes now landed without thinking on the side of the room that faced the Pacific Ocean. "The first pieces I ever composed, at twenty, I imagined I might play with my grandfather if we ever got a replacement piano. Back then, it was he who told me, half a lifetime ago now, that the secret to patience was finding something else to do in the meantime." She paused. "I wish I could tell him that it was very good advi—"

Her inability to continue in the middle of the word caught her off-guard.

Almost every interviewer, on the phone or in person, had asked her to recount the exact moment when she knew she would leave China behind, as if in every life there had to be an epiphanic moment of transformation. But if she truly wanted to convince them that it all had been fumbling, awkward, and riddled with false starts, she would have offered them this evidence. Before she left China with the delegation in 1979, she'd gone to her grandfather's grave, the same way she'd always done. She brought a bag of sunflower seeds, his favorite snack. The bag she brought that year was the same size as always, no bigger. She dusted off his gravestone, and spoke to him as she'd always done, and not as if she was going to be away for a very long time.

His was a gravestone with no replenishment of sunflower seeds for eight years now. She wanted to convey this vision to the crowd somehow, but the words required would not come out. They were lodged in her solar plexus, and she was suddenly flailing, changed from a jolly hostess one instant to someone who choked on words to end a toast.

"It was very—" she tried again.

Just then Viridiana moved toward Dawn and took the glass from her hand.

"I just turned twenty-one, okay? So I'm going to butt my way into every toast I can," Viridiana said to the room, which, along with its collective chuckle, seemed relieved that the festive mood could go on.

"When I play Dawn's music," Viridiana continued, "I feel like I'm part of something very ancient, but also very new at the same time." She paused to give the room time to absorb this, for the guttural noises of assent to die down. "Her music makes me aware of the time before I was born, of places I have never been—she makes my life larger." Then she held up the glass with one arm and wrapped her other arm around Dawn. "And this, I say, is her true gift to the world."

There were murmurs of assent. As people applauded, Viridiana squeezed Dawn's shoulder once before releasing her hold, and Dawn only had time to mouth a *thank-you* before Viridiana slipped back among the other guests. Dawn was now left alone in a small and quivering pool of limelight trained inside herself that dazzled and bewildered her.

The dumpling munching and chatter continued. Except for Edmund, who rubbed her arm in passing, no one during the course of the evening asked Dawn about her grandfather, and she was glad of it.

Edmund had been right: "From the Gobi's Shore" was nostalgic. But it was nostalgic not for a place or regime, but for a kind of youthful certainty that life must be so. The last time she felt that certainty was when she was walking out of the concert hall where Padushka played, when she couldn't wait to announce to Momo what her destiny was going to be.

She had been given credit—by the press, by her peers—for having seized her destiny, when it had been an accumulation of favorable accidents. She knew that everything that made up her biography, down to the most prosaic detail, could just as well have been otherwise.

Perhaps she had written "From the Gobi's Shore" for a hypothetical life not lived. She knew that in a world in which even a small flutter nudged her off-orbit just a bit, she might have lived on the edge of a desert, might have been a mother to many children, and might have been looked over by a man with bronzed arms who sang in a tenor voice as he labored with his hands.

Fan Mail

IN EARLY MARCH, IT WAS VIRIDIANA'S IDEA TO GO ICE SKATING to celebrate the end of a grueling week of recording, and she wanted Dawn to come with her.

"But you know you can break a wrist, right?" Dawn said, shaking her head. "Or sprain it."

"I am good at skating," Viridiana said, "so the chances are small—and the psychological benefits huge."

That recklessness. When Viridiana performed, it was channeled into a fearlessness that separated the good players from the excellent ones. But offstage, it burst open at the seams and spilled out without rhyme or reason. Dawn saw it in the way she leaned over the railings of her balcony to point out something on the street below, the way she walked too close to the burning cigarette of a stranger on a sidewalk.

"How about a movie instead," Dawn suggested, "with lots of explosions? I always find that relaxing."

"Thirty minutes of gliding on ice—that's all I need," Viridiana said. She used to take lessons, she told Dawn, and it was such a different way of moving about. "I miss this so much. My manager will be coming back into town next week, so this is my only chance!"

There was no changing her mind, it seemed, but the thought of a concert violinist ice skating made Dawn so nervous, she couldn't even call it by its right name. She kept saying ice "staking" this, ice "staking" that, which only made Viridiana laugh.

"I'll 'stake' for only twenty minutes, then," she bargained, "if you treat me to dinner afterward."

Dawn sighed. She thought that if she refused, Viridiana might go regardless, which wouldn't have been any better. She thought this was probably the reason child prodigies sometimes ended up astray in life: brimming with all that brightness with nowhere to go.

They went to a rink near Ocean Beach. Once on her skates, Viridiana was overjoyed to discover that she hadn't forgotten how to skate backward. And in that position she kept a good conversational distance from Dawn and couldn't stop giggling.

"If you ever have fans asking what you'd do with your life if you didn't play the violin," Dawn said, "I think the answer would be obvious."

"But see, no one *ever* asks me that." She was now swaying a little, looking over her shoulder and putting her arms out, as if she was getting ready to launch into a spin. "I wish they would."

"Don't even think about doing a jump," Dawn said. But even she had to admit that Viridiana looked genuinely happy, and also beautiful, gliding that way.

"When people write me letters," Viridiana said as she continued gliding, "most of them are young players asking me things like, 'How do you follow your dreams? I'm having trouble with mine.'"

Dawn nodded, but it was difficult to keep up with Viridiana this way. She checked her watch: ten more minutes.

"I've been getting letters from someone," Viridiana continued, "and he's the first person who made me want to write back."

"Not love letters, I hope," Dawn said, trying to ease her own nerves on the ice.

Viridiana rolled her eyes. "They started in English but lately he's switched to writing to me in Chinese."

"Promise me—no jumping," Dawn said.

"He wrote me about Padushka. His visit to Beijing must've been something."

"I remember it well," Dawn said, but what she was about to say was derailed by the fact that she stumbled slightly on the ice. Viridiana reached out her hand.

"I'm fine—but can you skate forward, please?"

Viridiana twirled around once, with ease, to show Dawn that it didn't matter which way she faced. "I could show you one of his letters," she said. "You'd enjoy them, and I'm also dying to find out what the Chinese letters say."

None of Viridiana's words fully registered with Dawn, and in fact were immediately forgotten, because she stumbled again, and this time landed on the unforgiving surface of the ice.

When she got up, it was Viridiana who seemed to relent, and she asked if Dawn was hungry. The thought of finally being able to usher Viridiana out of the rink gave Dawn such relief that she perked up.

"Just one more lap around, V," she said, "and then I'm taking you to dinner."

⚮

March 21, 1987

Dear Viridiana,

I'm writing this letter in my car, driving somewhere between Cheyenne and Laramie. This morning I found a male elk grazing on the shoulder of the highway, as if the flow of traffic posed no threat to him whatsoever. Elk or no elk, the landscape is new to me, and feels quintessentially American. As I was driving, I wanted to tell you this: I think that the immigrant must be like an improviser of music. He must take a template alien to him and, while bound by rules, turn it into something of his own. In this the improviser is the opposite of the composer, who has time to consider all his options and all possible architectures of sounds and silences. Design from scratch is not an option available to the immigrant-improviser. He must make his next move in real time.

I've always imagined that only here in America could we (my wife, daughter, and I) live together without pity or sadness. Nothing in my life has happened the way I planned it, but here I am still making more plans, to work out something so that my estranged wife and I might be able to spend Junie's twelfth birthday with her—now less than a year away.

In my last letter, I told you about my last-minute music lesson for my daughter, and you may rightly wonder why I was so desperate to make her into a violin prodigy. This is partly because shortly before I left China, my wife gave birth to a stillborn baby, a boy.

While in the delivery room waiting for that birth, I made a promise to Junie that the second child wouldn't change how I felt about her—and I meant that having an able-bodied child wouldn't make me love her any less. But even though our second child didn't survive, he did change things. He changed everything. I became fiercely determined about Junie's destiny in a way I wouldn't have been if it weren't for the second baby. (I keep saying "second baby" because we left him unnamed. But somehow I think my wife has a secret name for him, and it's one that she will never tell me.)

After the second baby, I realized that maybe having a "normal" life for Junie would be impossible. But then I thought—if not a normal life, then why not a spectacular life?

I wanted her to become someone people looked at with awe. I thought about the looks I got from strangers when I took Junie to public places, how people looked at her first with astonishment, *then turned to look at me, with pity. I wanted to change those looks into ones of admiration and marvel. When I think of the new legs Junie might have in the future, I always think of the electric violin you played on at that mega-concert on TV. The Italian luthiers certainly never imagined a violin could be made out of crystal, but in your hands, the crystal violin was just as alive, made music just as stunning, and I will never forget seeing you play that for the first time.*

I didn't let my wife see the dead baby. At the time, I thought that it was the right thing to do. Looking at Junie's legs every day reminded Cassia of what was missing, and that led to grief, each day. I thought that maybe this time, because there was no life to begin any memories, that she would be better off not knowing what the dead baby looked like. I would've kept the sex of the baby from her too if I could.

But this morning, while driving the last stretch of road with a storm gathering, I thought: Is it possible that grief too is like music? Maybe once grief begins, you cannot simply cut it off. Rather you have to let it run its course the way an aria comes to its last note. You cannot stop grief in its tracks any more than you can cut off the aria at just any point you deem convenient.

And maybe, like someone said, love is a wound that closes and opens, all our lives.

The Swerve

AT THE NEVADA-CALIFORNIA STATE LINE, MOMO SAW THE TREE-tops on the interstate median scintillate with ice. It was as if he had left winter behind on the plains, only to reencounter it here. The road was steep, and the Subaru climbed reluctantly. He worried that it might give out, but in the end, the Subaru prevailed. From the summit on down, Momo felt a sense of relief; now he would be coasting all the way to San Francisco.

It was there—past the summit on the west side—that it happened. It came without any warning. One moment he was on a flat stretch of road, and the next moment, he felt the car veer sharply toward the center divider. He tried to steer it back to the right, but the steering wheel was no longer calling the shots. The car hit the concrete divider at a fifteen-degree angle, and because Momo was still steering with all his might, it responded belatedly and turned all the way around. Now pointed in the opposite direction in his lane, the car kept moving, first against the direction of traffic, and then its momentum pushed it across the shoulder.

By the time the car stopped, it was leaning at an angle in the shallow ditch by the road.

Momo had to shut his eyes against the topsy-turvy view of the outside before he could unbuckle himself and reach over to shove open the passenger-side door and wriggle out from it.

It was only then that a jolt of panic set in: *I could have died.*

Since the ditch was shallow enough, he was able to maneuver

the Subaru back on the road. He pulled into the next gas station to assess damage: a substantial dent to the left side, a bruise on his head. His shirt was soaked through with sweat.

He had been very lucky. There had been no cars behind him, or there would have been head-on collisions. The mechanic at the shop, seeing his bruise, gave him coffee to calm his nerves, and when he took it, he saw how badly his hands were shaking.

Black ice, he learned from the mechanic. Happened a lot in these months when the cold returned unexpectedly, and most people couldn't see these patches on the road. "Might as well be careful," the mechanic said as he sent Momo on his way. "Plus, this car of yours doesn't take well to erratic steering, ice or no ice."

Momo saw the tinseled tops of the ponderosas differently after that; his wonderment at their beauty was more guarded now. He remembered that Larry told him about a party of pioneers in the previous century who reached a peak in the Sierras and eventually starved to death by the shore of a lake. Momo tried to imagine their last hours, huddled against despair.

Every few miles he pulled over, got out, and ran his hand over the road surface, just to make sure there weren't any more patches of this black ice. He did this five or six times before he felt he could move ahead without a constricted feeling in his solar plexus.

He stopped at a roadside diner just to hear voices in conversation around him. When he made small talk with the waitresses, they agreed that the road conditions were terrible.

And then suddenly—or so it seemed—the road he was driving on became a bridge. The bridge spanned a body of water, and across it, skyscrapers glinted before him. He knew that there was no more ice on the road. Things didn't freeze so close to the bay; that very possibility had vanished because of the geography here.

He had finally arrived.

Three Letters

Cassia and Cyrus walked out of the house toward the bus stop. It was a Tuesday in early spring, and the arboretum and petting zoo were free.

The two of them stood at the confluence of two hilly streets, with a stop sign no one bothered heeding. But today, Cassia saw that a car actually came to a stop. This was so unusual that she had to bend down and look at the driver.

Then she saw that it was Momo.

"What—?"

In the car, he appeared older and more tired. He also had a large bruise on his forehead.

He rolled down his window. "I asked the Wilders where to find you," he said by way of explanation and greeting.

Her first instinct was to ask about his bruise, but she suddenly found herself angry—to just show up like this with his unkillable optimism—for what?

"Can't you see I'm working?" she said. She was now even irritated at the Wilders, who could have at least called to inform her, or ask, in the first place.

"Bring the boy into the car, and we can drive around," he said.

By now, two cars were honking at Momo from behind. Cassia was sure that neither of those cars had ever seen a car stopped at that stop sign on the road.

Cassia said, "You'll have to find a parking spot and take the bus with us, then. We are going to the park."

Momo parked and joined them at the bus stop. He squeezed the boy's cheeks and legs.

"Look at you!" Momo said in a voice that told Cassia he was determined to ignore her unfriendliness. "I'd love to munch on such a chubby arm like yours."

Cyrus, who was just now smiling at Momo's pokes and prods, suddenly stopped smiling. His features began to rearrange themselves in a slow but resolute slide toward what would be the face of crying.

"All right, hey," Cassia said quickly to Cyrus, bouncing him. "He's just playing. He's not going to really eat you."

"He understands Chinese!" Momo said.

"It's either that," she said, "or he just has a sixth sense about certain things."

"You've changed," he said.

"I should hope so."

"You have a sharper tongue now."

"I'm not going to Chimney Bluffs with you," she said. "But you already know that."

"Then why did you come this far? To America, I mean."

Because I needed to ride on the coattails of The Other Woman to change, she thought.

"I do have an explanation," she said. "But you need time to absorb it. Plus, since you didn't tell me you were coming, you could at least give me more time."

"All right," he said.

Cassia could tell he was trying to be patient. This led her to say, more quietly, "Just give me a few more days."

It would have been very uncomfortable for them to meet each other without Cyrus, Cassia thought, and here the poor child is serving as the Ambassador for Estranged Spouses.

The three of them spent the afternoon in the arboretum. They made an odd threesome—one of the adults looking disheveled like a day laborer and entertaining a toddler, who listened to the woman give him directives in her native language and didn't seem to notice that he wasn't Chinese.

Momo did not make Cyrus cry again for the rest of the day.

⚹

When Momo and Cassia met again, it was on a bench above the ruins of an old bathhouse. From where they sat, they could see the surf crash onto giant boulders out at sea.

Cassia handed Momo an envelope. "I wrote down a few things," she said. "Things you should probably know about us before we decide what to do."

From the envelope, Momo took out three sheets of notebook paper with Cassia's handwriting on it. Why was it that writing things down was always easier than saying them to someone next to you? And yet it was.

On the first sheet Cassia wrote:

Two weeks ago I asked someone to drive me to Stanford University. The only reason being that the father of a boy I once loved studied there, years and years ago, and I wanted to understand a little more of that life. I call him a boy because we were both so young at the time that there is no other word for it. He died years before I met you. I still dream about him sometimes.

Momo thought that there must have been times when she was on the verge of telling him this. He could see now how years of living together with someone could lead to this numbness: when he heard and even acknowledged what she said, but did not let these things touch his inward self, the part of him that mattered.

He said quietly, "So I wasn't your first."

"Keep going," she said.

On the second sheet of paper Cassia wrote:

The person who drove me to Stanford is the man I'm currently involved with. I wasn't looking for anyone, and I certainly didn't do it out of revenge. But it still happened, and I think you should know. I think he and I will eventually go our separate ways, but I don't know how long it will last. Maybe months, or not even weeks. Maybe years.

"Who is he?" Momo said, and could not hide the rancor in his voice.

Cassia spoke as if he asked an entirely different question. "All I thought was: when a doorway opens before you and stands open, there is no reason not to enter."

He shook his head, as if to reset a thermometer that had registered a fever. There was heat rising from the pit of his stomach.

"What you are telling me," he said, surprised at himself as he said it, "is that I'm not your last."

Cassia looked away. "There's one more."

Momo tucked the second sheet of paper behind and started on the third sheet. On it were only two sentences:

I brought with me to America the ashes of our child in a tin can. Since that time I have hated you for not letting me see him.

Momo looked at those two sentences for a long time until the characters became a strange assemblage of strokes. His eyes went out of focus after a while, and came to fixate instead on four pale yellow flowers on a patch of grass in his line of sight, just beyond his hand holding the three sheets of paper. These flowers became etched into his mind's eye.

When he thought to speak, he saw that Cassia had been weeping quietly, watching him looking, in his own way, at those flowers.

"We . . ." he said as the weight of that pronoun settled on him, "we wanted you to rest."

⚓

There had been a debate that day outside the delivery room. About whether to give the lifeless infant to Cassia so that she could see him for the first and last time. Maybe even hold him briefly. The doctor was strongly opposed to this idea. There had been an emergency C-section, and the patient, he said, needed to rest and heal and not be exposed to even more mental trauma. The word was *ciji*—something often bandied about in psychiatric wards. It's never good to expose physically weakened patients to more *ciji*, the doctor said.

The other faction was headed by Momo's mother, who said they should show Cassia the baby. She and Momo's father had been visiting to help out, and after they heard the news, rushed to the hospital with Junie sleeping on her grandfather's shoulder.

"If you don't let her see the baby," Momo's mother said, "there'll be a hole in her heart, and it will be agony every time— every time it beats." She turned to her son and seemed to search his face for signs of courage. "I know this is true. Tell them."

Momo knew he was called upon for a major decision, but couldn't budge from the hallway bench. He had been sitting on this very bench when the nurse came to tell him that the baby had been suffocated by his own umbilical cord.

His future life with Cassia—into middle age and beyond—

flashed before his eyes, and the vista it showed was echoing with silence. For the first time in his life, he did not know how to fill that silence with upbeat words.

His father chimed in. "Let *us* take a look at the baby, then," he said. "We will look at the baby on her behalf."

It was the kind of conciliatory thing Momo's father often said in their family, after decades of bickering about things large and small—a halfway solution tossed out to give each side hope that they may yet prevail.

Momo's mother didn't argue this time. She looked at Junie, asleep, whose cheek was smothered against her grandfather's shoulder. "Let's do that," she said to the doctor. She took hold of her son's elbow to get him off the bench.

They were ushered into another room. They stopped in front of a counter. There was something lying in an oblong enamel tub. All traces of natal blood had been washed off of it. A small protruding genital was there between the legs to confirm that it was, indeed, a boy. The umbilical cord that had been wrapped around his neck was gone. His eyes were shut resolutely, as if he refused to be defiled by the world, and was finally granted that wish.

Momo needed only one hand to hold the dead baby, but he used both hands out of respect.

This was the three-generation assemblage in that room that day: Momo and his parents, along with his two children, one sleeping, one not alive for long enough.

"I think Cassia should see him," his mother said again.

Momo shook his head slowly. It was the most resolute he'd been that day since the nurse asked if he was the relation of patient number 17.

"She needs rest," he said to his mother, aping the doctor.

Now, Momo put the three sheets of paper away. He had made

his decision that day, and he was now looking at its consequences, surrounded by yellow wildflowers in San Francisco.

He could see now that on the day Cassia arrived in San Francisco and asked him over the phone what he would do if her plane crashed, it had been a mistake for him to dismiss it out of hand as if they were the jitters of a jet-setter. She wasn't looking for vapid answers like, *I would never remarry*, but the question had been a test after all. What she was really saying was that the distance between them took an act of faith to close. She was asking him how far he was willing to take that act.

"I didn't want to see your face when they'd give you the baby," he said to her now. "Not that time, not ever again."

She considered this. "It would have been heartbreaking, yes, but it would've been better, still."

"The doctor wanted you to rest," Momo said, "but that was just his job. It was my job to make sure there'd be no hole in your heart."

"It would've been nice to know what he looked like."

"His toes fanned out a little bit," Momo said, "like an amphibious animal. His eyes and nose were still kind of scrunched up, not very good looking. His face . . . looked like my dad's when he's taking a dump."

To Momo's surprise, Cassia cracked a smile. "I can actually see that," she said.

There was a slightly reckless feeling between them, the kind of lightness you feel because there are so many broken vases around you that it doesn't matter if you let another one drop.

He asked if it was his parents who gave her back the ashes.

"I asked for them the last time I went to visit Junie," she told him. "To fit it into my suitcase, we had to switch to an Ovaltine can. And even then, it didn't fill up halfway."

He did not expect this detail to hurt him, of all things.

"Maybe I also felt that it was the least I could do to take him along," she said, "seeing that he never went anywhere."

"We are entitled to our dreams for our children," Momo said.

For a month after the second delivery, the only thing that kept Momo going was the kinesthetic inventiveness of Junie. At the age when other children were learning to run, to clamber and skip, Junie too was moving around the world in her own way. She could even dance to music. She had a way of swaying and twirling that made you believe she was leaping through the air without ever leaving the ground.

Now, in San Francisco, Momo turned to Cassia, years too late, to say, "We can still do something about the ashes. Let's do something about the ashes."

Cassia tucked a strand of her hair behind her ear, as if to expose her face to the wind so that she could better assess the prevailing weather.

"Actually," she said, "I've been thinking about that."

The Vanishing Point

To any outside observer, the man and woman sitting on a bench above the ruins of Sutro Baths in the late afternoon seemed typical of tourists who came to the city. Both of them wore sensible shoes, and there was an animated air about them. He had on his lap an open map of Northern California, while she pointed to coastal features here and there. If one were to walk past their bench, one would have heard them discuss the best way to get to the Golden Gate Bridge and whether there would be traffic this time of day. Here was a couple in the process of checking off another item on their agenda.

All of this would have been true of Momo and Cassia. More specifically, at this moment, the two of them wanted to find an ideal setting for what they were about to do. Not on a beach where the sea breeze might blow back what you throw at it, and not at some spot where weekenders might come up to you for chitchat. They wanted a place where, if you were to walk toward its natural terminus, there'd be nowhere left to go except into the sea.

The best place for this, it seemed to them, was where the land became a tendril unfurling into the sea. The geography of bicoastal America provided several options for this. At the tip of the Florida Keys, say. From Montauk on the East Coast, or Provincetown. But starting from where they were, one place called attention to itself. On the map, the end of the landmass jutted out so much into the sea that there was a lighthouse there to warn seafarers against the land. It seemed cloven from the continent, and about as detached from the rest of California as anything could be.

"It doesn't look far from here," she said, pointing to the unlabeled vanishing point.

"It may be dark by the time we reach it," he cautioned.

"Probably better that way."

They dusted themselves off from the park bench. The idea declared itself and refused to be delayed by practical considerations.

As they drove north in Momo's Subaru, the Ovaltine can sat on Cassia's lap. It was beginning to show signs of rust. She had never taken it out of her suitcase after she landed in San Francisco.

Cassia found that her heart was not heavy. From the passenger seat, she watched the sun dip into the bay as they crossed the bridge, and it seemed to her that there was a flash of green when it disappeared under the watery horizon.

"Did you see that?" she asked Momo.

Momo did not. He was driving intently, his heart already gone on ahead to the chosen point of land, even if his eyes were dutifully glued to the flow of traffic. The road split into two counterflowing rivers, white headlights in one, red taillights in the other.

Momo was thinking that this might be the last thing he and Cassia did alone together. There'd still be outings with Junie in the future, but the two of them would never do something like this again. Because the second baby was the last time they had shared a dream. He had come here hoping to rewind their lives just a little, the way you could do nowadays with a VCR. But he saw today that to do so, they'd have to rewind very far, perhaps farther than the point at which their lives converged.

Beyond the bridge, where Cassia had never been, the road began to narrow and meander, and she marveled at the height of the mountains. When she told Momo this, he laughed. "Wait until you see the Sierra Nevadas," he told her. "I had a little car trouble there, and I thought—"

"What happened?"

"Well," he said, surprised that he was laughing. "It doesn't matter now."

They were still driving when they could see nothing except the part of the road lit up by the car's headlights. The landmarks along the way told them that they had underestimated the driving time. Fifty miles out on the switchbacks and regretting not having asked for directions at the last gas station they passed, they turned into the only establishment by the road, with a faded wooden banner that read CREPUSCULAR INN.

Miraculously, the innkeeper, a woman with long gray hair, was sitting in the reception area.

"No, you haven't passed it," the woman told them. "Everybody makes the same mistake. It's because once you leave the last town down the coast, this stretch of road takes a lot longer to get through. Just keep going, and drive safe!"

She didn't ask them why they were going out there at this hour; Momo thought that maybe she had already heard every possible reason.

By the time they reached the scree road at the turnoff, it was completely dark. The lighthouse appeared before them, stout though not majestic, still putting out a gyrating light. The light didn't help them see their way toward it, however. Momo left the parking light on in the car, so that they could find their way back.

In the distance, a foghorn bellowed. Momo wanted to say it sounded like someone was trying out a giant tuba, except it wasn't quite like a tuba either. He thought it was like the feeling you get when you opened the door to a large house that you knew no one had lived in for a long time.

Cassia cradled the Ovaltine can in her left arm, and could feel the powder shifting around in the unfilled spaces inside.

They passed the base of the lighthouse, then moved outward to where the rocky promontory met the sea.

"I think this is the place," Momo said. "This is the vanishing point."

She held the can out to Momo. "Do you want to start or should I?"

"We should say something."

Cassia stepped up to where an outcrop loomed over the surf.

"Dear child," Cassia said. The words came out calmly and did not catch in her throat. She had imagined and rehearsed this moment for weeks now. "I'm grateful for your company, even if it was for so brief a time. While you were with me, you gave me bigger dreams than what I was capable of carrying by myself."

There was a long silence punctuated by the waves crashing.

"We will take good care of your sister," Momo took over when he saw that Cassia was not going to say anything more. "We can't wait to see her grow up, and we know you'd be proud to have her as your sibling." He put a hand on Cassia's shoulder, at the base of her neck where he could feel the heat from her skin, because he didn't think it was right to let the child see them any other way, to let him think what brought him into the world were two adults not touching each other.

"Off you go, child," Cassia said, prying open the lid of the tin can. "Go see the world."

She leaned forward such that Momo had to wrap both arms around her waist so that she wouldn't lose her balance. She poured out the contents of the can. For a second some of the ashes flew up, mingled with the salty spray of the surf. The next moment they became indistinguishable from the waves.

Cassia pressed shut the lid of the empty can. Then she tossed the can into the sea too.

Fog had moved in by the time they got back on the road. It was dense enough to have a heft to it. Momo drove slowly, and his headlights seemed feeble against the fog.

By now, it was near midnight, and if they drove back across the bridge, there was no telling when they would get home. They talked about this and settled on returning to the Crepuscular Inn. Momo half expected the inn to have vanished; it seemed natural for it to disappear as unceremoniously as the fog had appeared.

But it was still where they expected it. They rang a bell on the counter, and the woman with long gray hair emerged moments later. "Let me show you to your room," she said.

The room looked like it was out of a novel set in the gold rush days. The innkeeper was informing them of practical matters (something about the plumbing, the wood-burning stove), but Cassia was thinking about the surf crashing beneath her at the end of the promontory, and about having felt no fear of falling as she stepped onto its edge. That fearlessness was only the briefest flash, like the green color she saw after the sun fell into the water over the bay, but that flash stayed with her. She tried to remember the last time she felt this way—unfocused and yet not bad, with something languid but hopeful coiled inside her such that at any minute, it could snap into wakefulness and energy. It was as if something that had been wound snugly around her core had finally been unraveled.

The innkeeper stopped talking for a moment. The smell in the air was a combination of smoke and wood.

"There are extra towels in the hallway closet," she said to them.

After the innkeeper closed the door behind her, Cassia and Momo were left staring at a four-poster bed in the center of the room.

"I will get the extra bedding and sleep on the floor," he said.

She shook her head. "The bed is large enough for three."

A small window in the room looked out into a velvet void created by the fog. Momo unlatched it, and the moist cool breath of the bay seeped in.

They washed up, undressed, and got into bed like two obedient children observing bedtime.

"We accomplished something today," he said.

Momo thought he'd have trouble falling asleep, but exhaustion crept over him almost immediately. He woke in the middle of the night in need of the bathroom. After he finished and turned off the bathroom light, his eyes already adjusted to the brightness, he found the darkness around him so total that he had to grope his way back to bed. Now he heard, more clearly than before, the foghorn from out yonder, and it gave him a maddening feeling he couldn't classify. With his hand outstretched, he found one of the posters of the bed frame and knew he had arrived at his side of the bed. Years of sleeping away from each other had made him forget how quietly Cassia slept. A sting of jealousy struck him now as he suddenly remembered the fact of her lover.

He slid under the covers, trying to not wake Cassia, but his hand brushed against her by accident. She instantly turned toward him. He was so surprised that when their foreheads touched, then their lips, he could not remember who he was and whom he was embracing in the darkness.

In a place where its history was so alien to them as to be charming if indecipherable, they felt, ironically, more at ease with each other and with themselves; the weight of their shared history, unable to find its place in this setting, simply melted away.

Without this mutual knowledge and its weight, he was and was not the man who dragged a child out of bed in the middle of the night to recover his own musical youth. She was and was not the woman who pretended that her newlywed husband could channel her lost love.

For a moment in this cabin by the sea, all their former selves, their ordinary and extraordinary life, in their resigned courage and folly, became translucent and flight-ready.

Momo recognized the smell of her skin, which hadn't changed. They made love not as a couple used to the routine of it, but not like lovers either. From the moment he entered her, Cassia felt as if another woman was receiving the body of another man, and she was both herself and also that woman. As their breathing quickened, his fingers gripped the base of her neck where he had earlier touched her on the rocky promontory. She understood exactly how the bony ripples of his spine turned into tremors in her own body, how her body's shiver brought on his own shiver. For a brief instant, she felt like she understood more than that too.

Later, as their minds slowly returned to the tender indifference of the cabin, they were afraid to loosen their grip on each other, for fear that they would not recognize themselves if they let go, or the person they were latched on to.

Elk

IN THE FOREST SLOPES NEAR THE CABIN WHERE THE TWO OF them slept, a five-year-old male elk, not unlike the one that Momo spotted on the other side of the Continental Divide, was grazing on the slopes leading toward a mountain roadway. It was coming into the height of its physical powers and would soon reach nine hundred pounds. Unlike its brethren, it was not prone to being startled and was wandering farther and farther from its habitual grazing ground. It was often alone in these adventures, which meant that it had the better pick of grass and the occasional chomp at the bark of trees.

This morning the elk was biding its time on the steep slope. The sun had not yet come up. The fog of the previous evening had stayed entrenched in the hills. From where the elk stood, there emerged a faint moving light out in the distance, up the slope from the ravine. As if prompted by that light, the elk proceeded to move up the steep slope. As it did so, dry branches rustled under its hooves.

The faint light came from Momo's car, as he was trying to drive back across the bridge ahead of morning traffic so that Cassia could get to Cyrus before Melinda and Bernie left for work.

It was still dark on the road. Momo felt as if it wasn't him driving the car, but that instead the two of them were propelled forward in a close-quartered alcove carved out from the fog. There was a congenial silence in the car. A strain of melody from a violin solo rose up in his head, unprompted, and he hummed along.

The elk had by now moved to the top of the steep forest slope and nibbled at a stem of grass there. It stayed for a moment at the top of the slope where soil met asphalt. There was a low guardrail there, and the elk made no sound whatsoever as it stepped over the rail onto the asphalt.

⚘

When Momo rounded the bend of the road, the first thing he saw in the headlights was the underbelly of the elk standing in the middle of the road.

He didn't have time to register what it was; he reacted swiftly because in his muscle was the memory of having hit black ice, and in his mind, the discussion with Larry about veering away from oncoming traffic. His steering wheel responded in time, but much too sharply, and the car veered sharply to the right. The Subaru tore through the low guardrail and headed straight for the steep slope above the ravine where the elk had earlier grazed.

As the car became airborne over the ravine, Momo understood exactly what had happened. That he—along with Cassia beside him—was falling. Just like the time when he was a small boy and rolled off the roof of his home in Trout River, he felt clearly that time slowed down, became stretched out to allow him to ponder things that would've otherwise taken much longer. There was enough time to understand that this might be the last moment of life, though not enough time for panic, remorse, or plans of contingency. There was still the same congenial silence in the car, during which he could feel his chest cavity fill with gratitude over the fact that, in this brief interval of weightlessness, he just might have time to reach for Cassia's hand.

So that was exactly what he did.

Tendrils

ON HER TWELFTH BIRTHDAY, FEBRUARY 29, 1988, JUNIE WATCHED as a stranger appeared at their door in Trout River. She carried with her two skinny suitcases. Her manner of dress was enough to distinguish her from all other adults Junie had seen, but even though the stranger brought with her a strong whiff of Elsewhere, when she came into their room, it was not intrusion Junie felt, but curiosity.

After the stranger greeted Junie's grandparents, the first thing she did was to come over and look at Junie. She bent down, braced her hands on her knees, and trained her full, expressive eyes on Junie's face. It was not a passing glimpse, no: she really *looked* at her. She seemed to be probing into Junie's entire childhood and was trying to predict her future too.

Junie was accustomed to adults looking at her a certain way. Their eyes usually scrutinized her lower body—from knee to wooden toe—while in their head, they replayed the story of Junie's life, as previously relayed to them by some neighbor or cousin or meat vendor, and which they will continue to relay to their in-laws or children or neighbors. Disaster. California. Orphan.

Now this stranger was looking at Junie, and her eyes said that she knew about all that, but she was beckoning Junie's own story too. Her gaze was so steadfast that Junie almost wanted to look away. But only almost. She saw that this woman liked looking at her, and that what she saw made her both happy and sad, but at the end of it all, the happiness prevailed.

The woman straightened up and walked over and talked with her grandparents for a while, softly, in the manner of adults who didn't want to be interrupted. She brought out a few pieces of paper in envelopes to show her grandparents, which Junie overheard her say were given to her by a friend. Her grandparents didn't read the letters, but the woman seemed to be explaining what was written in them. As she did so, Grandma wiped away tears, and Grandpa sighed once or twice.

When Junie felt that she had waited long enough, she walked over to them on her wooden legs.

"Who *are* you?" Junie asked the stranger.

Once again, it was always the simple questions that stumped them.

"I am . . ." the woman said, thinking. "Let's just say I'm someone who also grew up with grandparents."

"How did you find us?" she asked the woman.

"By accident, or almost accident."

That was clearly not the whole story, Junie knew, and she waited for the woman to explain.

"I'm here to show you something," the woman said.

When she unsheathed the two instruments from their cases, Junie's heart skipped a beat, for she knew she had seen this before, somewhere in the haziest edge of her memory. One instrument was bigger than the other, but both had the same curves, the same warm-colored wooden varnish.

The woman tucked the smaller one under Junie's chin, stretched out Junie's left arm, and slipped her fingers around the instrument's long neck. It was just the right length for her arm.

"It smells like a forest," Junie said, remembering the time the components of her legs were scattered on the floor of this very room among wood shavings.

The woman took up her own instrument and placed her bow on one of her strings. Junie did likewise, and was delighted at the vibration that followed.

"Now I'm going to make sure my violin is in tune," she told Junie.

Junie watched as the woman put her left hand on the nautilus coil at the end of the violin and, using her index finger and thumb, coaxed one of its black plugs to turn. She did this as naturally and nonchalantly as if she were tucking a strand of hair back into place. And with that, the strings were loosened, then tightened.

She saw that the woman was playing two strings at once, and heard the pitch coming from one of the strings rising slowly. Whatever she was doing to the string, the two commingled notes began to sound sweeter every second, as if closing a gap in Junie's mind. Junie could find no words to describe the change in the sound, except that it was as if an empty glass bottle was being slowly filled with water, stopping just at the brim, no more, no less.

Acknowledgments

The line on page 5, "to love someone is to figure out how to tell yourself their story," is drawn from a line in the opening chapter of Rebecca Solnit's *The Faraway Nearby*, and it reads, "To love someone is to put yourself in their place, we say, which is to put yourself in their story, or figure out how to tell yourself their story." These words have resonated with me deeply.

The line on page 238, "And maybe, like someone said, love is a wound that closes and opens, all our lives," is drawn from a line in the story "The Last Thing We Need" by Claire Vaye Watkins, which reads, "Sometimes love is a wound that opens and closes, opens and closes, all our lives."

My tremendous gratitude goes to Caroline Eisenmann, for being the Ideal Reader and the fearless champion every writer dreams of. I am indebted to the keen editorial eye and unflagging commitment of Zachary Knoll, who worked with passion and abiding care to make this book the best it could be, and to Nita Pronovost for her editorial guidance and support throughout. I cannot imagine being on a better team. Thanks also to the rest of the team at Simon & Schuster, Elise Ringo and Heidi Meier, for their expertise.

Before this book was even a draft, Lee Gowan asked me such astute questions that they could only be answered by producing a better version of what I had, and then more of it. For that—and for all our subsequent conversations on distilling words from life—I will always be grateful. In the first novel-writing class I ever took, at the University of Toronto's School of Continuing Studies, Shyam Selvadurai's comments on the beginning fragments of the story encouraged me to keep going, and also led to the novel's first title, *The Importance of Floating*, which shaped its subsequent trajectory. I'm grateful to Peter Ho Davies, whose Bread Loaf workshop was nothing less than transformative for me, and whose work—and incomparable humor—continues to inspire. I'm indebted to Garth Greenwell, whose workshop at Disquiet showed me not only how to pay attention to art but also how to *be*.

I am thankful to MacDowell for twice giving me the time, space, walking trails, and delicious hot meals to tackle difficult tasks in the novel's revision; to the Toronto Arts Council for its artist grant, and to Cyndy Hayward, Jeff McMahon, and Darice Grass at the Willapa Bay Artist-in-Residence Program for gifting me with a paradisiacal June.

No amount of chocolate can express my gratitude to Joe Palumbo and Victoria Barclay from the Toronto Writers Centre, who read this book in manuscript form and, with great generosity of spirit, helped me figure out how to get to the next draft. To the talented and hilarious members of my Toronto writing group of ten-plus years, Margaret DeRosia, Keith Rombough, Meghan Daividson Ladly, Franca Pelaccia, Diane Terrana (who also generously read my very first draft): you are irreplaceable.

My deepest gratitude to Yanzhi Meng, who over the years gave me more forms of support than I can count, but the most important of which was to remind me again and again that it all just takes time. Thanks to Jess Fenn and Sara Mang for writing with me under one roof (with and without small rodents) and for fortifying me with your talent and drive; to Caitilin Griffiths for sustaining me with caffeinated conversation and for nudging me toward a deadline that made all the difference. To Chet Van Duzer, for sharing your resourcefulness, enthusiasm, and for the bigness of your imagination. To Chen Sabrina Tan, for telling me about your favorite books beginning in our SSP summer at Ojai, and for showing me, over the subsequent decades, how to be a more attentive reader and how to inhabit unfamiliar worlds and try to walk in other people's shoes.

About the Author

Born in Shanghai, Linda Rui Feng has lived in San Francisco, New York, and Toronto. She is a graduate of Harvard and Columbia and is currently a professor of Chinese cultural history at the University of Toronto. She has been twice awarded a MacDowell Fellowship for her fiction, and her prose and poetry have appeared in publications such as *The Fiddlehead, Kenyon Review Online, Santa Monica Review*, and *Washington Square Review. Swimming Back to Trout River* is her first novel.

Visit *lindaruifeng.com* to learn more.